STAIRS
OF
SAND

By

Eileen Granfors

Stairs of Sand

ISBN 10: 978-1461109495

ISBN-13: 1461109493

Key words: novel, family, borderline personality disorder, drug abuse, dance, mothers, daughters, grief, healing

Other works by Eileen Granfors:

Some Rivers End on the Day of the Dead (novel, The Marisol Trilogy), 2010

And More White Sheets (poetry), 2010

Flash Warden and Other Short Stories, 2011

For Your Daughter
By Yvette Johnson

Best we believe in something, even if it's how the
sand breaks beneath our feet, even it's tree
sap or vapor in a wall,
we best believe in something to carry us when
our knees grieve.
take the moment when you sail away,
an imprecise evening
and when you do that, you burst and how sudden
you feel, how first
because the land is slipping off into moonlit
water and you know
you are the diamond, the turning leaf.

STAIRS OF SAND

"How many cowards, whose hearts are all as false

As stairs of sand. . . "

Bassanio in Shakespeare's *The Merchant of Venice*

CHAPTER 1: ZOOZLE

The Whidbey-Port Townsend ferry carries few passengers this late on a July night. The nearly empty ferry mimics my completely empty me. I lost my job last week, and everything else before that.

I'd meditate, but Mel is singing too loud, "Don't Worry, Be Happy," trying too hard to make me laugh. She's serious about us making some Internet porn for cash, pronounced with a long *a*. I've told her no way a million times, that I'd rather be homeless and starving or dead.

A crewman walks by, giving us a lecherous leer, calling out, "Hey, you girls. Haven't you heard of curfew?" We're both in our late twenties, and we both look twelve. Mel flips him off and slides closer to me. I push her away.

"Zooz, girl, I'm freezing," she says. As one, we look at her feet in terry-cloth flip flops. She moves over and touches the hollow in my throat, right where a lump of misery is clogged. She tries to zip my windbreaker across my tank top. "You feel like ice. Let's sit in the car. Quit trying to be Wonder Woman." That's how I mock my mom's self-perception of perfection. I shake my head.

"Take the keys. Get warm. I need the air."

Mel wanders back and huddles in the car. I pass by her as I walk to the ferry boat's stern, riding low to the water. Mel has wrapped a blanket across her bony shoulders, head tucked into her chest and the blanket is up like a hoodie. She often looks vulnerable, like someone I should protect. It took me a while to learn that was her act. Everybody acts a role. I'm totally tired of mine, and it's only been 168 hours since I was atop a shining star, dance teacher at Port Townsend University, now placed on leave, basically code for fired.

I study the waves, watching the ferry's wake in the darkness. That's like me, one bubble among millions. My heart aches more because it's a foggy night, and I can't see that far ahead. I love our rare sunny days in Washington. If I close my eyes on a sunny day, I can make myself believe I'm still a little kid, surfing in California with my Grandpa Joe.

As the ferry chugs into the channel, a tall, skinny, old man in a tweed sports coat comes to stand near me. His Newfoundland retriever, huge, black and white and unbelievably furry, sits between us, wearing a pink halter. "Guardian Angels" is scripted across the back.

Lately, I don't much talk except to Mel. I make an exception since he has a dog. "May I pet your dog?" I ask him.

"We'd love that, wouldn't we, Jacques?" He rubs his dog behind the ears.

I sink to my knees to pet the dog, who is tall enough to look me in the eyes when I do. His gaze is direct and soft with affection. Though he's wet in the misty air, it feels wonderful to put my head on his. My heart uncurls one nanometer.

"Hi Jacques," I say. Jacques smiles. He licks my face, my new short hair, spiky with hair gel. I push my hair with my fingers, then rub the dog's slobber and my hair gel on my jeans, and I smile back.

"His full name is Frère Jacques. But we cut it short." The old man grins with the pride of a father. "I'm Phillip McKillop." He takes off his hat and sweeps it across his heart.

I scratch the dog some more. "Hello, Phillip. I'm Suzann, Suzann Zimmerman." I don't know why I don't tell him Zoozle. "I used to have a dog, a little guy, part spaniel, part Pomeranian. My ex has him now." Javier has Boo, Javier has a house, Javier has a new life. Me, I've got Mel. I've got a roof over my head with Big Daddy, Mel's meth-making friend, which was cool until I stopped doing meth. Now, I wouldn't want a dog around Big Daddy. I don't want me around Big Daddy.

"Bye Phillip. Bye, Jacques." Holding the dog has tightened the knot in my throat. I can't swallow it down. Despair claws with more powerful digs into my stomach. I look off into the dark night, back towards the car where Mel is tracing patterns on the fogged windows. What escape route should I take from this huge mess I've made? I can't run home again. My mom wouldn't want me there and she won't come here, she's made that clear enough. Life with Mel is all I've got, and now I am certain I don't want that either.

Across the dark water, I see houses on the shoreline, alight with the business of living. I visualize my old life with Javier; my heart squeezes around my thoughts of Grandpa Joe in Imperial Beach. Grandpa likes to brag how it's the most southwesterly city in the United States. It's right on the border with Mexico. He wins bets when people don't believe him. "Gotcha!" he laughs every time.

The ferry churns into a wave, and my happy memory of Grandpa's folksy stories about the ocean's waves and the currents lurches into the voice and image of my first dancing teacher, Francis, his acne-scarred face and peppermint breath, his oily hands moving my body into postures, saying "do that turn again, repeat that step, the arm like this," each time touching my budding breasts or my inner thighs. I scrape my fingers against my pockets, trying to get the hair gel off because oil on my skin makes me shudder. The scene with Francis morphs back into Mel, whom I followed from my amazing appointment as a dance professor to emergency medical leave to the drugged-out living dead. I sold my condo for drug money. Dumb, so dumb.

I am through with do over's.

I walk to the other side of the boat, away from the crewman and Mr. McKillop. I unzip my boots, aligning them underneath the life preserver ring. The boots are the right size for Mel.

I clamber over the chain guard and dive away from the ferry into the sea.

The cold water burns my skin, and numbness makes my body feel as heavy as my wet clothes. The current is strong, pulling me south. My ribs hurt from where I hit the water so flat, and it's hard to lift my arms. It's even harder to keep my head up with the chop of the waves. I sink and swallow water. Floundering, I pop back up again. In the distance, there's the ferry.

Then, I see Jacques. He has followed my leap and is paddling towards me, maybe ten yards away.

I sink again, the waves and tide working together to push me under. Something in me tries to begin swimming towards him, as if I am suddenly awake. I remember it's better to lean back to float and conserve my strength against the cold. I'm grabbed by the neck of my windbreaker. It's Jacques! I reach for his vest straps, and he pulls me with sure, steady strength against the current.

"How's the dog?" I mumble, my closed eyes blinking open. I'm warm, the lights are bright, I have IV lines running into the top of my left wrist. A nurse looks at me, frowning. I don't know if she's angry or concentrating. She's pushing an amber liquid into the IV bag. It burns as it hits my bloodstream, and then it doesn't burn anymore. Unthoughts hum through my brain.

"Dog?" the nurse asks with a skeptical lift of her eyebrows.

Another woman steps from the side of the room and reaches to stroke my face. She's large and frowzy, her hair a wild, hennaed mass of frizz.

"Penny?" I say, not believing my new psychologist is here.

"Zoozle, how are you, my dear?" Her forehead creases into caverns of concern.

"I only remember a big dog. Where's the dog?"

Penny shakes her head at me. "You and your dogs. The dog is fine. Rest now. Your mother is on her way."

I try to sit up, but the pain in my ribs flattens me. "No."

"Your mother and you and I should talk."

We've had this conversation before, Penny and I. A chat with Mom is not something I can do. Besides, Mom hasn't even responded to the information packet I agreed to let Penny send. I picture Mom tossing the diagnosis and information straight into the trash, pronouncing it medical horse shit.

"Maybe I'll be ready for Mom next week. When can I leave?"

Penny hedges. "Mmmm, the doctors will tell you. I wouldn't want to guess." She looks towards the windows, and I see for the first time that they are cross-hatched with something like chicken wire.

"I'm not suicidal, Dr. Huizenga. Do you remember that old Julia Roberts' movie, "Sleeping with the Enemy"? It was like that, a dive to freedom." My voice is feeble and hoarse. And I know I'm lying again. Meth taught me a lot about lying and stealing and pawn shops and unemployment. Yeah, all that really endeared me more to my mom. Only Grandpa Joe stuck with me, saying I was surely lonely without Javier.

"Rest now, Zoozle. I'll come in the morning. You can ask your doctors about your release. And you'll feel better when your mom has come. You'll see."

Since my mom and I haven't spoken since Spring Break in March, I doubt she is going to make me better, but I'm tired and I give up fighting that issue.

"What about Mel? Can she visit?"

"No one except relatives," the nurse interjects. I had forgotten she was still in the room.

Dr. Huizenga stands up straight, adjusting her massive purple knitted purse. "Mel called me after they fished you out. You're lucky the dog was a Newfie. His owner almost had a heart attack." She pats my hand and leaves.

I am starting to remember what it felt like to hit the water, and how I tried to use the current to stay afloat, how my ribs ached and I couldn't lift my arms. Salt water, the cold, the big dog, Jacques. I want Jacques.

The drugs send me, smiling at the image of Jacques, back into delicious oblivion.

CHAPTER 2: JOLENE

Why is it that my daughter's scrapes turn my life into scraps? Aren't most parents done with all this hand-holding after the kid finishes high school? Here we are moments from push back, and a flight attendant leads a gaunt woman and a gangly kid with a Barbie backpack towards the rear of our packed plane. The woman on the aisle of my row paws into her flowered carry-all, tossing lipstick, a compact, and magazines onto the unoccupied middle seat between us. Seated by the window in my favorite safety zone, I err. I look up. Worse, I smile. Smiling is part of the public me; my students always comment on how I smile when I return tests or give quizzes.

"Ma'am," the flight attendant points at me, "Could you please move here?" She gestures vaguely across the aisle towards a solitary window seat, "to assist this mother and her daughter?"

"I'd prefer not to." I begin to lift my hair off my neck, remember I have a new shorter hair cut, adjust my glasses instead.

"It's right over here, it's easy." The flight attendant bites her lip and tries to keep her chipper attitude.

"No, I'd rather not." I look unblinkingly at her, just as I have out-stared the bravado of teenaged brats in my classroom for thirty-four years, always with that smile plastered across my lips.

The flight attendant begins re-tucking her white blouse into her khaki shorts and glares. "Ma'am, we need someone to help a little so we can get underway."

"Maybe these late-comers could sit across the aisle from one another? These two people," indicating men in suits seated on the aisle in front of me, "could move to the center seats. It's easy." This time, I smile consciously and flip through my CD's in their patent leather case.

"So you won't help?" The flight attendant frowns, her shoulders slump. Like a music box dancer, she turns, leaning up two rows, switches on a perky smile, and a young soldier by the window gets up. She gives him a fawning, approving grin. "Thank you so much, sir, for being helpful. Everybody benefits when people help." Her voice is loud.

My seatmate leans over to me. "Good for you. They always ask us, don't they? As if we're easy marks every time." She has a Midwestern twang. "You have such a pretty smile, no wonder she picked on you."

I note her pink scarf and blonde rasta-beaded hair. "The sanctity of motherhood is way over-rated in this country. In the last six flights, I've moved to accommodate some mother and a kid on every flight. Why don't they plan ahead? Besides, I barely slept last night. Family 'crisis.'" I try to toss this remark in as if it were a joke of long standing.

My seat mate nods, rattling beads. "I need the aisle seat to hop back to the lavatory all the time. But I'm with you." She picks up a travel magazine. The plane's window is cold against my cheek, and I settle my *pashmina* around my shoulders, hoping for a nap. I will need it.

The sacred mom and daughter once seated exclaim in noisy excitement, as if surprised there are airplanes at an airport. I rearrange my neck pillow, bashing the seat in front of me with both knees.

I fall into an addled sleep, accosted by visions of my daughter, Suzann, the daughter I have bragged about so often. I picture Suzann at five in her first tutu, pink with golden threads, her dance teacher, Francis, grinning behind her; on stage, receiving bouquets as the lead ballerina in the spring recital when she was sixteen, her grandpa beaming and cheering too loud. In the athletic director's office, signing for her dance scholarship at seventeen.

Eight years later, when I came north for a visit, she lived in that filthy apartment, her arms and ankles pocked with scabs and infection sites, falling asleep at the wheel in a meth downer, almost killing us both.

In rehab, bored and calling me incessantly to complain about the program and where was her mom anyway? In the psychologist's office, spilling the family history. And now, in the hospital? A fall off a ferry? Really?

Good God. Why is it that Suzann, at twenty-five, is unable to go forward without calling her mommy? Isn't it time she grew up?

I awake with a bounce of my head as the plane bumps into clouds somewhere outside Seattle. My stomach feels queasy. The flight attendant answers my call button, chatting her way down the aisle, with a special focus on the mom and kid in front of me.

"Yes?" she asks, snapping the button off.

"I was asleep when you came through with drinks. Could I get a ginger ale with ice. Please?" I try to sound neutral and kind, but she frowns.

"Sure." She flounces away and returns with the ginger ale, a warm can, no ice. With the soft drink in hand, I list an agenda for the next three days, meeting with Suzann and her therapist to talk through some issues all the while worrying about the classes I'm missing, the lesson plans left, the probably incompetent sub.

Rental car, Seattle traffic, my favorite boutique hotel. It's late, and I'm exhausted. On landing, I called the hospital. The nurse said Suzann is resting comfortably for the night, so no need to come tonight, to my immense relief.

I love this hotel, though it's two long blocks from Pike's Market. The hotel's masseuse was booked, so I place my breakfast order card on the door, pour a glass of wine, and slip into the soaking tub. An hour later dressed in jersey jammies, I take a sleeping pill, and it's lights out for me.

In the morning, I reluctantly pull myself upright from the down duvet at room service's discreet knock. I call the valet for my car and gulp down two cups of hot coffee, choosing one cranberry muffin to indulge in on the drive to Whidbey Island Hospital. Showered and dressed, I pick up the car keys from the doorman and leave an ample tip.

I'm way too early, not anticipating the easy traffic heading north from Seattle. I don't really want to arrive before talking to Suzann's doctors; her moods fluctuate from rage to neediness to indifference. She's mercury breaking into blobs in the old-style maze.

As I turn from the freeway towards Whidbey, a small village emerges from the mist like salt drifted into the shape of clapboard houses. I start up the road, the fog still blocking the feeble sunshine. I drive too fast, my one bad habit. Evergreens loom along the two-lane highway, and my anxiety returns, roiling into painful heartburn and the first grain of a headache.

The sun breaks through as I swing the car into a U-shaped parking lot, edged by a redwood building with window boxes askew, yellow petunias cascading in ruffled loops. Leaving my raincoat in the car, I am cold in my silk business suit. A quick walk through the chill brings me to the reception desk. A volunteer traces my route on a small map to Suzann's ward.

I buzz to enter. The nurses, busy at their computer monitors or talking to doctors, hurry on their soft-soled shoes in an efficient flow.

A beefy-armed woman sits on a bench near the nurse's station. Dressed in a sheer, sleeveless, turquoise rayon blouse and a voluminous bronze broom-pleated skirt, she raises her arm to beckon me to sit by her.

"I'm Dr. Huizenga, but please call me Penny. You are Mrs. Zimmerman, yes? Right on time, of course! Zoozle has told me how important time is in your family! And she looks so much like you. I'd know you anywhere! That same smile." She grins broadly. "You would be so proud of how she speaks of you."

This remark sets my phony-alert into high gear.

Penny Huizenga repositions herself on the bench, patting at her red hair upswept into a 1950s *chignon*, searching for the pen behind her ear.

I look anxiously towards the door of my daughter's room.

"We will go in soon, Mrs. Zimmerman. The other doctor will join us shortly too." Penny pats my arm. "Are you tired from the trip? I know you are worried sick as any mother would be."

"Yes, I'm tired. Yes, I'm worried," I say, thinking I'm also tired of being worried about this adult daughter and her constant crises.

"Zoozle is in amazingly good physical health. But her mental health, as I wrote to you, is precarious." Penny seems to hesitate a moment too long. "The packet I sent you on Borderline Personality Disorder applies to Zoozle's diagnosis — we've been working together this last few months. She needs your unconditional, supportive love. The childhood loss of her father may be at the root of this. She is going to need supervision too."

"I don't understand, Doctor. How does one supervise a grown woman?"

"Before going in, I am suggesting that you and I agree Zoozle will come home with you for an interim of intensive treatment, therapy, and healing. I have a colleague in the San Diego area who will work with her. and with you, for you are the key here."

I walk to the drinking fountain. Having Suzann home again would be a test. How could I possibly supervise her during the work day? What am I getting into here? Why should I have to do this for a grown-up child? Except that she's my daughter, my responsibility. The last time I saw her, on Spring Break, we snarled and snapped until I left early. She needs money. She needs more money. Add to that her commentary on my diet and exercise, as if she's some specimen of physical health, and you have mother-daughter dynamite attached to a very short fuse.

"Yes, of course, I want my daughter to achieve a full recovery." This is completely true. I want her back on her feet, living the life she was meant to live. Just not under my roof, please. "By the way, Dr. Huizenga, her name is Suzann."

"Oh that! Not to worry, Mrs. Zimmerman. She may be choosing this new name to go with this part of her life. You'll find out what she wants to keep and what she can leave behind as she works through recovery of self."

A young Asian woman, skinny like a stalk of asparagus complete with a shaggy layered hair cut, stethoscope hanging from her jacket pocket, hurries down the hallway and into Suzann's room.

"That's Dr. Tran, Zoozle's doctor," Penny notes.

After a few minutes, the doctor comes back to the door and waves us in.

"Suzann would like to see you now," the doctor smiles.

CHAPTER 3: ZOOZLE

I can't fake I'm sleeping when Dr. Tran was talking to me like two seconds ago and said I can be released today, no special meds needed except aspirin. Unless I want to check into a mental facility for a bit. Dr. Tran seems a little young and a lot naïve.

Penny and my mom enter the room as if they're bosom buddies. Mom looks thinner, a little more fit, but the skin around her eyes is dark like one of those old paintings of big-eyed kids. Just what I need, my shrink allied with my mom

"Oh, Suzann. Look at you." My mom starts crying.

"I'm fine, Mom. Sore around the ribs is all."

My mom looks as if she's ready to have a stroke, her face gets red and her eyes are kind of squinchy.

"I gave Suzann a choice about her release," says Dr. Tran. "I'm advising that she check in for observation at Simitoc Mental Health Center for three to five days. She is also free to leave, but no driving for two weeks."

Penny comes closer to the bed. I try to scoot up on the pillows to convince her I'm fine, but the ribs are aching, and I don't make it more than an inch.

"Zoozle, I agree with Dr. Tran. However, I would say, fly home with your mom and check into Bella Vista's day program in Mission Viejo. That way you have your mother's support."

"No way."

Penny moves back to line up with Dr. Tran. She tries to catch my mom's gaze, but Mom is staring at the windows.

Dr. Tran puts out her hand to me. "You are a lovely young woman, Suzann. I'm sure you will make the best of your life. Good luck to you. Remember what I told you." She leaves with rapid tiny steps. I can almost hear the swhoosh as she zips out the door to the next patient on her rounds.

My mom's focus comes back to me. "Suzann can come home with me if she chooses. Bella Vista isn't far from us. She can enter a day program there, or stay in residence. It's her choice."

I'm shocked. My mom has read the information? She's agreeing to go to therapy with me? She's always made the decisions that work to her advantage.

"Yeah, that sounds good, Penny. I'll fly home with Mom, and we'll take it from there." I again make the effort to sit up better, and by grabbing the bed bars, I pull upright. If I find that I can't take it down south, I'll split. "Penny, I appreciate what you've done for me. I can hug, but not tight, okay?" Penny's hugs crack my bones under normal conditions, and right now, a gnat would leave a bruise.

Penny approaches and kisses my cheek. "You are strong, Zoozle. You can do all you need to do." Her eyes flick towards my mom. "Go with the flow."

An orderly comes in with a wheelchair, and he helps me out of bed and into the bathroom. He has given me a bag with clothes Mel brought to Penny so I don't have to wear my old salt-crusted jeans. They're in the bag too, and I throw them into the trash can. Is it as easy as that to throw away that other life too?

One last look in the hospital mirror, my brown eyes looking almost black, the bruise on my chest purple as eggplant. I touch the sore rib, surprised that it doesn't poke out through my skin because it feels like a spike in my torso. I ease into a t-shirt. The jeans are a little tight, so I must have worn them back in the meth days. Or they're Mel's. I take a big breath and go back out for inspection.

The orderly has me sit in the wheelchair, which is actually a relief because I'm a little woozy. Penny pushes, and we parade down the hall and out through the main lobby.

On one of the couches, there sits Mel. She jumps up, and a pile of leaflets she was reading slips off her lap. She runs to me, almost tripping on her jeans hems that drag the floor in a raggedy fringe. She stumbles towards the wheelchair and me. Penny reacts just in time, pulling me back.

"Zoozle Schamoozle. God, girl, I was so scared. What the fuck . .,um. . ., hell did you do? Are you okay? Can I take you home? Big Daddy gave us rent for *nada* this month!"

My mom steps in front of her. I start to introduce them, "Mom, this is Melody Cookson, and. . ."

"Yes, I know. The one and only Melody. Such a pleasure. To meet the idiot that ruined my daughter's life." My mom looks as if she's going to vomit.

Mel's eyes fill with tears. Penny grabs my mom by her jacket sleeve.

I turn on my mom as well as I can turn, mostly moving my head, feeling furious but unable to get up and walk out. "It's not Mel, Mom." The things I've done with Mel were not caused by Mel. When Mom and

I fought over Spring Break, I was the one buying meth in the local park, shaking down my mom for money as often as I dared, pocketing the change from every grocery run I made up, gum, Tampax, candy. And then Mom exploded because I asked what trainer was she working with that taught her about the nutritional value of pizza? I shake my head. "Mel, I'll send for some of my stuff, okay? I'll be in Southern California awhile."

Mel swipes at her eyes with her hoodie sleeve, blows her nose into the cuff, and shrugs her shoulders. She turns to walk out the doors. She stands on the door pad so that the door stays open, and a cold wind blows in. Other visitors in the lounge glance up, some pulling their jackets around them.

"Bye Zooz. Call me. I'll be here." She leaves, and that sandbag drags at my stomach again. I wanted Mel gone, and now she's going, and here we go again. I do not want to lose Mel. No one else understands about me as Mel does, certainly not my mother. And I agreed to go live with my mother?

Penny walks out to the parking lot with Mel.

I have to get on my feet. I think I can.

Before I've gotten too far with this thought, I remember the car. It's my car, and I am going to need it, and I know Mel will hock it the first time she's low on funds. Even now, she honks the horn as she exits the lot and waves a single digit in my direction.

"Mom, I can't go with you," I tell her as she puts the brakes on the wheelchair at the curb. "My car, I have to get my car down there."

Without hesitation, she says, "We'll ship it. As long as you know where the title is. I'll drop you off to rest at the hotel. While you rest, I'll take care of all that. Call Mel and tell her to be home by noon."

She parks me at the curb and jogs off to the parking lot. I should call Mel. Instead, here come Mr. McKillop and Jacques. Jacques has on that pink vest. He is my Guardian Angel.

"You're in the nick of time, Mr. McKillop! I was just leaving. And I'm going to San Diego." I try to stand on my own, but that's not happening, and I ease myself back into the wheelchair. Jacques has put his paws over the side of the chair, panting huge doggy breaths into my face.

"Oh God, Jacques. You wonderful, wonderful boy," I whisper into his shaggy coat. He accepts the compliment by slobbering on my cheek.

"Suzann, you gave us a scare. Were you testing Jacques for water fitness?" Phillip tries to make a joke of it, but I can see he's still shaky about me.

"I'm okay, really." I put my hand out to him, keeping the other wrapped around Jacques. "I'm going to stay with my mom for a while in San Diego."

Phillip nods. "Very good. Here's my card if you're back in our area. Visit us, we'd like that wouldn't we, Jacques?" Jacques has caught something in his master's voice, and he barks with enthusiasm.

"I'll do that. My mom wants to meet you." Even if I'd rather keep my saviors to myself, I owe Phillip and Jacques.

Pulling up to the curb in her rented Taurus, my mom steps over to me with her clipped steps. She takes in Jacques and Phillip and with a sudden lunge, she hugs Phillip, saying over and over "Thank you. Kids these days, honestly, I can't explain them." Jacques pushes between her and Phillip, practically knocking my mom on her butt. This makes me laugh, which hurts my ribs. Phillip introduces himself and Jacques, hands her a business card, and Mom gives him one of her school cards. My Uncle Bill, who's principal of the high school where she's worked forever, bought the cards for the whole staff so they'd be seen as professionals, like lawyers, which seems like a reach. Who ever heard of a teacher with business cards?

"Jacques and I have to go on in now. We do rounds three times a week. All the patients love Jacques. We'll never forget you, Suzann. We have a convention in San Diego this fall. I'll call you." Mr. McKillop takes off his cap and sweeps it across his heart as he did on the ferry.

What a gentleman, I think. "Me too," I say, wishing I had talked to him longer on the ferry before I started this next big mess in my life.

"Let's get a move on," my mother interjects. With that, she sort of dumps me into the car, pushes the now-empty wheelchair back to the lobby, and drives us off together to resume a life under the same roof. Like that ever worked out.

CHAPTER 4: JOLENE

Meeting that gutter snipe, Mel, is the one way to get Suzann out of town. Suzann gave me directions to some coffee joint near their house. I'll pick up the title to the car and a couple of boxes of Suzann's most precious possessions, and then we'll wash our hands of this shadow life she's been living. Out with the old, in with the new.

The guy from the shipping company will pick up the car at the coffee shop. I like their accommodating style. Ms. Mel had better be on time.

Suzann was sleeping on the pull-out couch in our suite. I took her phone to forestall phone calls to her druggie friends. By tomorrow, we'll be on a flight home. I hope she'll see once we're there what she needs is structure. If Bill pulls some strings, we can get her hired in the district even if it's answering phones. Anybody knows work is the best therapy.

My favorite thing about Seattle, the ferries, now seems painfully slow. Finally disembarking, I can get to the meeting place in Poulsbo in under an hour.

The drive goes well, and I pull up to Cuppa Cuppa, pleased that it is both a bakery and coffee house. Suzann's car is nowhere in sight. I call Suzann, but the room phone is busy. I pick at my cuticles, realize it, and pull out a tablet instead. I make a list of collective nouns. Some people do crosswords or Sudoku, but I prefer working on lessons. As a teacher, there's never time to waste.

The striped chairs, garden table, and jaunty awning of Cuppa Cuppa suggest a gaiety I don't feel. I enter the shop and order espresso and a chocolate cupcake with peanut butter frosting. I'll make the most of a miserable situation though Antonio will triple my work out after weigh in next week.

For the thousandth time, I twist to check the clock on the wall. Mel gets one hour, no more, before I call the cops and report the car stolen. My coffee and cupcake are long gone, and I can't risk another cup of caffeine. I call Suzann again.

"What?" she asks in the snarly tone that means she's not in the mood to chat, at least not with me.

"No Mel, that's what."

"She'll be there."

"She'd better."

"Don't sweat it, Mom."

"We could be home by now if we weren't all tied up with your car."

"So go to the airport, and I'll drive down in two weeks."

"Absolutely not. I'll chase her back to Port Townsend if I have to."

"I'm sure you would, Mom."

"Can you call her?"

"Duh, you took my phone."

"But the room phone was busy a minute ago."

"Since you'll check the records anyway, would you believe I was talking to Grandpa Joe?"

"Oh."

"He's glad I'm on my way back."

"Fine. We'll arrange to visit him. Back to Mel. Do you want me to read her number to you?"

"No. You took my phone, Mom. Live with it or call her yourself. She would sure hate to keep you waiting." Suzann disconnects.

A car pulls up, but it isn't Suzann's. The side carries a magnetic sign, "We Ship Your Shi. . .pping." The driver is a paunchy black guy wearing a horizontally striped rugby shirt. He must weigh 380-400 pounds. He puts his hand over his eyes and gazes around.

"Mrs. Zimmerman? George Sevier, here." He laughs at his rhyme. "I have the paperwork for you to sign, you just show me the title, and we'll deliver that car within five days."

"Excellent, George. Slight hang-up. The car isn't here yet. Let me buy you something."

George's face lights up, the sunshine reflecting off his round cheeks. He strides over to the cupcake racks. "Why, that would be one huge pleasure," he says to me as he points at a double-decker strawberry-lemon concoction. "With a bottle of water, please," he adds, as if he's sticking to a diet. I pay the cashier. The cupcake disappears in two bites.

He pats at his mouth and grins, pink frosting on his teeth. "Let's sit here and go through the paperwork," he says. Mel screeches into the parking lot, leaving enough rubber on the pavement for the cashier and George to gasp.

She is dressed in the same outfit she had on at the hospital. Grabbing two shopping bags that seemed to weigh her down, she starts towards the café as if oblivious to any time constraints that might exist in the rest of the human world. She trips on the curb. Neither bag spills open. Checking her knee where her jeans have ripped, she grabs a sweatshirt from one bag and pats at a bloody spot.

George is out of his seat and to her side in a flash of bouncing belly flesh. He helps her up, picks up the bags, and they enter together.

"Ms. Cookson, this is Mr. Sevier. He's handling the shipping. As long as you have the title with you, our business is concluded."

"Sure, Mrs. Zimmerman. Hold on. It's in my purse here." She fumbles in a tiny little denim bag that couldn't contain more than car keys and a coin purse.

"Hold on," she repeats, while I fume. "I'd like to talk to you."

"No, not interested," I say with a stern look.

George watches the two of us. Getting our bad vibes, he buys Mel a coconut cupcake and a second one for himself.

"For you," he says, presenting the cupcake to Mel. She twirls the cupcake as she licks the frosting from bottom to top. I take three deep breaths to avoid an explosion.

Frosting gone, she nibbles the cupcake as if it were a truffle. She crumples the paper and slinks to the trash can. Returning to her seat, Mel again forages in her purse. At last, she produces the title document and the car keys.

"I have things to do," I said. "Thank you, Mr. Sevier. Ms. Cookson, Suzann will be out of communication. I'm on my way."

With that, I turn the keys over to George, take my paperwork, and hurry to my car as if escaping something virulent and dangerous.

I hit what I think is the remote lock of the Taurus. It's the panic button, and the horn sounds in a swell of blasting beeps. Mel walks to wait at the bus bench and laughs a horsy laugh. George waves to me as he turns to talk to Mel. A battered van with a moon-faced, smiling Asian driver pulls into the parking lot. Mel runs over and climbs in. Friend? Lover? Relative? Pick up? Pimp? Fine, I think. Do what you want with whomever you want as long as it's not with my Suzann.

After a delay at the airport, we are home and settled into a pattern of mutual tension. Suzann is too silent; I am too chatty. Soon, I feel trapped in this arrangement for an adult daughter, and then guilty to feel anything but loving. I know what the books say I should do; I just can't do it.

Suzann's car arrives. I give her back her phone. She attends the day program at Bella Vista. I know because I check, and I attend a few sessions with her, a basic waste of time, but required.

I chant Antonio's proverb of the week from yoga class to the rhythm of popping corn and a steady rain outside, "Overcome anger with love, overcome anger with love." The comfort of Suzann's t-shirt quilt on the couch urges me to hurry. Suzann has headed off to Blockbuster, promising to come back with something good. Maybe that renewed gleam in Suzann's eyes means she will reach for a talisman, the delicious joy of watching *The Princess Bride* together as we did when she was little.

The VW squeals back into the driveway, its door slams and Suzann zips into the living room, deftly palming her cell phone. She feeds the DVD into the player and hits *play* as I hurry from the kitchen, the popcorn steaming. I arrange my expression into a welcoming smile. Suzann tucks herself, chin on knees, at the far end of the couch. She shifts, sliding towards the floor. Her low-rise jeans ride even lower, revealing her thong underwear, an inch of butt crack, and a phoenix tattoo that spans from hip to hip. She begins clicking her tongue stud against her teeth as the credits to *Showgirls* scroll by, with a warning, "This film is NR for adult content, explicit nudity, language, and adult situations."

I sprawl on the couch with the popcorn bowl set to share. But the film's title scenes make me squirm, and I jerk upright. I stare at a fixed point in the direction of the t.v., but not at the screen's demeaning images. My mothering failures are written all over Suzann, from head to toe, from eyebrow ring to toe ring, in the three visible tattoos and two piercings and God knows how much else in between that I prefer not to know about.

Infuriated by her film choice, I collapse into the couch's corner, hiding my clenched fists under the quilt, tensed and unsure and angry at this intentional insult.

"Do we have to watch this trash?" I ask in a neutral tone.

Suzann shrugs. "Do what you want. I like it." She fast forwards. "This is where it gets good."

I boil over at this insult to our family values. I pick up the remote and hit the stop button. She starts to flounce out of the room, stops, and says, "You are the worst mother. You don't respect me. You think I'm ten. And when I was ten, you flushed my goldfish down the toilet." She breaks into sobs.

Should I answer? Almost twenty years ago, and we're still fighting about the stupid fish because I had told Suzann she could walk over to the school's Halloween fair, but she was NOT to bring home a goldfish. Of course she brought home a goldfish. "Your goldfish?" I ask.

She glares at me. "You wouldn't let me play video games. You said they killed brain cells."

We stare at one another, two women, related by experience and genetics and all that life is, separated by different visions of what life should be. Our doors slam simultaneously as we sequester ourselves in our respective bathrooms.

I sit straight-backed on the bathtub's cool tile rim, facing west. I picture Suzann theatrically collapsed like a dying Juliet on her plush lavender bath mat, facing east. Ironically, a common wall separates the bathrooms.

Were it not for the wall, we could see one another's pain.

I lean forward, peering through my graying bangs to assess the toll of this latest skirmish. I frown at the crow's feet edging steadily outward. I stretch my muscular arms and unmanicured hands in a yoga movement towards the ceiling, reaching, reaching. For what? Resettling my hands in my lap, I steady myself on one-leg, balanced like a short heron, confronting the small oval mirror.

Edging a red stool from the corner with my left foot, I step up to complete my critique and ignore the increasing volume of sobs from the other side of the wall, sobs which reveal that though Suzann pushes my buttons, I immaturely push right back. We are both adults, but I am the mother. I must do better.

Wrenching the door open, I roll out my Swiss ball, motivated to sweat myself into some shade of emotional balance.

A brainstorm hits me then. Sending her to help my daddy, her Grandpa Joe, for a couple days would give us both some breathing room. I can arrange it with her therapist who has been preaching about giving back as a path towards healing. Daddy doesn't have to know I need the break more than Suzann does.

As I make this decision, I hear her bathroom door open, the sounds of rummaging in her bedroom, and the front door slamming. The VW sputters into gear.

Has she read my mind? Or is she disappearing into her old life in Washington? Every day is a new piece of the puzzle with this woman, this daughter, whose name I chose: Suzann.

CHAPTER 5: ZOOZLE

Yep, we're home now. At least my car got here. My room has a new look, new paint, lavendatrice Mel would call it, and a bedspread Grandma Janie would love. I don't plan on being here longer than the treatment program requires, and then it's back to Port Townsend for me. Mom looks at me with this hurt, baffled expression all the time, and I can't take it. It's like I'd rather be in group listening to everybody else's dysfunctional emo tales than home with the look. I had role-played the right words to spill my guts, to achieve release from the toxic past. But then I faced this mom, marching around like a half-crazed disciple of the Dalai Lama. Jesus, mantra this, Mom: "Your little Susie Q is dead. Susie Q is dead." I want to circle the date on the calendar that Susie Q died.

Why doesn't my mother see me as I am now? Why won't she use my new name, Zoozle? Why is it a crime to prefer "The L Word" to "Dancing with the Network Stars"? Or to talk like normal people. *Fuck* and *bitch* don't mean *fuck* and *bitch*, anybody knows that, except my mom who freaked over "Showgirls."

I'm out of here.

Tribe 8's wailing lyrics rattle the VW's windows, and I sit at the red light, bobbing my head to the syncopation of the raindrops and my fingers' beat against the steering wheel. Racing up the onramp and then south on the 5, I call Mel. I haven't talked to her in weeks, but she acts as if we chatted this morning. She's high, babbling a mile a minute. I ask her to meet me in Imperial Beach when she can, tell her it's close to the border — two weeks, two months, whatever works—we'll have some fun. I give her Grandpa Joe's address when she asks, knowing she'll never find it.

Why not hang out with Mel? I've finished my addiction steps except the part about apologizing to those you've wronged since my mom has wronged me longer than I've wronged her. I'm clean, and I need a friend. I can't do things my mom's way, and why should I? I'm far enough along in the program. I know I can help Mel.

I arrive at Grandpa Joe's by eight. He's ready for bed.

He opens the door an inch, sees it's me, and says, "Hi honey. I thought you'd come last month for the Sand Castle Contest. Your mom said you were busy. She just said you'd show up here. Here's your favorite couch, like old times. How long can you stay? Call your mom, would you?"

"I'll stay a few days, Grandpa." He nods and then doesn't bug me with a million other questions. I don't call Mom.

The next day drifts easily between us. Though it's August, San Diego's infamous overcast tightens its grip on the afternoon. My grandpa's little trailer sports graffiti across one side. Grandpa says the gang tag means "Good people, don't shoot." He teases a lot. We're both wearing our long-sleeved flannel pajamas, eating ice cream and M & M's, watching tapes of "The Three Stooges." This has been our ritual since I was about two. When Grandpa fast forwards, the vcr's whir competes with the hum of his oxygen pump. His single-wide trailer clings to the sand above the jetty in an RV park at the southern tip of the harbor. Chilled breezes blow steadily from the west.

"Should I get the mail, Grandpa?" I squeeze his cold hand.

"That's okay, honey, my oxygen tubes reach that far. It's good to get some exercise." Looping oxygen cords around his arm like he's winching up an anchor chain, he wobbles upward. "I get a little dizzy. Call me Dizzy Izzy." He's had two heart by-passes. The doctors have given him less than a year.

I follow him through sliding glass doors onto his narrow porch. A rotund Buddha graces a café table between two deck chairs. Grandpa pats the Buddha's belly as he shuffles past. "This here keeps all them Bible thumpers away." He chuckles and makes a hexing cross with his fingers. He reaches the mailbox, ten yards in about three minutes. "Nothin'. Let's go in."

He trembles back into his recliner. "We'll watch the news until the Our Meals Ain't Deals gut wagon comes by. I wonder what's for chow?" He flicks at a digital clock illuminated with three-inch red numbers. "It ain't your grandma's cooking. Jolene, my queen, Lord, that woman could cook." He picks up the remote, but doesn't click it, seemingly lost in a reverie of Grandma's chicken and dumplings.

I linger outside. Seagulls swoop over the bay, sandpipers probe the wet sand, dripping fog shrouds the trailers in a palpable gray. The sun shines so weakly, it looks like the moon. I'm not Zoozle or Suzann, the Great Disappointment, here; I'm *honey*. Without my tongue stud and eyebrow ring, my face feels lighter, it's easier to smile, to forget about how much my life sucks. I look back into the living room. "I wish I could stay with you forever."

"Aw, honey. Today's as important as forever." Grandpa Joe smiles, closing his eyes to rest before dinner.

Today after a fifth night with not even twenty minutes of sleep, I'm sprawled, sweating, on a mildewed, bumpy love seat. The heater is pumping full blast, Grandpa Joe gets up to pee every half hour, and there's the incessant click-whoosh of his oxygen pump. My head throbs. I love my grandpa, but if he tells me one more time about his Marine platoon's beer-swilling bulldog, to hell with AA, I'll chug the Bud in the 'fridge. I would cruise some crank, but that's a step backwards in my manual, *Twelve Steps for Meth Heads*. Worse, Grandpa jokes about everything, even dying. Worst, the only thing he won't joke about is drugs.

He feels faint from low blood pressure and wobbles around. He takes longer every day to walk to the mailbox, trailing a mile of oxygen line. Right this minute, he's chatting there with his liver-lipped friend, Simon, who's chomping on a huge, wet stogie. They're wheezing, which passes for laughing when you're that old and that sick. I slap a UDubb (UW) cap on sideways, proud alum that I am. My hair gel is stickier than usual from the trailer's heat, and even the pink-tinged spikes of my short blonde 'do are drooping like meringue gone flat. I tug my sweats over my shorts because it's windy out, and the air hits my bare arms like that first dive into a wave in April. I reach for my hoodie too. I holler that I'm going to drive to the pier and walk a bit, and I'll bring back lunch and a video. Grandpa says he'll make popcorn. I'm lucky. This time, they don't break into a cough-addled chorus of "5 foot two / eyes of blue / has anybody seen my gal?" The song fits me to a *T* and makes me blush, except my eyes are brown, like dark caramel if you believe Javier, which I did for a while.

I skip down the stairs, nod to Simon, keeping my distance from his cigary embrace, and put the bill Grandpa Joe proffers into my jeans pocket. I blow them both a kiss, listening for their delighted snorts. The sun nuzzles the top of my head, as Javier used to, only sunshine feels safer.

The parking lot on Seacoast Boulevard is studded with weird plastic sculptures that someone thought would look like surfboards, but they are more like pool noodles coated in shellac. The lot isn't crowded, and I park, backing in for a quick exit.

I stroll along the pier, leaning over to watch the swells roll by, inhaling the salt air and the tar-scented planks. Wind surfers crash through the breakers and leap high off the foam into the sea.

This is where I belong. Maybe Grandpa Joe will give me his trailer to get started, when the time comes. But I can't think about living in a world without my Grandpa Joe. He's like the sun shining into the cave where I've been living.

Grandpa has had two attacks this summer before I got here, and when there's another one, the hospice—not the hospital—the *hospice* says he has to come in there for what they call palliative care, to die. That's pretty harsh.

Port Townsend is beautiful, but nothing important ties me there, just the job next semester, with strings attached to sobriety. Javier moved on to Gonzaga in Spokane. I don't need him back anyway.

I walk along the beach and dig a pit in the sand to use as a backrest, a trick Grandpa Joe taught me when I was about three. I doze. The aloe of pickle weed drifts into my dream. I was a happy kid, before my dad died, before my mom and I went to war with one another, before all that other stuff happened that Penny preaches about my pushing past.

I jerk awake as the tide rolls in, cold water touching my toes. Hot and sandy, I glance at my watch, knowing Grandpa Joe is already frantic for his lunch and movie. The VW's motor is balky, as it always seems to be when I'm in a hurry. I don't want to flood the engine, so I take some time, relax my shoulders, and try to avoid grinding the starter. No luck. A cluster of tanned, long-haired surfers is leaning against the lifeguard tower. They watch me struggling and a muscle-toned old guy calls out, "Hey, need a push start?" The younger ones laugh and thrust their hips like MTV dancers. The old guy is about Grandpa's age, with a grizzly white beard and deep creases of tan.

"Dude, thanks!" I get out and together we push the car towards the driveway's incline. I jump in, slide the gear into second, and surfers one and two put their shoulders into the effort. The VW hops to life, and I wave out the back window. My car sputters into the intersection of Seacoast and Evergreen, and a driver turning left blares his horn at me. I double salute him. The surfers laugh like crazy. I head on down a block past the trailer park. Not wanting to chance another stall, I leave the car idling, and run in to the video store, where I rush to the classics shelf and grab *The Blackboard Jungle* and *The Big Heat*, starring Glenn Ford. I'll point out Grandpa's resemblance and make his day.

Fifty minutes of freedom have aroused my endorphins. I picture them rising from my scalp into the sky like visible notes from the concerto I'm humming. I hear distant sirens, probably some bicyclist hit on the Strand. The sound diminishes, heading north. My phone rings, and I panic about Grandpa. It's Mel. I should have sworn off talking to her, like I've sworn off meth. That Whidbey doctor said a new staph infection could go straight to my heart.

I need to get a new phone, dump this one and dump Mel. Stupid that I called her and told her to come here. I let my voicemail take the message, putting her off. Maybe she doesn't even remember that I asked her here. I feel too good right now to feel bad.

At the drive-through of KFC, a giggling teen takes my order. She is pushing her bangs back under her cap when I drive up to pay. "It's my first day on this job, and you're my first customer!" she laughs.

"Really?" I smile back at her, weighing a couple of sarcastic remarks, one against the other, dump them both in a brain file for later use. "You're doing great. And you look very nice in that hat." I lie. It's fun to be nice. The KFC order takes just a minute to fill, and I start back up the street. My phone rings again, Mel again, like a sand flea stuck under the leg binding of my bathing suit. I switch the phone to off.

When I turn the corner back into the trailer park, Simon is standing with two neighbors outside his trailer. He reaches out to me with one hand, keeping the other on his walker.

"Suzann, your grandpa. Joe had an argument with a skinny girl. We went inside to get away from her, and he had another heart episode. His defibrillator went off. That girl, she wasn't making sense, talking about meeting at the zoo. I called 911, and Mitch. But I didn't have your number," Simon pants.

"She was skinny? Dark hair? Oh God!" I grab a bar of Simon's walker for support. "Where'd they take my grandpa?"

"The ambulance guys said the hospice center. That's where Joe told them." Simon drags a long hand over his veined face, his bulbous nose made redder with exertion. I rush ahead into the trailer, and Simon follows.

"Where's the hospice?" My voice rises an octave.

Simon shakes his head. "Some place near downtown." Simon inches his way out, looking disgusted.

Inside, an iron skillet rests like a tumbled tombstone on the kitchen's linoleum floor surrounded by kernels of unpopped popcorn spilled like bird feed. God damn me! My stupid walk, my stupid car, my stupid movies. A paper taped by Grandpa Joe's phone has the hospice center number along with Mitch's and Art's. I call them, but both phones lapse into their answering machines. God, where is everybody? Why wasn't I here? The smell of the chicken makes me nauseated. I jump up, take the KFC boxes out to the trash bin, come in, call the hospice line. I'm on auto-pilot, staring at the once-familiar room. I throw myself into Grandpa's chair. How is he? Where is he?

Is Mel around here? I peek out the window. I swear if I see her, I'll kill her.

After a few rings and transfers, some guy, Derrick or Eric or Fariq, answers. "My grandfather, Joe Franklin, he should be there. Some time in the last hour?" I try to walk to the door with the phone, before a tug reminds me it's a land line. The phone teeters on the end table, and I push it back. "What's his condition?"

The guy says he just heard from the ambulance crew that they're still en route and it's too early to know, something about the hospice is always open, no limits on visiting hours. I'm about to reply, when Grandpa's brother appears at the door. He's taller and younger than Grandpa Joe, a reminder of what Joe once was. He walks in without knocking and waves to me as I hang up. "Hey, Suzann! I thought we could go to lunch."

"Mitch. I called you. Grandpa's not here. He was with Simon, they were playing dominos, and he said for me to get lunch, and when I got back, he'd been taken to the hospice center. By ambulance." My words tumble out so fast that I'm buried in the wordslide. Mitch looks first bewildered, then defeated.

Tears well up in his blue eyes, so much like Grandpa's eyes except the color's not faded away. He begins sweeping the kitchen, putting the skillet back in the cupboard. He straightens up slowly, as if his back aches. "We knew it was coming. Are you okay?"

"No." I turn away so he won't try to hug me.

"I'm going over there. Coming with me?"

I hesitate, deciding if I should go see Grandpa or stay and face off with Mel. I shake my head. I cross my arms and hold myself together. "Pretty soon, Uncle Mitch. I'd better wash the sand off my feet and change clothes. Tell Grandpa Joe I love him."

He says, "Call your mom. I'll handle Winona, Art, and Bill." He doesn't know about Mel, me and my druggie friends, my brilliant ideas, my fault, my fault, my fault.

I collapse on the porch. The trailer is footsteps from the bay shore and just twenty yards across the peninsula to the ocean. Years back during winter storms, breakers roared across the highway to the bay, crashing through the man-made berms of protective sand.

Smacking my code into my cell, I listen to Mel's messages. She has arrived in San Diego by air because Big Daddy thought she could make a buy in Tijuana, and we could drive it up to him. She hopped the trolley to Hollister and Palm, about five miles from here. The second message is garbled and hysterical. She says she'll see me after a tour of TJ. I can picture her running away, leaving my grandpa breathless and panting for help before the crowd gathered at Grandpa Joe's place.

I've already reconnoitered Grandpa's medicine cabinet, so I know what goodies await behind Door #3, and I head for the bathroom. There's not much: a giant bottle of Tums, a straight razor, and after shave. Old Spice. Javier's scent. Up high, a bottle of Percocet, prescribed for my Uncle Mitch.

With Grandpa's razor, I cut two teensy strokes across my inner thighs. Relief floods in as blood trickles down. I haven't cut since I started seeing Penny, earning a gold star. I like Penny, but what's she know about being me? I pat tissues on the clotting cuts. To postpone the pull of the Percocet, I flop face-first into the bath mat. The mat's entwined colors, rose and crystalline, splash my memory. Once, I pranced through my first solo recital in a frothy rose tutu. Me at nine. Sixteen years ago.

I pat my bony chest, etching its heart tattoo with my ragged thumb nail. God, me and Melody shared some laughs in those first crazy days together, "Zooz, pass the Grey Poupon!" And then the crashing, crushing rush of meth zooming like a propellant through my veins, making me invulnerable, invincible. Maybe I do need Mel's presence, her knowledge about the real me.

My mother won't be any help, she'll freak out, blame me, even if she doesn't know about Mel, which she will if Simon shoots off his mouth as usual.

Mom still ignores my new name, Zoozle. *Zoozle* sounds hip, sexy, alert, alive. Zoozle Zimmerman! Mel was calling me Suzanne, then Zuzann, then Zuz, and we both said *Zoozle* at the same time. Goodbye perfect, boring, insipid Suzann, formerly Suzie Q. Suzann Marie Zimmerman-Quintanilla. That's me. Or used to be until I exchanged the hurt child for the daredevil, laughing Zoozle.

I sit up, skimming the rough ridges along my ankles, peeking at the new cuts. Needle scars compete with self-inflicted razor lines: these from the lows of my messed-up marriage to Javier, those from the highs of meth to blur the divorce proceedings.

Muscle memory floats my arms up into ballet's fifth position. There's a puckered crater under my left biceps where the surgeon excised a staph infection from dirty needles. Chi-rist, he took a chunk out of there.

They said there would be bumps on the rehab road. Here's to bumps. I pop two Percocet and crash on Grandpa's bed. He's never coming home. I have phone calls to make, Mom, Mel to tell her to just go back to Washington. I can't deal with either of them right now, and why should I?

I should get over to the hospice. Except first, I need a little rest.

It's about 5, evidently a.m. God, my whole head is pulsating like some parasite is burrowing its way from my left temple through to the right. I start to call out, "Javier?" when it comes to me that I'm in Grandpa Joe's bed.

Grandpa Joe isn't here. He's not on the porch. He's not at Simon's. I start to pull at my hair because now I remember. He's at the hospice center. I need to get there. I slip into Grandpa's tiny little shower, using his sliver of soap that smells like childhood vacations, no exotic citrus scents or phony spices, just plain soapiness. I throw yesterday's sweats on. Forget the gel for the hairdo. My mom has certainly arrived and will be rampaging at me no matter how I look so why waste time trying to please the unpleasable?

There are OJ cartons in the fridge, those little eight-ounce ones. I take a couple of extra strength aspirin, because that's what I need, extra strength, and shamble to the car, trying to memorize the directions. I should call first to make sure he's still alive, but I'm too chicken.

I navigate there in less than twenty minutes since it's out by SDSU where I had a wild weekend or two during college. Not seeing my mom's car in the parking lot lifts my spirits. At the reception desk, I sign in, and an angular woman in a business suit gives me directions to my Grandpa's room.

They wouldn't give me his room number if he had died, would they? I rub the tight pain in my left chest.

The corridors are painted a sunset orange. I pass doors that open onto a grassy children's play yard complete with a red plastic playhouse and a swing set. At the end of the south corridor, I turn left to the open door of my grandfather's high-domed room. Floor-to-ceiling windows overlook a steep, chaparral-covered hillside. The pungent mesquite outside drifts in through the open, screened patio door. The hospice feels inviting, not stinking of cigarette smoke and b.o. as my rehab hospitals did.

No machines clutter the room-- no heart monitor, only the oxygen lines. The oxygen is turned to peak capacity. Grandpa Joe is propped up in his bed, chatting with a statuesque black nurse's aide. *Chloris Ikemefema*, her i.d. tag says. She reminds me of an aging Nubian queen from *King Solomon's Mines*, except for her hands, which are large and strong.

"Now, Mr. Franklin, how'd that bath feel to you this morning?" Her voice is low and mellow, like a jazz singer's.

"I'm a new man." Grandpa Joe winks at her.

"You can have a bath any time of day. And don't you let any of those other aides come give it, ok? You're some man, Mr. Franklin," Chloris flirts, the fuchsia moons of her earrings clicking as she shakes her head. She has crooked teeth, but her smile is shining.

Grandpa Joe wheezes a laugh. "You do a good job. But next time, I'll take care of my privates." Grandpa Joe waves me in. "Hi honey. This is Chloris. She's in love with me."

"Yes, sir, I sure am. Good morning to you, young lady. You share Mr. Franklin's good looks!" says Chloris. She wheels her cart from the bathroom, doing a cha cha step as she backs out of the room in a whirl of red hibiscus print.

I lean in to hug my grandpa. He has been shaved and wears his favorite, thread-bare flannel pajamas.

"Ain't this place something? I was afraid to come, but I like it here. It's better than a fancy hotel—it's free."

"Well, that's good. How's the food?" What else can we talk about in a place where he has come to die?

"We can order anything we want anytime. It's chicken and dumplings for lunch."

I shake my head and pull a leather chair closer to the bed. "Who else is coming today?"

"If there is a God, Winona won't come. My sister is losing some brains every day. Whew. . . I wish she had my mind or I had her lungs. Anyway, Art and Mitch will come. Your mom called, and she'll get here. Traffic." He sighs.

Grandpa Joe rumbles a belch and pats his taut stomach. "Could you bring me my enema bag from the trailer tomorrow, honey? I like it better than the ones they use at any hospitals. Whoo, I need some relief soon."

Anxious to help, I jump to my feet. "I'll go tell the nurse right now."

"I don't want to be Lester the Pester."

"Let me ask."

At the nurse's station across the hall from Grandpa Joe's room, Chloris is rearranging supplies for her cart. The nurse glances up from a chart he is updating. His shiny black hair, chopped into bangs and a bowl cut, fringes a friendly round face. Noting his muscled arms, I think of the guys who paddled our tourist catamaran in Waikiki when I was ten.

"How can I help you?" he asks.

"I'm Mr. Franklin's granddaughter, Suzann." The name *Suzann* feels like a glutinous mass in my mouth. "My friends call me Zoozle," I add quietly.

He points to his name tag. "Eric Puhalo."

"My grandpa says he needs an enema." My cheeks mottle with hot spots of embarrassment.

"Sure." He looks as if he wants to say something else to me, but turns to cabinets behind him. "Why don't you wait in the lounge for about twenty minutes?" He points across the hall.

At the hospitality center, I pour a coffee and flip through the DVD's and CD's in the racks, reading the credits, admiring the covers before choosing Glenn Miller's music and Clint Eastwood in *The Unforgiven*.

As I return to the room, Eric is leaving, chuckling. Grandpa Joe sucks on an antacid, smiling as if he'd pulled a fast one in school. "Whew. Better!" he confides.

I divert him before he provides the minute details of the enema. "Do you want to watch a movie or listen to music, Grandpa?"

"Nah. Last night they were playing some chinky chant with bells. It made me ding-y. I told them to shut it off."

"It's supposed be soothing." I lick my dry lips, change the subject. "Eric seems like a good nurse, huh, Grandpa?"

"Since Korea, I haven't talked to many Chinamen. I like him. And that Chloris is my kind of woman. She could make a dead man laugh."

Tears flood my eyes. Grabbing a tissue out of my pocket, I walk over to look out the door.

"Did you clean up the kitchen, honey? I dropped that pan. The doctor said I should've known not to lift something so heavy." He closes his eyes against such foolishness. "A frying pan ain't heavy."

"Mitch and I did clean up. Simon, um, he said something about a girl?"

"I don't remember nothing except I was fixin' the popcorn and then bam, I was on the floor." He looks around the room, out the doors at the hills. "Next time when you come, honey, bring my notebook from the drawer, would you? The one with all my plans and papers?"

"Let's call Mitch to bring it."

"He never answers his phone. On Friday, the ambulance guys had a heck of a time reaching him." He reaches to itch his shoulder. "Could you scratch my back a minute?"

He smiles and relaxes as I rub his shoulders and back. My fingernails are ragged, and I don't want to pinch his skin with them. We are quiet together. I read the book I have in my backpack, *The Confessions of Nat Turner* by Styron. My mom sent it with me when I had so much time at Bella Vista between sessions with the doctor and my group. I'll try to finish it while Grandpa Joe sleeps.

Eric steps in now and then to check on things. He tells me, "Your grandfather cracks me up with stories about the Marines. He said he would've ended up in jail if he hadn't met Janie after the war."

"Yeah. They were a perfect couple." I tamp down the emotion that edges into my voice.

Mitch and Art arrive. Mitch gives me a long look, and I think he's going to call me derelict in my duties after not coming here yesterday, but he just kind of tilts his head in an absent-minded way and takes a chair on the other side of the bed from me. He leans his face into his hands. Art, my youngest uncle, slouches his lean frame silently by the windows facing the hillside. He is recently divorced and more taciturn than ever.

We make some small talk, but mostly we watch Grandpa Joe. He rouses himself when a squad of doctors marches in and lines up. They

introduce themselves, all five of them, and one, Dr. Sanjit, asks Grandpa
if he gives his permission for his defibrillator to be turned off. He does
(what choice does he have? He can't stay in the hospice if he doesn't).
Dr. Sanjit is very solemn, about thirty, but already gray at his temples. He
de-magnetizes the device. Another heart episode, and Grandpa Joe will
be gone.

Before noon, Winona peeks into the room. She's dressed in a
baggy red-plaid corduroy jumper. She bustles in, a Bible protruding from
her pink paisleyed carry-all sharing space with her blond bichon-poodle,
Poochie. The dog wears a patient, resigned expression. Winona absent-
mindedly rubs his fur the wrong way.

Grandpa Joe reaches out to the dog. Winona drops Poochie on
the bed where Grandpa Joe can pat him, and she opens her Bible to
Revelation. I don't feel like hearing a sermon. I grab Poochie when
Grandpa's hand quits stroking his silky fur and take the dog for a walk
out on the children's patio. Poochie is a hit with a bald kid in a
wheelchair and his tired, valiant parents thank us for stopping. Poochie
smiles for his admirers. His two top front teeth are crossed, making him
look even more like a mop-haired little kid in a fur suit, one who needs
braces.

We wander past the parking lot and down a brick staircase into a
eucalyptus glen where it is shady and cool. Chloris is sitting on a bench
swing, her muscled arms tracing Tai Chi movements. Poochie runs
straight to her. His front paws snag in her sock. As Chloris reaches
down to disentangle him, she flings her shoes and socks off, and her
honeyed laughter surrounds us. She seems to smell of eucalyptus.

In the dappled grove, her shorn lamb's wool gray hair contrasts with the ebony of her skin, a chiaroscuro print come alive.

"*Soodhawoow.* Somali for welcome," she says. "Lord, my feet ache. You caught me, how do you say, taking a load off?" She rubs her long toes; her nails glint with metallic gold nail polish. Poochie wanders off, sniffing.

"My feet ache all the time too." I point to the bunions on my big toes. "Dancer's feet. Gross, huh?"

"They're beautiful. You're Suzann?"

"Yeah, Suzann to the family. I prefer Zoozle."

"I love that sassy name! Zoozle! Well, Zoozle, dear, you call on me if I can help you or your Grandpa in any way in the next little bit."

"Little bit?"

"*Little bit* can mean a few weeks. Most of our patients are here less than a month." Chloris takes my hand and rubs my cold fingers. She seems to smell of eucalyptus and cinnamon.

I had thought Grandpa would be here for six months or so. My stomach clutches; my heart hurts. "How can time run out so fast?" I squeeze her hand. "How can you work here when people die all around you and you know that's going to happen every single day?" I feel fragile in a new way, as if my body's nerve-endings are exposed to cold air.

"It's part of life. Your grandpa accepts that. And I do too." She's quiet a minute. "That doesn't make it any easier for you, does it? But he's very much at peace with this."

"It's not fair." I am thinking it's not fair for me to lose the only one who believes in me. It's not fair because Grandpa Joe brings joy to every day. What kind of family will we have when he's gone?

"Maybe it is fair. Maybe it's best. We don't know." Chloris reaches her arms towards the treetops. "What's fair is that we've got this day."

"I feel like I should stay here 24/7. But I'm so tired."

"You have to take care of you, too. The dying need time to themselves. They need time to think and remember, not family noise constantly. It's right not to be here all of each day."

Slipping her socks and loafers on, she rocks the swing, and we sway another minute in the quiet, the freeway a white noise behind us.

"Gotta go." Chloris lifts into a stretch, up, up, up towards the sunbeams. "Take care, Zoozle."

Returning with my mind playing idea tag, I deposit Poochie on the couch where Winona has settled. She's still mouthing Bible verses. Mitch sits forward closest to the bed. My stomach flips as I fear again he might question me about Mel and my not showing up yesterday, but he doesn't. My failure seems worse now with what Chloris said about Grandpa's short time left.

I kiss my grandpa and tell him I'll be back later. He gives me a wink and says, "Don't forget the stuff we talked about." He likes to create secrets.

Outside, a breeze blows fresh and shea-butter soft. San Diego is beautiful. I hope Heaven is just like here.

I'm feeling better when a horn beeps, and I jump out of my skin as if I've stepped on a snake. It was only a tentative tap, but it broke my mood. Dr. Huizenga says I have a typically high startle reflex from my PTSD and borderline diagnosis.

The doctor must be right. My mother has arrived, and without a doubt, I'm dead meat.

CHAPTER 6: JOLENE

As I swing to the backseat to pick up my purse, who appears behind my car? Suzann. I tap the horn, and she jerks as if I had used a cattle prod. I don't like seeing her react like a jumpy druggie, especially not here and especially not now, after the hours I've endured since yesterday.

"Where were you?" she asks me.

This is what I do not tell her about the past twenty-six hours and why I am only now arriving.

Mitch called. I will not allow myself to cry. I have to act, stay in motion, get things ready. I should have had a suitcase packed, lesson plans in place, but I had been refusing to accept that this day would come so fast.

All I wanted after school was a little time for my yoga and maybe some *gobi alou*. Instead I got the phone call. Daddy in the hospital. Where's my darling daughter when she should have been with him? Probably drunk in Tijuana.

I type in hyper-gear, the first week's worth of lesson plans, contacting my favorite sub, Jim Dowd, who doesn't get into fights with the kids and can make them do their work even if he won't grade it. He emailed that I could drop the lesson packet off at his house near the school, but I'd rather be alone, not deal with all that sympathy. I'll trudge all this junk over to my classroom. Books are flung open all over my den,

I'm sifting through files on the computer and in my cabinets, trying to get hard copies for Mr. Dowd to run off. I rummage through the videos. Thank God for videos on sub days. My own collection assures that I don't have to fight with the library. I choose a Romantics biography (boring! Make them take notes) and a documentary on the way *Frankenstein* has been used through the years. You do what you have to do in these situations. AP kids are equal parts delight and curse. With the sub, he'll think they are a delight while letting their cursed texting and god knows what else slip right past him. I think cellular phones are going to be the last straw when I do my plus-and-minus list of taking early retirement or not.

I race back to the school, annoyed by the traffic build up in the subdivision. I never go there during peak traffic hours. Maybe the traffic mess is why the parents are so crabby when they talk to me. It is eerie being here after hours; I usually arrive early but leave the minute the bell rings or even earlier, since my last period prep gives me an excuse to be off campus. I go over everything on my desk. There is no way Mr. Dowd could miss what he needs to do with which class and when. If I stay longer with Daddy, I'll send e-lessons.

I hurry home to pack, trying not to think that this is it, the last step for Daddy. He has been failing, but this is the end. He accepts the end with such dignity, even with a laugh.

I Google the directions to the hospice and try to reach Suzann on her cell. No answer. I call Dad's trailer. No answer.

Mitch answers at the hospice room and tells me the situation is under control. Wait for morning, he suggests. Daddy is sleeping peacefully.

I go to bed early, set the alarm for 4 a.m., and begin the hour's trip by 4:30.

Traffic slows, then stops. I put on satellite radio and try to relax. My yoga chants are not working.

The red freeway signs announce a road closure where the interstate narrows and Pacific Coast Highway ends. Local radio reports that some idiot wants to jump off the overpass after a bank robbery. CHP has everything cordoned off. I wish I could get out and drop kick the guy off the bridge.

Traffic is stacked up, people are out of their cars talking to one another, and no one can move. Of course, I hadn't checked the traffic report before we stopped when I still had an option to take another route. We sit. And sit. And sit.

Too much time to think of the ocean glistening off to the west, of summers helping my mom by babysitting my baby brother on summer afternoons so she could work part time. Usually, Art napped. I was ten. At thirteen, I took care of that three-year old for an entire week, day and night, when my parents had to go out of town. My dad didn't think it was a good idea, but my mom said I could handle it. They didn't ask me what I thought. An image of Art surges from my memory unbidden, how he clung to me with his sticky hands at the screen door while I watched my girlfriends parade by to the beach, with their towels and beach bags, a pack of boys flirting with them. Bill was supposed to help out since Winona was at a church camp retreat. Bill was older, but he didn't. He had a great time, working and surfing and out half the night. It was a nightmare week that changed my attitude about being a parent, being in charge.

And I'm about to enter a different nightmare. Will my family be there to support me or will they keep their distance? They wrapped themselves in silence when Mom died. None of us dealt with that very well.

Traffic still isn't moving. An old guy in a convertible travels with a black dog in the passenger seat. I smile, thinking of dear Mr. McKillop and his dog—Jack? Jake? Jacques, oh, my brain. I wish I could have spent time in Seattle with someone besides Suzann or with Suzann without her problems. Those days passed long ago.

In their dented-up van a group of surfers turns their radio up, and hands begin pumping to the beat. I had always wanted to go on a surfin' safari with the Beach Boys singing about California girls, but I was helping Mom, or working, or taking summer classes to get ahead in credits.

When Suzann was little, we didn't take enough time for beach days. It was always dance, dance, dance... competitions, lessons, practices. . . for what? We should have spent more time on the beach. We should have spent more time with my parents. Now there is no time, and now there is no Suzann, not the one I raised.

A horn blares again, and I grit my teeth, my reverie vanishing into the concrete and metal stretched out in front of me. The surfers start calling across to the punkers honking their horn. Farm workers in the back of the pickup in front of me cat call in Spanish, laughing and punching one another in the ribs.

Someone pitches a watermelon out of the surfer van. Splat, it hits the punkermobile, and the punkers duck. They come up soon, lofting white balls. One hits my car—white bread smushed into golf ball-sized ammunition. All around me, people either bob low in their cars or join the food fight. Before I think to roll my window up, a tomato, not quite ripe or squishy, sails through the window and bounces off the steering wheel into my lap. I throw it with the strength of anger, and it whaps off the high-back seat of the guy in the convertible. The driver raises the top to his car, walks around to the dog's side and leashes the dog up. The dog wags his big tail, and now that they face me, I can see it actually is Mr. McKillop and Jacques. With the appearance of the dog, a truce breaks out. The surfers and the punkers get out of their cars to talk to Mr. McKillop and to pet Jacques.

Embarrassed about the tomato, I slink down on my seat. I'll call later to apologize. But he catches my eye and approaches me. I lower the window.

"Your smile is a welcome relief from all of this, Mrs. Zimmerman. We meet under the most unlikely circumstances!" Phillip sweeps off his golf cap and extends his hand. Jacques puts his paws up on my car window.

"I can't believe it's you." My cheeks are burning.

"We're on our way to the Guardian Angels convention. Just our luck to be nearly to our destination and endure this stoppage. What on earth?" Mr. McKillop puts his golf cap back on his head.

"We have to wait for a police escort through the area. It's a mess, and I'm in a hurry." I explain to him briefly about Daddy, tell him the name of the hospice, avoid mentioning Suzann.

"Why not come out and smell the breeze with us?"

"Let me make a couple phone calls first."

"Certainly." He walks back towards his car with Jacques.

I call Mitch, already at the hospice and talk to Daddy. Dad laughs about the traffic.

"Here I am fighting for one more day and this guy wants to croak? Ain't it always like that?" He sounds tired. "That makes me think of Winona. Boy, she's not as sharp as she used to be."

"Daddy, I'll get there as soon as I can. I think they're going to start leading some escorted groups off the freeway, if the traffic reports are right."

"That's good, Joleney, honey."

"Is Suzann there?" I ask.

But Mitch has taken the phone back. He says Joe is drowsy again. Mitch is anxious for me to get there. While I am on the phone, a first group of ten cars is escorted off the freeway. I wave goodbye to Mr. McKillop and Jacques. He waves as if he were saying, "Cheerio!"

After another forty-five minutes of sitting and several more traffic breaks that didn't include me, the traffic is released, like minnows pouring into a lake from a tight channel. The freedom pulses through my foot to the gas pedal though I slow as I pass a CHP patrolman.

He follows me for half a mile, and just as I think I am in the clear, his red-yellow flashers blink. Breathing deeply, I wait. My heart pounds. Traffic slows. Drivers ogle.

The cop takes off his sunglasses as I lower the window, my hands still on the wheel at the proper ten and two angle. The bones in my knuckles stick out in white ridge lines.

"Good morning. License, please."

I fumble for my wallet, my hands shaking.

"Do you know the speed limit?" he asks. His face is square and tanned and young. He has the manners of a well-trained school boy, catching me off guard.

"Yes."

"And you were going how fast?"

"80."

"Why were you knowingly breaking the law, ma'am?"

"Do you really want to hear my story?" I have had enough tickets in my life to know a story has never once done any good.

"Sure." He looks at my license, types into his computer, and returns to lean against the car. I have my insurance card and my car registration ready too.

Telling him the story of my dad's hospice stay, I keep it simple. I acknowledge my fault and wait for the ticket.

He asks me for the address of the hospice, and I show him my map. He returns my documents and puts both hands on the window's edge.

"Ma'am, it won't do your family any good to lose you too in an accident. I'm going to skip the ticket this time. Please drive safely." He salutes and returns to his cycle, waiting to see that I can merge safely into traffic.

"Thank you, sir," I say, and then repeat to myself over and over. And for some reason, I think of my mom, and I thank her too. She must have been watching over me. Easing the car into traffic, I drive as if an electric shock would pop me a jolt if I ease past the speed limit. After a few miles, the officer exits near Sea World and the Hilton.

I finally make the switch to Highway 395 and into San Diego's Balboa Park and Hillcrest district. It is quiet on the streets. A homeless guy limps through the picnic grounds, a place my cousins and I used to lunch when we went to the zoo all day. The scent of eucalyptus hits me hard and I begin to cry, for all the losses of the past few years, for my mom, for my daughter, for my dad.

Turning onto University, I try to read my printed directions, but I cannot drive and read. Which way? I park at the drug store, not wanting to stop. I turn the car around and go west a few blocks to Third Street, inconveniently one-way, necessitating an extra turn down a narrow street with cars parked hood-to-trunk with little room to maneuver.

I miss a stop sign. I slam on the brakes. A red-faced man is gesturing foully at me. All I can do is shake my head and mouth the word, "Sorry." God, so many people are so rude.

I find the hospice then, right on the end of the street as Mitch had told me. Did the architect have a sense of irony in his perfect imagery, the dead-end street? Approaching the cul de sac at the front, I pass up the parking lot where the cars are stacked bumper to bumper. I don't like my car caged in any more than I like that trapped feeling for myself.

Further away, I drive around twice before spotting a place I can navigate this car into. The next car I get is going to be small and maneuverable. I turn off the ignition, check myself quickly in the mirror, smooth my hair back, and tell myself that this is the way life has to be. And then I see my daughter. I ready myself for a secondary battle. Why am I overwhelmed in this role as her mother?

CHAPTER 7: ZOOZLE

My feet turn my reluctant body even though I'd rather follow my heart, jump into the VW, gun it and drive south, like to TJ for tequila shooters. I would swallow the worm with more enthusiasm than talk to Mommy Dearest right now.

Mom slams her car door, reaching out to hug me half-heartedly. She's never been into hugs, so her Anne Klein perfume ratchets up my emotions, and I wish I could just collapse and let her carry me off to a warm bed, as I've seen T.V. moms do with their baby girls. I begin, "Where have you been, Mom? Listen, about yesterday," but she cuts me off with a curt "Not now."

I pull back, stand up straight, daring her to say one word about how I'm dressed or about my hair or my missing eyebrow ring. Like she should talk with her blond hair all scraggly in a pygmy-sized ponytail. She's got on gray slacks that are baggy in the butt and a gold UCLA sweatshirt, rather than her schoolmarm uniform of blouse, v-neck sweater, and jeans. She owns about 150 of those teacher outfits. She sets her alarm pre-dawn as a rule, but today must have been even earlier to drop off lesson plans for the coming week at school. She drives me crazy, but even I admire her ability to organize and get a job done. Her students write her grateful emails from college. Every single one of them is forwarded to me with a happy face and the header, "Isn't this nice?"

I snap back when she clears her throat. Pale with worry about Grandpa, she's asking me to go in with her. It's a little weird coming back in when I left a minute ago. Eric raises one eyebrow when he catches my glance, and mouths "Your mom?" Wrinkling my forehead in pain, I make Grandpa Joe's hex sign behind her back, infuriated that I'm still so obviously her mini-me, a genetic fact that once felt like a merit badge. Now her presence turns me into such a brat.

Mitch is helping Grandpa with an early lunch. Lying back against his pillows, Grandpa has eaten about half a bite of dumpling.

Winona is on her knees in the corner, invoking Christ's love to save sinners. Poochie sits facing her, his head cocked to one side.

When Mom hugs her dad, his smile lights up even though his eyes are closed. He knows her special scent too. He whispers, "Joleney, honey, I'm glad you're here." His eyelids flutter open.

She launches into some story about the freeway. I take Poochie back to the eucalyptus glen where we can chill. I draw my legs up onto the swing and watch Poochie, wishing I had a ball to throw to him. He has found an empty potato chip bag that he's wrestling with. After about forty-five minutes, I pick him up, rub his round belly, and walk back to the room where Grandpa Joe is snoring, Mitch has gone home, and my mom is staring out the patio door. She doesn't turn when I come in, but Poochie noses her ankles and she seems to shake herself awake. She offers lunch out. Winona refuses our invitation, probably thinking she's earning martyr points.

I tell Eric we're going out to grab a bite in case Grandpa asks where everybody went.

My mom has years of experience in lie detecting with me, so this is going to be a tough one to pull off. It's hard to breathe, the air between us is so thick with question marks. I wish we could sit on a bench or go back to the eucalyptus glade and cry our guts out in equal grief. But she would want to prove she's losing more than me, that my grief pales in comparison to hers and my grief wouldn't count at all. Nothing I do counts in comparison to my mom, unless it's mess up because God knows she's perfect herself. I even heard her tell Grandpa Joe way back when that she was a perfect child. He smiled that smile of his, and it made me giggle, but then I forgot to ask him about Mom's mischief.

Today it's better to stick to other subjects even if my heart is wrapped in chains.

My stomach growls, and we set off.

Reticence tightens between us all the way from the hospice to the deli, two blocks south and two blocks east. Though she is barely taller than I am and has the morals of a Victorian, her brisk pace tests my endurance, and only pride keeps me from whining, "Mom, wait up!" the litany of my childhood. A glimmer of a memory, my dad holding one hand, my mom the other, stops me in my tracks. After my dad died, Mom was always hurrying away from me, as if checking things off on her day planner was her mission in life. Until Javier and then Mel, I walked alone or behind my mom, trying to catch up.

She crosses a street just as the light changes, stranding me on the opposite curb. Tapping her watch with one finger and beating on the walk button with the other hand, she makes no effort to mask her impatience. Naughty, slothful me to have missed the light. On green, I trot across. Jesus, could she treat me better now and then?

The forced march ends at the deli's door. At this post-lunch hour, it is nearly empty, with a foursome of college girls in one booth, their books and lap tops open with barely room enough on the table for their veggie plates. Two of them are holding hands; my heart squeezes with jealousy at their carefree happiness. A gangly man-boy lounges at the counter, circling ads in the newspaper, talking on a cell phone and twirling a straw in something green and frothy. His suit is too short in the sleeves and pant cuffs.

We seat ourselves in a pillowy red naugahyde booth right by the window under a sign painted on the glass in fat yellow letters that spell HOT PASTRAMI backwards from my view. My mom swallows and purses her lips for a yoga breath. I gulp the iced water the bus boy brings and sit back to savor the deli aroma of coffee, bacon, and chicken soup.

Our bald waiter is five foot-sixish. He's not attractive, but he seems to think he's pretty cool from the tone of his cocky greeting, "Hello, ladies!" Curly, strawberry blond hair squirrels out of his unbuttoned blue denim shirt.

I want to say, "Can it, fool," but instead I order, looking down at the menu. "I'll have the spinach salad, dressing on the side. And a whole wheat bagel."

"A grilled cheese sandwich and fries for me and a chocolate malt to go," says my mom.

"Nice nutrition, Mom." She doesn't react.

The waiter nods and saunters off, arching his neck like a stallion as he pauses to flirt a little with the unpaired college girls. Mom starts again, "Daddy loves his chocolate malts," but tears lace down her cheeks, and she shuts up.

I gaze out the window. "Look at the traffic. Hillcrest is such a congested neighborhood. You wouldn't think that from the hospice rooms, would you, with the canyon and all? Grandpa saw quail there this morning."

My mom wipes her eyes and straightens her shoulders.

I suck my upper lip and turn it under to chew on. "I finished that Nat Turner book by what's his name. Oh, yeah, Styron, William Styron. It was cool." I'm ready to give a full book report if asked.

She doesn't react and instead hits her opening gambit. "Suzann, I wish you were more considerate. Not hearing from you about Daddy's condition. . . ," she looks out the window as if one of the homeless guys could supply the appropriate words. "If Mitch hadn't reached me, well, what if he trusted that you had made the call like you told him you would? What's wrong with you, Suzann?"

"Would you please, please, please, call me Zoozle?"

She looks at me, more tired than I've ever seen her with purple hollows below her eyes. She announces in a flat voice, "I don't have a daughter named Zoozle, a pathetic, unemployed drug addict. I have a very successful daughter named Suzann. And she doesn't have pink hair."

"Guys like a little pink, Mom." The crude remark goes right over her head. I don't want her commentary on my choices. I crack my knuckles, a habit my mom hates, and wait a beat. "Never mind, whatever."

I make an accordion of my straw cover. "You know you hate for me to call you at school. Was I supposed to leave a message with the secretary? Considering that you unplug your classroom phone during class and all?"

She grits her teeth. The rant begins. "Why not? Call Dorrie? Bill and I both needed to know. This is life and death, not just some breakdown of your car, or you're worried about waiting at the airport because of a flight delay. You should have called me the minute you knew it was an emergency. The important thing is, what I need to know is, why did you even leave him alone?" It has taken her almost an hour to get to the only question matters.

"How many times do I have to tell you?" I ask as if we've discussed this a hundred times. My voice pitches into a shrillness I don't like. Mom looks around to see if others have noticed. "He wasn't alone. Simon was with him. He was fine. He told me to go get a movie. God, Mom, why do you always blame me for every single bad thing that happens?" I glance around the restaurant, relieved to see our waiter with our food headed our way. Mom shuts up if there's an audience so that we can masquerade as the Brady Bunch.

I throw in another wisecrack. "If you'd learn to retrieve your voice mail on your cell phone, I could've left the message on that. It's not exactly hard to get your voice mail messages. I heard the Washington Zoo taught orangutans to do it."

Our waiter hears only "orangutans do it" and starts singing in a ridiculous falsetto, "Birds do it / Bees do it" as he sets our plates in front of us. Mom flashes a smile at him. I could hug this guy for the comic relief, except he might take it as flirting.

After he sidles back to the counter, Mom and I eat with no further attempts at self-improvement. It's not a comfortable silence where you just feel in harmony with one another and the world, but the tense kind that echoes in your head like practicing leaps and landings without music in an empty studio.

She polishes off the grilled cheese sandwich and about half the fries. My head is beginning to ache again, and I ask Mom for aspirin. She looks at me with exasperation, her eyes sparking anger. She hands over the aspirin, clearly relieved that I'm not asking for oxy or something.

It's time to finish the Grandpa question before she ramps up the anger again. "A hospice guy said Grandpa wouldn't even be awake until today. I had to get some sleep from the past few nights helping Grandpa. You know how he is, needing something half the night?" I toss in the closer, "Or I guess you don't know since you haven't stayed over with him lately."

The last hits the guilt target bull's eye, and she suggests that we go back. Not me. I'm going to the trailer. She offers dinner, she's just down the highway at Loew's Resort, walking distance, but I tell her I'm meeting Eric—*as if*--reminding her that he's Grandpa's nurse.

That kind of information gets her off my back. If there's anything she wants besides Grandpa to be young again, it's for me to remarry and not be such a pain to her. She won't ask Eric anything about this fictive date. I hope.

And so it goes for the next eleven days.

My mom visits sporadically, balancing trips downtown with subs and lessons and work. At the hospice, she grades papers. Does she understand Grandpa Joe is dying?

I spend time with Eric on his breaks sometimes when Grandpa Joe is sleeping, which is mostly what he does though he has lucid moments too. Eric is an Iraq war vet. That's where he promised himself he would help the dying. Chloris meets me in the glade around lunch time where she teaches me relaxation techniques and positive thinking. I've been bringing little picnics to share with her—hummus and pita bread, PJ&B. I like to surprise her, which is easy since she and her Auntie cook their traditional foods. Chloris has shared a few with me. I have developed a taste for spicy dishes from Somalia.

As I approach Grandpa's room on the twelfth morning, Eric is backing out with a cart. He closes the door part way and brushes at his eyes with the back of his hand. My heart rate triples.

He sees me and twists his blue scrubs top in his hands. "Hey. Let me update you. We've added a morphine drip to ease his breathing and a catheter. He refused diapers —- over his dead body he said." Eric pushes the door open with his hip. "We've been having a few laughs this morning." Grandpa Joe is pressing back into his elevated bed, a smile twitching across his lips.

"Hi Grandpa," I say quietly, kissing his cool cheek.

Grandpa's eyelids blink twice. "Hi honey. I was just telling Eric about the Chinaman, who hated the bulldog our platoon had in Guam." His trembling fingers pick at the bed covers.

I shake my head and drag a chair closer to the bed. "You keep everybody laughing, Grandpa." It's hard to speak, my chest is so tight. He opens his eyes to look at me.

"I brought your file again and my little notebook. So we can go over things like you wanted." I brandish my pen and notebook, eager for distraction. I have the checklist we made last week, but Grandpa Joe may want changes.

"Oh, goody, honey." He tries to clap his hands, but they rise less than a quarter inch above the sheet. "You was always a smart one. I'm glad you're early. It gets pretty crowded and noisy later." He rests a moment. "I'm feeling better on account of this." He shows me the button in his hand. "They gave me the button last night. I push it when I need to. I was feeling so loopy, I asked if maybe I could go home tomorrow. But they said no. I hope I'm not losing my mind like my sister is."

I swallow hard and look at the I.V. bag, its tantalizing, mind-numbing morphine. I want to joke about sharing his I.V. needle, but Grandpa doesn't see anything funny about drug use.

He falls quiet, then rouses himself. "No church service, honey. Just a prayer by the grave."

I have to fight to keep my chin from wobbling. Biting the inside of my lower lip works. "Okay, Grandpa. We won't make you go to church. Why not be buried in your jammies if you want? Since it's a closed casket." Grandpa chuckles and hacks.

"My brother's got my clothes. Mitch chose something so I'll look spiffy. Religion or no, I'm countin' on meeting up with my Janie." His eyes mist over. "Would you bring my Old Spice? It's Janie's favorite."

He gets back to business. "Now all the bills are paid because I don't want to leave any debts. I'm no cheater. Mitch will clean out my hut. You can live there, honey." I open my mouth to question, but Grandpa musters the strength to wave the words away with his pinkie finger. "Nothin' would make me happier. Is Mitch here?" Grandpa's eyes close again. He points to the water pitcher. My own hands tremble. I splash water on the sheets. Grandpa manages a sip.

"I'll tell Mitch and Winona. No damned lawyers either. I have everything set. And don't let those graveyard people try to rob us twice. I have the receipt right here." He reaches for his wallet on his bedside tray, gives up, and points to it. "The receipt's in there."

"I hope you'll say something at the grave. Twenty-five words or less. Let Winona read that shepherd verse, or she'll hog the show. I'd be all moldy by the time my sister finished." He cracks himself up and begins to cough. Eric pops his head in the door, concerned, backs off when I signal we're okay.

Now I can't seem to breathe either. "What else, Grandpa? Rest and think a minute. I'm going to buy a Coke." I'd prefer cocaine. Just for today. I scramble from the room, trying to hold myself together.

Two hours pass. Chloris comes in and out with a hot sponge bath and a vase of daisies. I provide ice chips for Grandpa and spoon out tiny bites of cherry gelatin and of soupy chocolate ice cream. Grandpa flails at the catheter when he's sleeping. The extended family begins to drift in and out of the room.

Uncle Art stands at the foot of the bed. Winona flips through her Bible, stuffed with letters, reminders, sticky tags, and chooses a verse to read in the corner. She left Poochie home today. My mom hasn't arrived. All voices are hushed except Grandpa's when he rouses from morphine dreams and Uncle Bill's when he hurries in, wearing a custom-made suit and an oppressive cloud of *Gucci Pour Homme*. He arrives last, to hold court among the family underlings, to pontificate on the outlook for his promotion in the school district and his recent good publicity for the high school. After asking, "How's my dad today?" he glances at his father and goes on with his monologue. They've had issues since Bill was little and Grandma's obvious favorite. Grandpa Joe appointed Bill as executor of the estate since Bill cuts through red tape like a plastic surgeon attacking cellulite.

I've been contemplating the nature of time since May. I don't understand it. My mom is a time freak, perpetually early, running through life as if mere speed of performance can outmaneuver flaws of character. How often had we arrived at a recital or competition so early that I practically hyperventilated waiting to perform? So where is she now? What is she waiting for? I have too much time. Grandpa, not enough. What did he say with a chuckle last week? "Resistance is futile."

By late afternoon, the family has left, and I prepare to go. Maybe I'll walk north along the Silver Strand, the highway that divides the ocean from the bay. Or bike to Coronado. Maybe I'll stop at Kinko's to check my email. Maybe I'll. . . I don't know. There's no escape except the forbidden one. Maybe it would be okay to use one more time to survive this pain.

"I'll see you in the morning, Grandpa," I whisper, petting his hair, stroking his face. "Do you want me to turn on the radio for the Padres game? Or Rush?"

Grandpa smiles without opening his eyes. "Not tonight, honey. Keep reminding Winona. And promise me. . . ." He nods off. I wait, but he's sound asleep. Remind Winona that he did love her? About the trailer? Promise to dance again? Promise to learn to cook? To quit fighting with my mom? To remarry? To keep the trailer neat? I would promise him anything right now and try to keep that promise too, no matter the cost to myself.

Storm clouds are blowing in from the south, a San Diego September surprise. Maybe I should spend the night at the hospice? I decide not to, all the hospice air of dying clings to my skin and I want to shower, and I should eat. I stop by Lydia's Café. The cilantro and spice shocks my appetite awake, and I splurge on two tacos and a tamale to go.

The rain bursts from the sky. I pull into my parking spot, grab my food bag, backpack, then check the mailbox for Grandpa, and rush towards the porch. I lose my grip on the food bag, which splashes into a puddle. Under the deck's awning next to the Buddha, Mel is lying on her back, facing the street, her knees pulled up. She looks like an orphaned rat.

Mel grins and twirls both arms windmill style to sit up. "How's your grandpa?"

"What do you think? He's dying. I can't talk about it. Go away."

She rubs her eyes. "Sounds like time to find some pharmaceutical help."

"No!" I shout. I grab her arm to pull her up. "You are not welcome here. Last time you came, you caused this whole mess."

Mel slinks into the pelting rain and retrieves the bag. "You invited me, remember? We can talk. You used to say I was the only one who heard you when you talk."

"Grandpa listens. I'm too tired to argue. Let's eat and crash." She shrugs and shivers as I unlock the trailer and put the styrofoam container on the table. She grabs Grandpa's quilt and snoops around the kitchen for forks, opens the 'fridge, grabs a beer Grandpa keeps on hand for Mitch. She offers to split it. I jiggle my water bottle. We finish everything — it was more than enough.

"Mel, in the night, I might go back to the hospice. If it's raining, stay put. But if the rain stops, you have got to go. I absolutely do not want you here, and my grandpa wouldn't either."

She reaches behind her, opens the 'fridge, pops the top of a second beer. "Sure, Zooz. Got any extra sweats?"

I toss her some from my pile of clothes, and after she changes, we sit watching television. Mel scrolls through the channels, looking for "Celebrity Rehab" or "Cops." Thunder rattles the windows, and lightning illuminates the trailer from the outside in. With every lash of rain on the windows, I hate the storm, which whirls me through thoughts of Port Townsend, Javier, my old job, my other life, which was actually good for a short while. I'm so tired. I sleep in fitful spurts with the wind roaring outside, Mel sloshing through a sixth beer. The cans roll towards the kitchen as thunder vibrates the walls.

I hope the flash and crash of the thunderstorm doesn't give Grandpa nightmares. At midnight, I am ready to drive to the hospice since deep sleep won't come. But I sit, immobile. Restless, I ready my backpack for morning, adding a *Reader's Digest* from 1999 and Grandpa's bottle of Old Spice. But again, I retreat to his chair.

JOLENE

It was a tedious day of parental whining at school with a week to go before progress reports, and what difference would it have made if I happened to miss a few more days? It took me until 6 p.m. to get to Daddy's bedside. I sit close, reading to him from the evening paper. He likes me to read the sports page and the letters to the editor so he can say, "Damn crooked politicians." His breath puffs in little bursts since dinner. He flutters his right hand and when I lean in, he says, "Phone Winona. And Mitch."

We try, but no one answers.

A small smile quivers on Daddy's lips. "In the morning," he says. He falls asleep. Nurses come in and out, and one, the tall black woman, suggests I pull the couch out. She arranges the pillows and sheets.

I doze, my temples pounding with grief. Then anger about Suzann intrudes, getting me up to walk to the patio doors. How have I let Suzann dominate my thoughts when these are my last moments with Daddy? He has seen her at her best and her worst, and he doesn't seem to think that one matters more than the other with her. And that time I reminded him I had been a perfect child, which I tried to be, he laughed at me, right in front of Suzann. He didn't care if she joined the San Francisco Ballet or the chorus line of the Imperial Beach Repertory. He thinks she's funny and sweet and good, like he is. He'll never see the way she filters information to favor herself, making me look like an extra in her personal drama.

Evening has turned to night with cracks of lightning. I drop onto the couch bed and somehow fall asleep, dreaming of summer days. A tap on my shoulder wakes me, and in my happy sleep, I reach up to brush it away, as if a lady bug has landed. It is Dr. Sanjit, kneeling by the sofa.

"Mrs. Zimmerman," he says, "I am sorry. Your father has passed."

I shake my head and press a hand against my mouth. This cannot be true, not so soon. The doctor offers his arm and walks with me to the bed. Daddy lies there, quiet as before, and when I take his hand, it is not completely cold.

Dr. Sanjit stands with a chart in his hand, initialing this and that. But his face, though fatigued, is soft with kindness when he looks at me and grasps my shoulder. "I offer you our deep sympathy. Would you prefer that I leave you for now? Please call us if you want anyone on staff for any reason."

Resting my head on Daddy's chest, I don't know what to do. There's no rising and falling, no wheezing breath, no laugh that I have loved, no life. I blot tears on his pajamas and inhale the crisp soapy smell, knowing these are my final memories and that I should call Mitch and Winona and Bill. I feel unable to lift the phone. But then I call Mitch, and he does answer, and I tell him, "Daddy died."

Mitch's voice sounds froggy. "We'll be there soon. I'll call the others. And Suzann."

Suzann? I want to say, no, Mitch, she can wait, but the connection is broken. I cannot deal with my grief and Suzann's too. I need to take care of me. I need to take care of Daddy and a funeral. I cannot be a mother and offer strength to Suzann when right now I am the daughter. I am the one who has lost her heart. I don't want her here. No one answers when I call back. I hope he didn't reach Suzann.

The gray-haired, foreign nurse steps into the room –she's Chloris. She's the nurse's aide Daddy likes so much. Liked. He's gone.

"May I bring you some coffee or some water?" she asks.

I open my mouth but can't find my voice.

"I understand. This hospice was honored to care for your father. Mr. Franklin was a special man." She turns towards the door.

"Wait, Chloris," I say. "Thank you. Thank you all so much. Daddy wasn't afraid to die. He was the only one of us who wasn't afraid."

"He accepted death, didn't he?"

I nod and try to hold myself together, but loneliness surges over me. "Chloris, would you sit with me for a bit? Daddy's brother is coming."

"Let me tell them at the desk that I'll be here." Chloris's shoes whisper on the carpet, and the door whooshes closed. The door has been open during all my other visits.

Returning to Daddy's bedside, I lift the sheet over his hands. They are cold, like clay before it's malleable. Chloris returns and pulls a chair over by mine. She takes my hand in hers and begins to sing in a low register, her voice silky:

"Hanfarkaan adiga ma makalesit
Lakin magahadi ua uaha"

She goes on a bit longer in this odd foreign language of chopped sounds and clicks. When she stops, I ask her to sing again. She repeats the song in English:

"This wind, now you can't hear its sound

Chloris hums a few lines as if she has forgotten the English words, and then goes on,

"Here to my face that looks like yours
My face that looks like yours."

"This is a Somali song, 'Hanfarkaan,' meaning 'wind.' Let us think together that is what your father has done, yes? He has left this home, but the wind brings his memory, 'a face that looks like yours.'"

Chloris pats my cheek, and I understand how she is the kind of person who is quiet in her soul. She believes that Daddy has left and found another life, a new life. What if even now he's leaping into the surf as he used to, catching a wave all the way to shore until his belly rubs the soft, marbled sand, shaking his head, the water drops flying, turning in a dive back under the waves to ride again? Sometimes, he used to watch Art for me and tell me to go play and enjoy the water. Mom would stay out in the breakers all day, not concerned one bit about us kids. My parents are together again, otter diving and resurfacing, catching the next wave and the next and the next. Their spirits are unshadowed by separation or work or worry or illness.

I let myself vanish into a vision of what was and what may be, what must be so, for in his simple way, Daddy was all that is good in my life. Could God deny him his eternal happiness for refusing to follow one church, one way, one belief? I long to be outside in the wind.

Chloris turns her head towards the door. Mitch and his wife, Kaye, and Winona come in. All are crying, but Winona rushes away, probably to the chapel..

"I will go with her," says Chloris.

Mitch and Kaye stand by Daddy's bed, then they kneel and begin to pray. I'm not comfortable praying with them. They finish their prayers with an "Our Father," which I join. We sit, quiet, lost.

ZOOZLE

2:30 a.m. The phone blasts. It's Mitch. His voice is hoarse and flat. "Joe passed. Your mom was here with him. Can you come out?"

I shower, dress, drive. It's not fair. I could have been there, should have been there, not my stupid mom.

It's still pouring rain, and I get drenched between the parking lot and the lobby door. Entering Grandpa's room, I wish I could hug my mom, Mitch, Kaye, but I can't. Their faces are tight and old with grief. The couch's sofa bed is pulled out, and the sheets are rumpled.

I've never seen a dead person before, but there's nothing scary. Just my grandpa, his jaw jutted forward. He would laugh at the way the night nurse positioned his false teeth, like a chipmunk. I caress his cold face and lay my head on his chest. Strange, how the dead feel like soft marble. "I love you, Grandpa," I whisper.

I don't know how long I hold him. Then I sit, unmoving, broken. I remember the Old Spice at last. In a final benediction, I pull the after shave out and pat Old Spice on his cheeks and jaw. Once when I was little, Grandpa let me use his Old Spice on my dolls. My mom scrubbed it off the minute we got home. Grandpa let me sit in his recliner with him and go through wedding magazines. We agreed on my wedding gown before my mom ever saw it. We both said, "That one!" and laughed. He winked before he walked down the aisle with Mom and me.

My mom has turned to the door, and I can hear her weeping. I will collapse if I let her console me, and after a moment talking to Mitch, I walk on out.

In the parking lot, I see Eric, arriving for his morning shift. "My grandpa went out the way he wanted to," I say, a forced laugh catching in my throat. "With a bang." I open my arms to encompass the electric sky.

Eric steps into my wide-flung arms and hugs me. He feels solid and warm, and I would love to stay here wrapped in comfort. He pushes me to arm's length and looks at me. "Chloris called me so I came in early to see you. And I called Mr. McKillop. But Zoozle, you have to know how we feel at the hospice. Good for Grandpa Joe. And good for your family too. You'll be okay, but it takes time." He sees my doubt. "Here's the hospice card again. Call us to talk, anytime, about anything. Don't handle this alone. I mean it. Seeking help is not against the rules, you know?" He walks with rapid steps into the main building. I wave at his back and walk away. I see Phillip pulling into the lot, parking between my car and Mom's.

I knock on his window, and he rolls it down. "Grandpa died. May I borrow Jacques?"

Phillip offers his sympathy and tells Jacques to behave.

"Before I bring him home to you, I'll call or text," I say. Jacques settles into the back seat, and I open the window so that he at least can enjoy the ride.

JOLENE

This is what I remember from the rest of that time at hospice.

Suzann walks in. Her eyes are red, and I check to see if she has that Mel girl with her, and sniff the air to detect any druggie smell. She walks to her grandpa, and I walk to the patio doors.

I know I should hug her, but I am incapable of moving in her direction, and she doesn't move towards me.

Mitch tells Suzann we will begin planning the funeral at Art's later in the morning. Suzann makes a choking noise, digs in her backpack, and gives Mitch some papers.

"This is what Grandpa Joe wanted," she says and leaves the room. "I'll be at the trailer. I'll come to Art's later, maybe."

Mitch and Kaye watch her and exchange a look, indicting me. "Where's Bill?" I ask.

"We tried his number and Art's."

It's only four in the morning. If his phone is off, there is no sense calling Bill until five or six. I hope he won't choose to orchestrate the details with us.

Mitch, Kaye, and I begin to gather things from the drawers and closet, from the bedside table, from the bathroom. Chloris returns to inquire if anyone else is coming before the hospice releases Daddy's remains.

Remains, I think, looking at his thin frame and fuzz-specked pajamas. This is not what remains. What remains is in memories, in words, and in deeds. This cold body is not any true measure of Daddy's remains. I do not share these thoughts with Kaye and Mitch.

Mitch has signed a form, and he tells Chloris that six o'clock will be all right for the hearse. "Do you think Bill or Art will be angry?" he asks. He cocks his head left and right as if his neck hurts.

"Art and Bill can handle things at the mortuary," I say. "Mitch, do you have to go home for Daddy's clothes?"

"No, I remembered them. Joe," his voice has caught on his brother's name, "had everything planned out." He stops. "Let's go through his list."

"I can't."

"All right. We'll wait."

Art arrives. Kaye opens a Bible and begins to read, ending with "We live by faith, not by sight. We are confident, I say, and would prefer to be away from the body and at home with the Lord." She puts a book marker in place. "That's Corinthians."

"Away from the body and at home with the Lord," I repeat. These verses comfort me in the same way Chloris's song did. I fall into Art's strong body. My little brother has become a huge man.

Art takes the seat by Daddy's bed. I tell him I will get Winona from the chapel, and we will all kiss Daddy goodbye. The walk to the chapel is brief; Winona rises with creaking knees. We see men assembled at the nurses' station, all wearing dark suits. I nod to Chloris who follows us into the room. Chloris again sings softly, the song of finding a new home. Mitch, Kaye, Winona, Art, and I kiss Daddy's cheek. The scent of Old Spice lingers. There is no more to be done. Slowly, we walk down the hall. It feels different this morning, the colors on the walls, the framed art, all these seem too bright and hopeful for the truth of the matter.

As the others settle into Mitch's mini-van, I am surprised to see Mr. McKillop's convertible with the top up, parked next to my car. Phillip looks up from a book.

"Daddy's gone." The syntax is simple, the words, difficult.

"I thought I should wait here after I talked to Suzann," he answers. "I'm so sorry, Jolene. Please, would you like to come sit with me a while?" He clears the passenger seat of dog toys. "Suzann borrowed Jacques for his good comfort. She feels at ease around him, freer than around people, at least that's what I think."

I step around the car's hood and sag into the seat next to Phillip. "I don't know what to do now," I say. "I've always thought I knew what to do. Even losing my mom and before that, Suzann's father, was not like this, losing Daddy."

"There will be a lot of details to keep you busy. It's the time after the details that's hard to fill." He puts a long arm across the seat, and I feel his compassion and strength. "I'm here for you whenever you need me."

"I need you now," I say, and the tears begin to flow as if there is nothing in anyone's power or comfort to stop them, not ever again. It is a soothing thought that for this moment I can lean on someone and not put on my brave face that's nothing but a mask.

CHAPTER 8: ZOOZLE

In the light traffic, I navigate back to what is now my trailer by the bay. With Jacques I walk in to find Mel still curled on the love seat. She turns over with a gross exhalation of beer breath.

"Zooz? It's too early."

"Grandpa Joe died."

"God."

"Yeah."

"I'll get up." She rolls off the couch to her knees, and Jacques licks her face. She yelps, "Jesus H. Christ, where'd you get the bear?"

"It's Jacques. Remember? Get moving."

She stumbles into the shower. I remove Jacques' halter and leash, and he jumps onto the bed, lying down with a sigh. I lean against the bedroom window's sill and open a window after tying the curtains back. I inhale a puff of morning that floats in from the sea through the jasmine. A few blossoms float into the room. They drop like frayed yellow ribbons to the gray carpet.

I rock in the bedroom's wicker chair and flare my hands open on my lap, like tiresome Winona. Will I end up like that, an old maid who talks too much, my gray-haired mane skimmed into a haphazard topknot, wearing the granny jumper over a baggy t-shirt? I look at the photos Grandpa Joe surrounded himself with. There's one of sixteen year-old me, a dancing trophy held aloft in my perfect ballerina's stance, my still-perfect dancer's arms, before drug scars and infections and surgery.

I sit down at the table to write the eulogy. I think about what it will be like to live here in Imperial Beach, the town my grandparents loved, that my mother loathes, too full of hippies, illegals, and druggies, she says, even though ninety-nine percent of the people are everyday, middle class workers or retirees. It's true though about the drugs: meth, pot, cocaine, I could buy a fix easily here.

Mel drips her way from the shower to the bedroom, nude. "C'mere. Let me make you better. You could use a little lovin'. Or get into your pj's and I'll make cocoa. We'll snuggle up with Jacques over there. Whatever you need, Zooz."

She has often made me feel better, but not today. Goose bumps erupt on her bony arms. "No. Get dressed. It's quit raining. You're leaving."

Mel wrinkles her forehead and opens her mouth, but throws on yesterday's sweats. "You shouldn't be alone, Zooz. The beach is good. I know some peeps there already who'll deal."

"No. No drugs. No more"

"Just for today and maybe tomorrow. You deserve it."

"No. I promised my grandpa."

"Well, he's not here, and I am. Who knows you better than me?"

Do I say who cares? Your help is not help. Do I force her to leave? I pick up Jacques' halter, and he jumps up at the sound of his tags. Mel follows as if she too is leashed to me. We walk to the manager's office and tell the girl at the desk that my grandpa has died, but I'll be staying. I accept her sympathetic noises as condolences. Jacques trots along with us. Full tilt, we charge onward. I target a little park on Emory Street, but affirm only that it still has no grass. From here I can see the corner where my great-grandparents had built their wooden home now replaced by high-rise condos. I take Jaques's leash off to let him roam free. Mel climbs the tall aluminum slide I loved as a child. It is so quiet, I can hear the surf pounding two blocks away. I remember Grandpa Joe's advice, "If you can hear the waves from Third Street, don't go in the water." My life used to be divided into decisions like that. Swim or don't swim. Go to the movies or go to the beach. Now it's too complicated. Keep Mel or throw her out? Buy drugs? Feel better? Stay clean?

"Come, Jacques." I leash him up again. I need to talk to Grandpa and Grandma Janie's old friend, Sal, catty-corner from Mitch and Kaye. Sal's sons are gang bangers, one in prison, two on parole. Those guys will have something to buy if I choose to let loose.

Jacques swaggers along. Any other day I would laugh at how he swishes his tail and barks as if he owns every neighborhood. I stop to ruffle his coat and bury my face in his neck fur and cry. The decision is made. I require chemical help.

We approach the Cisneros' house. The boys are home. An *El Blaxicano* CD is playing full blast from a truck stereo, the bass turned so high the Chevy jumps to the hip hop beat.

"Hey, Chicas. What's happening?" One of two skinny boys— Gil? No—Sal Junior-- the taller, older one with the three tear-drop tattoo, calls out to me, "Hey!"

"Is your dad home?" I stop at the curb. Gil, slim as a whippet, fresh-faced and untattooed, peels himself off the hood of the yellow truck and lags indoors. His baggy, unbelted shorts slip down four inches below his boxers. He returns with his father.

"Suzann, it is good to see you and your friend. Please come in and sit with us. Gloria will put coffee on." He waves the boys aside. They jump into the back of the pick-up truck. Mel begins to shimmy and shake. The boys laugh. Sal Senior smiles, but I don't.

"I came to tell you that my grandpa died today." Despite my best efforts to hold on, the tears flood out. Jacques leans up against my leg, and I kneel to pet him.

Sal pulls me up, enfolding me in his round embrace. "Ah, *mi hija.* I knew he was very sick." He shakes out a spotless white handkerchief. "Here now. Joe was a good man. He was very proud of you."

I hiccup. "He wanted to be sure you could come to his service. It's this week at Glen of Peace — you can call the place or my mom. Grandpa didn't want a long ceremony. We'd appreciate it if you could come." I look at my watch. "I need to go. We have a lot to do."

Sal waves goodbye. Gil follows me down the street. "Chicas! We know you use. Our white buds, down there, they got it now that they're back from Iraq. Good prices too."

I look where he's pointing to my Uncle Mitch's house. Mel knocks on their door and a scruffy, flabby guy, my cousin Mike, looks at us without recognition. He's woozy and wasted, hobbled by braces on his legs.

"What ya got?" Mel asks, as I look into the house to see if anybody there might know me.

"What ya want?"

I put my hand into my pocket, ignore Eric's hospice card and pull some cash, buy the bag. Mel's right. I need something in reserve to survive the next few hours, the next few days.

The dog, Mel, and I move on, to the beach and down the beach a mile from the pier to the jetty. The waves are breaking in huge, booming sets near the mouth of the Tijuana River. Three wet-suited surfers bob on their boards in the swells. Maybe I could teach Mel to surf. No, not for a week, no surfing after storms. I've already learned all I want to know about bacteria. I touch the jagged, empty pocket of scar tissue under my arm, a constant reminder of the power of microbes from dirty needles. Dirty water, no difference.

Jacques and I splash across the shallows at the river's mouth. The river water is warmer than the ocean. Mel doesn't follow us, which eases the tightness in me. Jacques is frisking with the seagulls in the kelp piles, arousing clouds of sand flies. I sit and dig my toes into the cool sand and squint south at the welded metal fence that extends into the sea, the secondary rusted chain link that marches out into the furious breakers. The border fences weren't in place when Mom was a child. She walked with her brothers all the way to the bullring in Mexico, and no one thought anything of it. She lived her childhood in such a time of innocence. I bury my head in my crossed arms and weep. I catch the scent of Old Spice on my fingers.

Time, innocence, the scar under my arm, the scent of Grandpa Joe. Promises unsaid, but left to keep. I rise, tentatively letting my left leg reach out into an arabesque. Jacques comes rushing at me. I hold the position. I am surprised at my steadiness after so many months without dancing. I pirouette, once, twice, three, four, five times. After the fifth turn, I am facing north, and I hurry back towards Mel's prone body. Jacques showers her with water and sand as he shakes his fur dry. She groans, but gets up to follow me. In my head, I compose my tribute as I walk:

"Grandpa Joe loved sweets and hated vegetables.

He loved his family and hated cheats.

He taught me that today is as important as forever."

A lifetime in twenty-five words or less. An unspoken promise.

We reach the trailer. I towel off Jacques, especially his paws and tail. Then with renewed strength, I walk into the bathroom, grab the bottle of Percocet and dump the pills and our new buy into the toilet. I flush it three times to make sure all the shit is really gone.

I pull Eric's number from my jeans pocket, flip open my phone, and text him, "WN2TLK." I leave my phone on. I know he'll get back to me.

First, I deal with Mel. I cross my arms. "You can't be here. You're not helping me."

"You'll feel better tomorrow. I'll stay with you."

"I don't want the drugs. I got rid of them."

"No, you didn't. You're not that straight."

"I did, and I am."

"Fine. We'll find more." She traces her arm tracks.

"No God damn drugs. Not today, not tomorrow. I was being stupid. I wasn't thinking. I am asking you to leave."

"Sure, Zooz. Tomorrow. Tonight, we'll lay low for a bit. After the funeral, you'll see."

What I see is the light that was Grandpa is gone now. What I see is that Mel is toxic to me. Jacques gives me a reason to escape, away from Mel's oppressive, tantalizing presence.

"I'm taking Jacques back to Phillip. Don't wait up," I say. "And I want you gone. Soon. Leave when I'm at the funeral."

"Thank you, your Majesty," she snorts and buries herself under a quilt on the couch. I'd like to curl up right there too, but I refuse.

Jacques needs to get home. Phillip should not have to worry because of me. He's a good man, Jacques is a good dog, and I can be a good me. No matter how wonderful it would be to slip back into her warm arms, both of us high and silly, Mel has got to go.

JOLENE

Art's housekeeper, Magdalena, opens the door, the cavernous entryway towering over her tininess. She drops her head to hide her tears and hurries away to the kitchen while Mitch, Kaye, and I settle ourselves at the dining room table, Daddy's notebook pages in front of us.

Magdalena brings in coffees flavored with chocolate and a plate of cinnamon and sugar-coated churros. "You must eat, *ninos*," she tells us as she has always told us, food being her answer to a teenager's broken heart, a grandchild's skinned knee, and our adult grief. We all reach for a churro and bite into the warm, sweet dough.

Mitch rubs his hand across his chin where sugar has sprinkled into his morning beard. "I didn't shave," he says.

Kaye shakes her head. "It doesn't matter." She pulls a tissue from her purse. "This is too much like when Linc died, trying to be a good Marine like his Uncle Joe and then the twins' injuries, following Linc's footsteps." She leaves the table with her coffee mug, and the sliding door to the backyard rattles open. A fresh wind scatters the papers we have in front of us, and Mitch and I bend to retrieve them.

"Moms don't recover from losing sons. Dads either," Mitch sighs. "I've felt every second of the five years without Linc." He stops, lost in thought. "Let's get to work."

Work works for me. We read Daddy's list, his choice of a graveside service and no open casket, no viewing. Daddy thought it was ghoulish when my mother requested the viewing. He stayed only a few minutes and said later, "That waxy thing was not my Janey." He wished he had not seen her like that as a final memory.

Mitch gets up to call the Marines to see about an honor guard. I look at Daddy's list, knowing I should be one of the speakers, but I see only Mitch's name and Art's and there it is in Daddy's writing, Suzann's name. Daddy chose Suzann to speak, but not me? I could read a poem. I could write a tribute. But I'm not there in the instructions. Bill isn't listed either. Winona is to read Psalm 23. Knowing Daddy, he wants this ceremony short. He complained at Mama's funeral, leaning towards me to whisper, "This is too long" and at Suzann's wedding too. My Daddy hated ceremonies and getting dressed up.

Mitch returns to the table. "They'll send an honor guard. We just have to phone with time and place. I'll call Glen of Peace to see if we can arrange for a Wednesday ceremony. How early, Jolene?"

"Ten?"

"That sounds about right."

"What sounds right?" Kaye asks, returning.

"Ten for the ceremony." She takes a seat across from me. But then she gets up again and disappears into the bathroom.

From the phone Mitch nods and then dials the church. Reverend Parchton cannot make it on Wednesday this week, but refers Mitch to his colleague across town, Reverend Suss. The ceremony is now in place as Mitch calls the Marines back with the time confirmed.

"I'll work on the computer, Mitch, to make the programs. What else?"

Mitch shrugs. "I think I'll take Kaye home. She'll want to get the twins to their physical therapy. I'll be back later."

The quiet of the house is what I need. I use Art's computer to look for a poem to put on Daddy's memorial program. The poem has to be about death, but it can't be morbid and it can't be too feminine and it can't be too fancy or too modern. It has to convey Daddy's sense of the world, his joy in life, his confidence even in death. I scan and dismiss Eliot, Graves, Donne, and Rossetti. Thinking of my classes and these poems I love to teach reminds me of Mr. Dowd struggling through Tennyson today. That's the key I need. Tennyson's "Crossing the Bar" is the answer. That sounds like Daddy, "let there be no moaning at the bar" and the line about "when I embark." I am proud of finding these words that are just right even as I rub my wet cheek against my sleeve.

Art has photo folders arranged on the computer by category, so it's not hard to find a good shot of Daddy to put on the front of the program. The front door slams. I peer out of the computer nook and find Bill flipping through the notebook pages on the table.

He looks up, his face is composed, and he does not open his arms to hug me.

"Mitch and I have taken care of a lot of things," I tell him. "Did you go to the funeral home?"

"Art came with me. He handed over the clothes. I think we should have a viewing."

"Daddy didn't want it."

"Well, he's gone. People expect it."

"I don't care what other people expect, Bill. I want to do what Daddy asked. Read this, he has it all written out." I point to the sheet of paper, and Bill scans it.

"I'm not listed to talk at the funeral? He must have done this list after the drugs kicked in."

"Well it's here. Mitch, Art, Suzann and Winona. Not me, not you. You know how Daddy liked to keep things short."

"That's not right either."

"Let's not worry about what we think is right. Let's follow Daddy's wishes, please, Bill? I can't handle conflict right now," which even as I say it sounds ridiculous since I can't stand conflict anytime anywhere, and the whole conversation reminds me I need to speak to Suzann.

"Who would know?"

"I would. Mitch would. Suzann. We're going to do this Daddy's way. If a man can't choose how he'll be buried, what else is there?"

Bill inhales and his nose whistles. I can't tell if he is laughing at me or giving vent to disagreement.

"Fine. What's left?"

"The reception, food and drinks and tables and chairs."

"Can you do that?"

"Sure. I'll finish the program and go to Kinko's and choose a paper for it. What about Nory?"

He ignores my question. "What about Kaye?"

"Kaye had to go home. I'll do it, or I'll have Suzann make the calls. Or Art. Where's Art?"

"He stopped at Mom's gravesite. He's having a hard time."

"Aren't we all?" I tear up again.

"Sure, Jo, yeah, we all are." He checks his watch. "Look, while you're at it with the program, put the funeral details on the family web site. That might save us a few phone calls. I'll handle the legal end, and you take care of the party."

"I don't think I'd call it a party."

"Party, wake, whatever it is. It's not for Tuesday, is it? I can't miss the Principals' Meeting, no matter what. You handle the *get together*, and I'll deal with the legal paperwork, and you make the change to the program. Nobody will know. Nobody's hurt. Fair enough?" He pats his pockets and jingles his car keys.

Nothing is fair when Bill is involved. Nothing is fair when death is involved. It's easier if I agree to his terms. I have work to do, and I'm glad he's leaving. I need to visit Suzann to make sure she's not getting herself drugged or drunk, but she has Jacques with her, and I know she'll respect the safety of the dog. I call her, leave a message for the arrangements we've made and post a note on the family's web site.

What I want most is to call Phillip. No one in my family offers me the comfort Phillip's shoulders offer. The intensity of my yearning to be back in his car, back in his arms, cradled and allowed to cry, shocks me. Pulling Phillip's card from my wallet, I pick up Art's phone.

CHAPTER 9: ZOOZLE

What I remember from my dad's funeral is that I got very tired of sitting still and very tired of people kissing me. Other than the exact day someone dies, I always believed the funeral day would be the worst. I'm wrong. It's the day before, when there's nothing to do but sit and think.

My mom is busy at Uncle Art's trying to help get the place ready for the big party after the funeral. How sick is that? They're worrying about things like what color table cloths and where the heat lamps should be and if sandwiches will suffice, while I am worrying about whether my heart is going to break in two.

I find that either I can't sit still or I can't get moving. I caught myself sitting here pulling my hair out, which Penny says relates to loss. I need to stop before I'm bald. Like when I was about eight, and my mom was busy with her job and trying to run about five committees at school and basically working all the time. I passed my free time reading *Heidi* and *Black Beauty*, all those little kid books. I began pulling hair while I read. It felt good to pull it and examine the roots.

When my mom was getting ready to braid my hair or wash paint out of it, she saw a bald spot I had created on my scalp. Rather than console me, she yelled out to my grandmother, "Hey look! Suzann's snatching herself bald."

I stopped pulling my hair for a few years, but who says such a thing to a little girl? Why wasn't she worried about the cause of my behavior instead of only the result other people could see? She would have learned that I felt lost, with my dad dead and her working nonstop, even when she was home. That's the whole thing with my mom – as long as we appear perfect even the huge defects of character don't matter.

In the midst of this meditation, I get a text from Eric, 'R U OK?" I call him and tell him no. He suggests we meet at the deli. He doesn't have to work until later.

I'm there in under twenty minutes now that I've learned to park at the Long's Drugstore lot a block away. Eric is sitting in a booth near the front window and waves me in. He has a beautiful smile, those perfect teeth, that dark-honey skin.

Eric scoots over, and I sit next to him. He hugs me. He feels strong and supple and safe. He's in his hospital scrubs.

"Hi." Nothing more will come out.

"What do you need, right now, Zoozle?"

"I need. . .I need something that's not stupid."

"Like?" He leads me forward.

"Like a plan. Every plan I've ever made was stupid."

"So plan away – I promise to tell you if it's stupid."

"I'm staying here. Not with my mom, not back to Port Townsend."

"Why not do it then?"

"Job?"

"Pet sitter?"

"Too boring. I like the animals, but I don't want to play with dogs all day."

"Dog walker? Everybody around here has dogs. You're pretty active. It takes tons of strength and concentration."

"Every dog I've ever known has been my pack leader. I'm a softy when it comes to dogs."

"So take a class."

"Too many bills due, probably yesterday."

"Let's go to my place, watch a movie. We'll go through some want ads. Chris should be home. It's time you met."

"Roommate?"

"Yeah, roommate, soul mate. We've been together two years."

"Oh." That's all I can think of to say.

The waiter arrives with coffees. He's the bald guy with the falsetto voice. Eric says, "Hey Gaylord!" and Gaylord punches Eric in the shoulder.

"Do not use that name for me here. I'm Lordman, remember? He taps his shirt, clearly embroidered "Lordman." "Why did MY mother have to have a crush on Gaylord Perry?"

"Who's that?" I glance at Lordman, who has a chipped front tooth. He is rocking from foot to foot.

"That baseball player, a pitcher. He was infamous for his spitball, but maybe my mom thought it was called a screwball. She named me Gaylord in his honor. I guess she knew I'd be a screwball."

We're all laughing as Lordman carries on about his mom. I feel less alone in my struggles, like maybe most moms are crazy.

"Zoozle here needs a local job. She doesn't want to move back to rainy old Washington," Eric tells Lordman. The more people who know, the better, but I feel weird having my problems broadcast in a coffee shop. "Among her other talents, she's a dancer."

Lordman snaps his fingers and shimmies his hips. "Dance?"

I nod.

"My condo manager said this girl, Dahlia, will be gone a while, staying with her mom in Texas. She took a leave after surgery. Dahlia taught dance at a junior college. Could you do that?"

The possibility is tantalizing. "Sure."

We pay for our coffees and walk to Eric's condo.

As Eric unlocks the door, a sleepy, deep voice calls from behind a shoji screen, "Honey, c'mon in here." I know that tone of voice. Javier used it enough.

Eric blushes and tells me to grab a drink from the 'fridge. He'll be right back.

The sleepy voice gets louder, and I can hear Eric's quieting murmur. A few words crackle through the screen, like "stray dogs" and "plans" and "day care." What?

Maybe I should go. I hadn't pictured Chris as male or mean.

Eric is still talking quietly to Chris even though Chris has slammed a door. A shower spritzes into action, and Eric slumps back into the living room.

"Don't mind Chris being pissy," he says looking over his shoulder. "He took the dogs to day care already and thought he was going to come back and sleep in. Or something."

The something is obvious, and I feel even more intrusive. "I can go." As I stand, tears fall. I've never been so on edge with my emotions in my whole life, well, not since the last days of Javier.

"Zooz, sit down. It's fine." This is a different Eric, all tense and uneasy. "The computer's over there — go check the jobs in the San Diego Junior College District."

"Wait. What?" I ask. My mind is not processing well today. And then I stifle a sob.

"Geez. Don't do that. I'm sorry. I'm too bossy. I'll navigate." Eric takes over the keyboard and brings up the junior college job page.

I push down the heartache. Sure enough, dance adviser is posted under openings. It's at Puente Rojo, about fifteen minutes east of Hillcrest. I fill out the application online, using Grandpa Joe's address, which makes me cry harder, and then I email Bert for a letter of recommendation to send asap. I know he's back at Port Townsend since the semester started weeks ago. I've got my girls' fall show tape in the car. I kept meaning to start reviewing it. I can send it to arrive before any interview.

We high-five, and Eric gets out *Mad Hot Ballroom*, a documentary about little kids learning to dance. We throw ourselves on the couch and watch and laugh and talk. I love how much the teachers obviously adore the children in their classes. Chris stalks into the living room, looks at Eric with a snarky expression and starts crashing around with plates and silverware as he empties the dishwasher. He's tall and slender but not skinny slim. He's wearing a Tommy Bahamas shirt and camp shorts and high top tennis shoes.

Chris grabs a duffel bag and leaves without speaking to us although Eric yells, "Later, luv." Eric sighs and explains that Chris is always tired, especially when he's unemployed like now. Eric and I sit awhile longer. Eric promises he'll be there for Grandpa's funeral service and he'll tell Chloris the time and place.

Despite all I have lost in the past few weeks, I feel as if maybe I will survive.

CHAPTER 10: JOLENE

Cyberspace has swooped away the memorial program for now, and Bill's secretary, Dorrie, acknowledged she will print it to show Bill and also post a note on the school web site and grades portal, which should help with the interminable phone calls and emails from parents I've been getting. Mr. Dowd has received my lessons, such as they are, for the remainder of the week. In my email, a note from Aden epitomizes my high school classes, *"Dear Mrs. Zimmerman, We miss you, and we are sorry your father died. Will you be able to get my recommendations in on time?"*

I have a printed copy of this email to show Phillip as well as the program. The program sticks out of my purse, taunting me with the text I replaced for Bill, ignoring Daddy's notes and Suzann's knowledge of them. It's not far to Phillip's hotel downtown even though downtown's one-way streets are as confusing as ever. I'd rather have met him at a restaurant, but he is waiting for Suzann to return Jacques. I hope she's in a hurry and that I can delay enough to miss her. If she has one of her tantrums in front of Phillip, who knows what she might say about me? He's aware that she's unbalanced. As far as I know, he doesn't blame me. God, what if the issues with Daddy's program turn Phillip's sympathies from me to Suzann?

Parking at the Little M Hotel works out, and I phone Phillip to let him know I've arrived. He says he's in the lobby waiting. My heart skips as the elevator descends with a clunk from the rooftop garage level. The oily smell of the elevator smells like my bicycle chain and sharpens my sense of needed repairs.

I check my hair in the mirrors overhead. *Haggard* is the word that first comes to mind. I'll need to make a style appointment before the funeral.

Doors open to a small lobby, two aqua sofas facing one another on a plush brown rug that contrasts with the terrazzo tiles near the main desk. Phillip's arm rests across one, Jacques sitting at his feet. Leaning down to the dog, Phillip is laughing, and then he looks up at the person across from him, Suzann.

I start to dart back into the elevator, but Phillip catches my glance, and Suzann turns her head. She sees me too. Her mouth turns down as she presses her lips together. She stays seated though Phillip stands up as I approach.

He hugs me, not as tightly as I'd like. Suzann looks off through the window. She moves over on the couch, and I sit next to her. My purse spills open, with the program. Daddy's picture calls out to be noticed.

Suzann picks up my hairbrush and wallet. I grab the program copy, but not before she knows what it is.

"Let me see, Mom," she says as she pulls it up into plain view. "I like this picture of Grandpa Joe." She pets it lightly with two fingers. "When was it taken?"

"Your cousin Lacey's wedding. While you were up north—you had a dance conference?"

"Yeah, I missed a lot of family stuff those years," she answers, paging through the program.

Phillip says he's going to take Jacques upstairs for his kibble after the afternoon's exercise. They're in room 1112.

I'm left exactly where I don't want to be, alone with Suzann. She is now reading the Tennyson poem, and I sit on my hands to control myself, to keep from pulling it away from her before she gets too far.

"That's perfect, Mom. I wish I remembered more of the poetry I studied." She starts to hand the program back to me, but begins to read over the listed speakers. "This part isn't right." She rereads it and jabs at the page. "What have you done?" Her voice is loud and high, and the desk clerk leans forward, eyebrows raised.

Suzann flings herself to the other couch, holding the pages out of my reach. I stretch for the program and say, "Bill thought we should re-arrange the speakers. I remembered how much you hate to speak in public, and I didn't want you to feel uncomfortable. So I agreed. Winona doesn't have to know I'm replacing her."

Suzann shakes her head. "Grandpa told me he wanted me to speak. Why would you take me off the program? I already composed my speech." She digs into her backpack. "Look here it is." She hands me what looks like one of those twenty-five words or less verses in a jingle contest. "Did you think I'd embarrass you?" She crumples her speech paper and tosses it towards the nearby waste can, commentating "Zoozle shoots and misses. As usual." Swinging her backpack to her shoulder, she knocks it into an urn. The urn wobbles. The desk clerk looks our way and taps numbers into a phone.

"Bill thought we shouldn't discriminate among the grandkids," I lie. "Remember when you gave that election speech in high school and your mind went blank?"

"Sure, Mom. I was sixteen. Maybe I've learned something in the years since? Have I grown up at all? You think I am just one total fuck up." She leans her head into her knees, and I'm afraid she's going to vomit, which would be a horror in an exclusive hotel like this. She regains her breath, though her face is a frightful pale greenish-white when she sits up again. "And who would care if I messed up? Just you. It's always about you, you, and more you." She stands to leave. I want to quell this now, but she continues. "And as if any of the other grandkids or cousins are going to want to speak. None of them even came to the hospice."

My cheek is raw and puckered where I've bitten it. The metallic taste impels me to speak. "You know the twins are injured. You know Bill's kids are in New York. The programs are already printed. Maybe you can say this speech at the reception?" I can picture Suzann pushing people out of the way at the funeral, underlining the fact that I can't control my own daughter. People will think my classroom has kids hanging off the light fixtures if this is the way my own daughter acts.

"It's not right. How can you ignore Grandpa's wishes like that?" She is practically shouting. She purses her lips as if to spit at me, and I flinch. Her voice gets even louder. "'Your shit smells too,' Mom. I remember that quote from that Nat Turner book. Does that prove I'm smart enough? You make me sick." She turns to leave as the concierge rises from his desk to talk to the desk clerk, who is pointing towards the couches. Watching Suzann push through the revolving doors, I feel relief that she's gone and want only to disappear as fast as possible. The concierge, the desk clerk, and several guests have all turned their attention elsewhere, but their disapproval hovers in the air. Why does it matter to me? I preach self-control to my students day after day, and I control so little in my life.

Bill has control over me at school and in the family. I lack confidence in my own daughter. Most of all, I act out of fear of what people think of me. Why else would I have been so strict with Suzann, right down to flushing her goldfish when she disobeyed me. Why did I remove her from her grandfather's funeral program?

I manage to get to Phillip's door where I knock lightly, and he brings me in, enfolding me in an embrace that is full and exactly what I need.

He tilts my chin up, not to kiss me, but to assess me. "How are you? Better or worse?"

"Worse."

"Let's go to the restaurant. No wait. I'll order room service. Come in and relax."

I slide off my shoes. Jacques jumps up on the couch next to me, taking up the other half. Phillip laughs and scoots a chair closer to us, reading a room service menu. He orders appetizers and soup. Jacques stretches and rubs his face on my rumpled slacks, leaving a trail of dog slobber. I bury my face in his soft fur.

"Suzann is mad at me," I tell Jacques loud enough for Phillip to hear.

"Yes," Phillip answers.

"She told you?"

"She said she should have been there when her Grandpa died. I think she's madder at herself than at you."

"Well, now she's mad at me with good reason." I explain about the program and Bill and the changes we made. I skip the part about Suzann's behavior in the lobby and de-emphasize that she is right. I do say she's a clueless, self-centered brat who has made a complete hash of her life. Hasn't she proved it time and again? This time, I'm at a loss of what to do.

"Can you explain why you gave in to Bill?"

I reach for Jacques, tip his furry face towards mine. "I was angry at being left out," surprised that I know this.

"Do you think Suzann feels left out now?"

"Probably." Looking at Jacques' trusting expression, I see a reflection of me in his eyes. I look old and bitter.

Phillip scrutinizes the program. "Did you email a copy of this to yourself, Jolene?"

I nod.

"We can change the speakers back, email it to Kinko's around the corner, and pick up the revision before the evening ends."

"What will Bill say?"

"What has Suzann already said? Who's right?"

"Suz."

"Exactly."

On Phillip's lap top, we log on to my Internet account, bring up the program and make the changes. Bill will not speak, Suzann will, just as Daddy asked. Winona will read Psalm 23. If certain egos take a bruising, so what? A confirmation tells us that the programs will be ready in an hour. Phillip massages my shoulders.

The waiter knocks at the door and rolls in a cart with gleaming silver dishes. Jacques leaps off the couch and comes to sit by the table as the waiter sets places and napkins. Phillip ties a napkin around Jacques's neck, and we laugh as Jacques barks his approval.

Potato, leek, and scallop soup, crispy empanadas filled with spinach, an array of cheeses, a tall bottle of sparkling water. My stomach growls, and Phillip laughs.

I point at Jacques. "That was him."

Phillip tips the waiter and signs the check, lifts his glass, and toasts, "In the spirit of Joe Franklin, I salute life and joy." I click his glass to mine, and we eat with murmurs of delight. Each scallop is tender, seared and flakey. The empanadas are hot inside, the filling like spanakopita.

There is more food than we want or need. Jacques gets several bites of empanada crust. Phillip gathers things on the tray and places them outside his door.

"Let's finish this bottle," he tops off our glasses, "and then we can walk over for the programs."

"How do I cover the changes at the funeral without causing a scene?" I ask, crinkling my forehead at the vision of Bill going ballistic.

"I bet it's no problem at all," Phillip smiles. He hugs me again, and I wish I could spend the night in his arms. I have to get home and clean up. I should try to reach Suzann to tell her that I know I was in the wrong and that everything is fixed now. Surely, a small confession like that would help our relationship.

For the moment though, I rest my head against Phillip's shoulder. I know I'll cry myself sick tonight. For this one minute more, I understand Daddy's joy in believing that death would soon put him back in his Janie's arms.

CHAPTER 11: ZOOZLE

On Wednesday, Grandpa Joe is buried next to Grandma Janie on a hillside in the Glen of Peace Memorial Park. Their policy allows neither grave monuments nor tombstones, only simple plaques over each grave. The hillside faces west, and the morning ceremony is bathed in sunlight from behind.

The sun soothes me as if Grandpa Joe's hand rests between my shoulder blades.

I chose an ankle-length black jersey skirt with an organdy, long-sleeved white blouse over a white camisole. I even have on black, high-heeled sandals.

Bill strides in at the last minute with Nory, finds no front-row seats remaining, and sits in the second row. He looks twice at the programs and taps my mother's shoulder. Mom shakes her head and puts her finger on her lips.

The service is short. Uncle Mitch's eulogy captures some of Grandpa Joe's best rhymes, puns, and jokes that have us laughing through our tears. Uncle Mitch concludes, "Very few of us live with such joy and die with no fear as my brother did. We'll miss him."

After Mitch, Uncle Art gets up to speak, but breaks down in tears. Even when my mom stands by him, taking his hand, he can not go on. Winona reads as planned without the fire and brimstone her church favors. I close the eulogies with my little speech. Looking out at the small crowd, I see Eric and Chloris together in the back row; they have been true friends to me. Sal stands with his hat in his hands, next to where Simon is seated, Simon's walker behind his chair. Phillip is in the last row of seats, Jacques lying with his head on his paws.

Mitch has arranged for a Marine honor guard and a rifle salute. Uncle Bill curls the folded flag to his chest. The hired-for-the-day minister in frayed vestments blesses the deceased and blesses the family. He glances at his watch more than once as people stand to share memories.

Escape from the family's party afterward is not an option. I have a role to play for a few hours more before I can return to what is now *my* trailer by the sea. Driving to Uncle Art's, I play the last tracks of *Evita* and choreograph a somber ballet.

Entering Uncle Art's home, I grab a cup of hot coffee in an art deco cup and a chicken salad sandwich from the simple buffet. No one else seems to be indoors at the moment except Uncle Art's ancient Mexican cook and housekeeper. Magdalena, barely five feet tall and dressed in her usual full-length peasant-style apron over a black blouse and black polyester slacks, busies herself in the kitchen arranging frosted sugar cookies on a tray, her back to me, and I sneak by to avoid crying in her arms. Chili-fragrant tamales steam on the stove, reminding me of Christmases past, the whole family as one.

Huge mission-themed chairs and tables dominate every room. White table linens on half a dozen tables invite guests into the sunny backyard where a chorus line of purple-on-purple and white-on-pink geraniums toss their showy flounces in the chilly breeze. Pole heaters help. Already about twenty people, all old, sit chatting at the tables. I know maybe a dozen of them. I settle by Mom, as she chats with Uncle Bill and Nory. across the table. Nory is fair-haired and elegant if somewhat overweight. Her size-22 white suit stands out like a formal gown at a tea party against the black blobs of the other mourners. She says she knows black is more customary, but white is the new black. Would somebody tell her black is more flattering?

"Suzann, your little speech was just right," Uncle Bill congratulates. "Grandpa Joe would be very proud of you." His words sound as hollow as the false bottom of a magician's suitcase.

My mom agrees. "I liked it too, Suzann."

"Thanks."

Uncle Bill resumes his conversation, evidently right where he had left off.

"I have everything set with the will. Things should settle in about forty-five days. The catch will be selling the car and the trailer." Dollar signs ka-ching behind his narrow eyes.

I jolt to attention. Under the table, I yank at my mom's skirt, but she moves her chair out of my reach. Mom hits her chin with her old diamond ring. She presses a napkin to the cut, which serves her right. She's a freaking two-faced pretend mother if there ever was one. First, she dumps me from the program, then she puts me back in, and now she allows Uncle Bill to manipulate the trailer away from me.

"Uncle Bill, Grandpa Joe said I could keep the trailer. Mitch knows." People turn to look toward our table. "Where's Mitch?" I holler, and other conversations around the yard stop. I'm thinking oh god, oh god, I cannot lose one more piece of myself. Grandpa Joe is lost to me, and now my own family wants to take away his house, our special place, my true home, my spot in the universe where I am me, and I am safe.

"Well, he didn't write anything like that into the will, Suzann. When exactly did this happen? The lawyers might say something else about it." Uncle Bill frowns at the hitch.

"He loved that trailer. And he loved me. He wanted me to live there." My voice wavers more than it did when I said my eulogy. "Don't do this to me, Uncle Bill."

"If Suzann says that was Dad's promise, then we shouldn't fight it." My mom certainly doesn't want me coming to live at home.

"What do you mean *if*, Mom? Like I would lie about a promise?" I push away from the table, ready to leave.

I spit out more words. "I've already put about a thousand resumés in at dance studios here in town. And one of the junior colleges, Puente Rojo, posted for a dance advisor. I just need to set up an interview. Please, Uncle Bill, help me with the trailer."

Nory listens. She looks at me as if I am one of the caterers' helpers. She checks her nail polish.

Bill puts his arm around me. "Don't worry. One way or another, things will work out for you."

I interrupt him. "I have to live in Grandpa's trailer. It was my only special place in the entire world. Grandpa Joe is the only one in this whole family who believed in me." I look at my mom. She is wringing her hands. She knows it's true. She believed in my dancing and my ability, but she never believed in *me*. "I love the ocean and the bay. I like walking around town. Don't worry, I've met some good people through the hospice staff." I collapse back into my chair, hug my arms and knees against my body, hide my face.

Uncle Bill has turned away to glad hand a few more relatives as they mill around the backyard. He turns back to me and grasps my shoulder. I flinch away. "Don't get your heart set on the trailer. I'll see what I can do. Nory and I have to go now. We have a flight to catch to Sacramento -- big meeting with the Education Commission." He can't resist adding, "The guv should be there."

With a wave, he and Nory trot through the chain link gate to their new red Camaro convertible, which is parked on Uncle Art's front side lawn. At the gate, they almost collide with Mitch, Kaye, and Winona.

Uncle Bill expedites the formalities of greeting them and continues to usher Nory to the car, his body language exhaling *close one*.

The others join us. Silence falls. Winona lets out a dramatic sigh and announces sourly, "He's going to hell, you know."

I could choke her. Mitch intercedes with a weary, "Not now, Winona. We all know your views on Joe and religion. Just not now, if you don't mind." Winona puffs out her reddened cheeks, scoots her chair sideways from the table and opens her Bible, flipping from flagged page to flagged page. She's intent on finding a verse to prove Joe's fate in the flames.

Thank God that Jacques and Phillip are here. Phillip puts his arm across the back of my chair and tilts his own chair back on two legs. He stretches. He caresses my wrist lightly. He has calluses on his fingertips.

"Hey, I liked what you said about Grandpa Joe."

I try to smile.

Mitch and Kaye agree. Winona gawps a moment, says nothing.

Phillip points at my napkin, with its untouched chicken sandwich. "Show me where the buffet is. I'm starving." He swoops the sandwich into his mouth as we leave, an easy escape.

We go to the dining room, stopping in the kitchen to talk to Magdelena.

"Your Grandpa Joe, he was my friend," she says. "I am so sad, *niña*."

"He loved you too, Magdalena." I put my arm around Magdalena's narrow shoulders. She barely reaches my chest in height.

Magdelena piles a plate high with tamales, sandwiches, potato salad and cookies from her reserves in the kitchen. "You need to eat, Ms. Suzann. You are too skinny."

"Thank you, sweet Magdelena." I kiss her wrinkled cheek.

Phillip pulls me out the front door with his left hand, balancing his overloaded plate and a napkin with his right. A cushioned garden swing faces the iron-railed porch. It is a quiet spot. He unwraps a tamale, bites a big chunk and smiles. He pushes another couple of chunks onto his fork and offers them to me. I gulp a piece and spill another on my blouse, burn my tongue, wave my hand in front of my mouth.

"Spicy!" I go back in, reach in the ice chest for beers, switch to colas, and return, handing one to Phillip.

"Tell me how you're doing, Suzann."

"I'm doing okay."

"Come on, now. There's more to the story." Phillip's persistence is both endearing and annoying.

"Call me Zoozle."

Phillip hoots. "What? Dweezle?"

"No, ZOO-zle. Like SU, but Zoo. Get it?"

"I guess. Besides that, what's happening?"

I gloss over the days at the hospice, the time I spent at Grandpa Joe's before that, a little bit about therapy sessions with Mom, how both of us were holding back more than opening up. I avoid telling Phillip about my real work in the past with Dr. Penny Huizenga or about Javier.

"It was so boring in this latest program, Phillip. I couldn't have my phone. Just group meetings, journaling, and hanging around reading these quasi-inspirational magazines, *Borscht Bull for Meth Heads*, or something. The Twelve Steps over and over and over. I think I made progress just to get out of there."

"And was it progress? The Twelve Steps work, don't they?

I squirm.

"Zoozle?"

"Yeah, I'm clean," I equivocate. Phillip puts his plate on the tiled table. He searches my face for truth or deception. Winona bangs through the front door, Bible in hand. She marches down the street in search of Mitch's car where she can finish her devotions in solitude.

"Don't lie to me. Are you staying?"

Clean or in town? I wonder. "I want to."

"So do it."

"I want to."

Phillip holds my hand, watching two neighbor kids shoot hoops in their driveway. "If you want to, you will." His wry smile wavers. "I've been there. Did you know that?"

I shake my head. "No way."

"Well, it's true. I went through some very bad years, using alcohol to cope when my wife, Ariel, died. I was older than you, but not wiser. AA made the difference. Don't think of life as stairs of sand, crumbling with each mistake. Think of mistakes as forgiveness in the form of water that turns sand into concrete. You can climb up your mistakes if you forgive them and reach solid ground."

Taking this in, I wonder about the world. How could this debonair good man have been anything other than what I see right now? "I need something concrete to lean on, for sure. Like, I'm supposed to inherit Grandpa's trailer because Grandpa Joe told me I could have it. But now Uncle Bill says he doubts the lawyers will honor the agreement." I pull my hand from Phillip's and fray the piping on the seat cushion. "It makes me so mad. Uncle Bill has everything he could want -- why can't he just let this one thing go?"

"It's probably not up to Uncle Bill," says Phillip. "Your mom and I can look into it."

"How long are you here? Do you have time for me to take Jacques back to the beach? He loved it. Right, Jacques?" His tail thumps against the porch's railing.

"Not this trip. I'll be back in a couple weeks. Your mom's going to have some hard times with her dad gone. Try to deal with her, okay?"

"I'm not sure. It's not just me causing problems for my mom. It goes both ways. You don't really know her yet."

"But I want to. Since I retired, I don't have any big deadlines in Washington to rush home to except our normal rounds. People perk up when Jacques comes to visit. I hate to disappoint them." Phillip drags a hand across his face, probably thinking of the long drive and my complicated family.

"Really, Phillip, could I take Jacques with me for one last walk? He would like it, and it would calm me down. I'll bring him back tonight to your hotel? About 8?" He gives me a smile and Jacques' leash. "You have my number. Tell my mom I took off. I'll get Jacques back before bed time." I hop up and let Phillip hug me tightly. Even though he is still seated in the swing, he is about as tall as I am standing.

"Alright, Suzann, I mean, Zoozle. Live the Twelve Steps, sweetheart. Heal." Jacques cocks his head, having heard "heel." Phillip laughs and gets up to wave and nearly hits his nose against the fuchsia pots hanging from the awning..

I'm carrying my sandals as I start walking along the sidewalk. I wonder if I can get the job and what I'll do if Uncle Bill rips the trailer out from under me. There's no room for me at Eric's what with Chris's attitude. Can I really feel any worse than I do right now? I am thankful to have Jacques to hug.

A car purrs around the corner. The driver scans the crowded curbs for a parking space. Javier is behind the wheel.

He pulls up in the driveway beside me.

"What are you doing here?" I know this is the wrong approach, but the best defense is a good offense. Uncle Bill preaches that philosophy, not that I want to be like Uncle Bill.

"Your mom called me about the service for Grandpa. And hi to you too." Javier is talking to me through the open window on the car's passenger side. With his sun glasses on, I can't really see his expression. His warm brown eyes are his best feature.

"I'm just shocked to see you. It's not exactly a good day." I hold on by being abrupt.

Javier rests his forehead on the steering wheel, and I could escape right now. But I linger. He says, "I loved Grandpa Joe. He liked me too. I thought coming down here was only right."

"Great. But you missed the service. My mom is still inside. Have fun." I pull my car keys out of my purse and drop my sandals in doing so. Javier laughs a little, and I say the way I always used to, "Shut up, okay?"

He gets out. He looks good, like he's getting enough sleep and exercise. He didn't look so hot when we parted in Port Townsend last April. He picks up my sandals and sits down on the curb. I sit near him, not close enough to be hugged or grabbed at.

"Always with a dog. Boo is fine, by the way." He looks at me, but I don't answer. Jacques decides to sniff Javier's crotch and paws at Javier's pockets.

"Jacques, stop it." Could he have done anything more embarrassing? But both Javier and I are laughing.

"Suz, we don't have to be enemies."

"So you say." I stand up, ready to flee.

"Hey, wait. What are your plans?" He looks up at me, and his expression reveals the anguish that characterized our married life, our backs to one another in bed night after night when I squirmed out of his reach, our façade of newlywed bliss in public.

"Plans?"

"Are you coming back north?"

"No."

He stands. He's so tall and he's so handsome with that black curling hair and he's wearing a suit. I always loved to see him in a suit; it was so rare. "I heard from Burt Rapshon. He says they miss you in the department and want you back."

"Really? I like it here though. Grandpa left me his trailer. I have a head start. San Diego suits me."

"It wasn't Washington making you miserable, Suz." Javier's eyes mist over in memory of our troubles.

"Thanks for reminding me."

"You look better." He smiles again, lights up the street. The sun has disappeared behind new storm clouds.

"The last time you saw me, I guess I couldn't have looked worse." I'm ashamed to think of the state I was in back in June, unable to walk, infections on my feet and ankles, my wrists, my underarms, out of my mind with boredom and withdrawal.

"You could. Before you went in, you looked worse. Are you through seeing that Mel and her crowd?" Javier knows my manias and my hysterical fits when the drugs were at their peak and my dealer was late or when I had nothing left to pawn. When I wasn't high with Mel, we were out at the pawn shops, taking in whatever we could for drug money. Javier didn't walk away from our marriage with much.

"My shrinks, the old one Penny and the new one here, insist, and so does my mom, and so do all my new friends. They're so right. I'm so done with Mel." And I realize in this moment, I am done with Mel. I will tell her tonight if she hasn't left as I asked her to. "Same old thing—she wants to live near me, sponge off me some more. She was fun though."

"That's not a good kind of fun." Javier hates Melody. Mom and Javier, they both continue to blame her. My troubles were not her fault. They won't believe it.

"Whatever. I'm learning to live again. I met some people here. They help." I think of Phillip and Jacques, Eric at the funeral and of Chloris in the grove, even Lordman at the deli. They aren't users. They'll help keep me straight.

"Cool. I like Spokane. It's beautiful and outdoorsy and I'm meeting people." He stops as if he shouldn't have said that. Javier stares up at the clouds, pulls his jacket tighter around him.

"Javier?" I look at him.

"Yeah?" He looks at me.

"I'm sorry about us." I swallow a huge lump. It's made of pride and sorrow.

"Me too."

"I didn't know when we got married that I couldn't handle it. Therapy has helped. Did you talk to anyone ever?" I want him to understand that it wasn't his fault that I am the way I am, not capable of making love unless I'm drunk or high, stuck in adolescence until I can free myself of the Francis secret I've kept so long.

"No, no I didn't."

"Well, you should. I guess I'd better go. I'm really tired. Be sure to go in and say hi to my mom. She's missed you." I almost add the word *too*, bite it back in time. "Come on, Jacques." Javier pats the dog, and Jacques bounds into my car.

On my way home, I wonder why it had to be this way. Javier once loved me. I tried to play the role, get married, look forward to kids, have a career. Therapy has helped me understand first, I have to deal with the past. Then I can have a future.

Though the weather is cold, I head for the beach with Jacques. He romps in and out of the water. I sit and sit and sit. At last, I get up, call Phillip and drive Jacques to Phillip's hotel. Phillip meets me out front, sweeps his cap off, opens the car door and envelops Jacques in a huge towel. We wave goodbye.

Evening. I am cold deep into my bones. I'm back from the hotel and the beach, alone in the trailer, and I pull Grandpa Joe's quilt up to my chin. I wish he had a fireplace. I used to feel so warm when I was here. Mel and Mel's junk are gone. She left a note for me, "Have fun, Zooz. I'm scoping out your cousins, so drop by if you miss me." She signed it with X's and O's. I put on soft flannel pajamas Grandpa left in his drawer and tuck myself into his bed, listening to wind gusting through the palm trees. The fronds rattle like bones. I'm scared, empty, still cold. Maybe someday I won't sleep alone.

CHAPTER 12: JOLENE

I'm longing for my solitude, an end to all this remember when. I wish people would quit descending on me to offer their regrets.

Each memory is cherished, sacred, wonderful and heartbreaking. I'm tired of crying.

Suzann, as usual, has created a scene, fought with me, riled Bill, and disappeared. Winona has wandered off, Phillip too. My chin has quit bleeding, but it's a good excuse to leave Mitch and Kaye, "Ice," I say, pointing at my cut. As I walk into the house, Phillip's shadow appears on the front porch. He's in earnest conversation from the way his shoulder tilts towards another man's. The other man is familiar in his stance, and – something sharp pokes against my heart— it's Javier, the son I never had. He is one more treasure that Suzann tossed aside, this good, funny, wonderful man. She never told me exactly why; she said "the marriage is over, he doesn't keep me safe," and that was the end of the conversation. How could he not keep her safe? He is tall, he is handsome, he is smart, he loved her. And he still loves me.

After a quick brush at my hair and a cold cloth across my puffy eyes and chin in the bathroom, I rush to the porch to join them.

Javier looks nearly the same as he did on his wedding day, a lifetime or two ago. The brightness I associate with his eyes is layered with fatigue.

I rush in to hug him, holding back tears.

"Madre," he says, using the name we agreed on once they were engaged. "I've missed you so much. I'm sorry about Grandpa. We always laughed a lot together even if he thought my dance career was a little," he flips his hand back and forth, "swishy?" Javier smiles his beautiful smile. "How are you?"

"Very glad you came. Thank you for making the trip." I look at Phillip, who has stood back. "Did you meet our own Guardian Angel, Phillip McKillop?"

"I did. And Suzann introduced me to Jacques as well." He brushes at the paw prints on his pants.

"Javier still lives up north, Phillip. Walla Walla, right?"

"Spokane."

"I can't remember facts today. I couldn't even tell people Daddy's birth year. I hope this senility isn't permanent." My fake laugh sounds like a crow's call. "Do you like it there?"

"Sure. I could use more sunshine. When we first moved to Port Townsend, Suzann kept me warm." He shakes his head. "She looks good."

What can I say to that? That's she as screwed up and stupid as ever? "Yes, better," I admit, but blink back tears at what used to be.

Phillip comes over beside me. He takes my hand. I feel as if he is pulling me back from a dark tunnel. "Don't be so hard on yourself. You're allowed to grieve."

At a shout of men's laughter in the living room, Javier excuses himself to say hello to the others. "I'll call you, Madre, before I leave town. Same cell?"

"Same."

I follow his progress into the house. A small sigh shivers through me. Phillip holds my hand more tightly.

"How about a walk on the beach or the esplanade?"

"All I can think about right now is sleep, Phillip. Maybe tomorrow. When are you heading home?"

"Jacques and I have a lot of friends to visit between here and Washington. We're not in a hurry. My cousin has a Career Day. She wants me to bring Jacques. It's at San Clemente High next week."

"The kids will love him! Is Jacques in the kitchen with Magdalena? I know he's a treat hound."

"With Suzann, er, Zoozle?"

I want to shake him. "Please do not begin using that Zoozle nonsense with me."

Phillip draws a finger across his mouth, zipping his lip. "Okay for now. Guess I should be going. Zzzz-Suzann is going to call before she brings Jacques back this evening."

The day has caught up with me. My head feels foggy. I really am not ready for Phillip to leave. "Phillip, will you come to my school — it's Bill's too — remember he's my brother and my boss, my principal. You could present a Career Day for my ninth graders?" It's a gamble, I know, but I want to secure a connection with Phillip.

"How soon?"

"I'm going back Friday to pick up papers, but I'll start teaching again Monday. Maybe you could come next Wednesday?" My heart is hammering. You'd think I was a ninth grader myself.

"We can be there. I'll go to San Clemente and double back to your school. What time?"

"Let me check the calendar — Bill throws in special schedules to show off his latest programs at assemblies or puts in a pep rally that no one attends. I'll call you."

Phillip pulls my hand up towards his chest and tugs me towards him. It is delicious to be held. He rests his chin on the top of my head. He hums "Someone to Watch Over Me."

"I'll watch over you, Jolene. Count on me."

Wonderful words, those, and one tense rope loosens its binding across my heart.

CHAPTER 13: ZOOZLE

A car alarm goes off at 4 on this Monday morning, the sound too far away to be mine, as if I would have a car alarm anyway. It could be a burglary or taggers. Who cares? I toss and turn, give up and sit in Grandpa's chair, doze off. By 8, I'm on the porch, reading the paper and crying as I smile at Grandpa's Buddha, hoping Simon doesn't toddle over for a chat.

A phone begins ringing, not my cell, Grandpa's. There's no message machine so the ringing doesn't stop. I rush inside to pick up.

It's Uncle Bill. His spiel, delivered in machine-gun bursts, leaves me no chance to interrupt. He's already checked with the lawyers. I cannot stay here. The trailer will be sold. Death bed promises don't hold up with the attorneys. I need to move out so they can haul the trailer back to the dealer, who will sell it on commission. Bill says Nory will check their rentals and see if there's something I can stay in, like they would do that for me.

He probably won't come through anyway since I tell him to fuck off and leave me alone. I unplug the phone and throw it across the kitchen into the bedroom. It hits the corner of the dresser with a muffled jangle.

I brew some coffee and stew in my choices. I call Puente Rojo, getting the first good news in about a hundred years. I can be interviewed this afternoon if I am available. I'm not in the mood to play perky dance adviser, but what can I do? I look at the outfit I wore to Grandpa's funeral. Maybe I can put a pin over that tamale blob. I get started. The next thing I know, I am dressed and on my way to Puente Rojo. It's a forty-minute drive north and east on busy freeways, but straightforward enough. Something else I love about San Diego is that I feel oriented in my directions: the ocean is west, the Laguna Mountains rise in the east, Mexico is south, and big, bad LA is north. You can practically see the brown layer of LA smog from where I am, 120 miles away.

The secretary told me to park in lot J. A surly, fat, frat boy parking attendant with a love-patch beard looks up from his cell phone game app, probably "Kill the Ballerinas" and sends me off into the hills, lot D. It's a ten-minute walk up about fifteen flights of stairs and I'm in my spike heels, having managed to get the cemetery's sod off with Windex and a sponge. I have enough time since my mom's scheduled training works in my favor when I have an appointment. I'm lots of dumb things, but late isn't one of them.

They have my paperwork, including letters of recommendation, and I brought the video of my girls' last big show in April. Was that last century? I'm hoping these people haven't made phone calls to Port Townsend or if they did, maybe they reached my friendly supervisor, Bert Rapshon, the dean, rather than Archie. Archie hates my guts because he knows about the drug stuff and he has to take me back if I pass the drug tests. The state of Washington is enlightened that way, calling addiction an illness rather than a flaw of character. Maybe they could write a letter to my mom?

I find the office and spend thirty seconds trying to get my hair to look something besides icky. My hair is growing. Only the fringes are still pink. My brooch from of one of grandpa's bolo tie ornaments and a safety pin covers the tamale stain on my blouse. The sum of me is that I look odd enough to be chic. Appearances count; just ask my mom.

A secretary leads me down a short, narrow hallway. All the walls are painted a flat gray, but posters of Broadway shows add color, if prehistoric musicals like *Bye Bye Birdie* turn you on.

A committee of three, two women and a man, sits around a long institutional conference table of faux enameled ash. The older woman points me to a green plastic chair at the head of the table. The woman's hair is wrapped in a gauzy beige turban splotched with grotesque burgundy roses; she wears a caftan in the same fabric. She is slight in build, her face stiff around the eyes and lips from either a stroke or anti-wrinkle treatments. The other woman is considerably younger, she has platinum blond hair bisected by four inches of black from the roots to the blond. Her face is tawny, and she seems to radiate energy that would be infectious on another day. She's wearing a low-cut black leotard and tights plus the school's red warm-up jacket unzipped. God, I used to be that young. Compared to her, I'm a walking ghost.

The man looks quite GQ, with his narrow face, long reddish hair, and an expensive business suit. The hair is killing me--it's swept back into a pony tail except for two curls hanging by his ears. I can't say how old he is, maybe a young forty? His tie is cubed in a pink and purple geometric print. His nails are manicured, and I slip my raggedy nails under the table.

We go through the regular opening motions, how are you, how was the drive, who's who. One important bit of information is that the new adviser needs to begin a week from today.

Leotard-girl, Veronica Slattery, throws out the opening salvo, "Why should we hire you? What's so special about you?" I'd like to tell her, you probably shouldn't count on me because I've messed up everything I've tried to achieve in the past six months, including my own suicide and babysitting my grandpa who is now dead and buried, plus I hate stupid conventions like interviews, but somehow something better comes out of my mouth, and they all smile. What I actually said was, "I'm industrious." I guess that kind of threw them. They act like I'm Isadora Duncan without the scarves.

GQ man, David Inman, asks me to summarize my approach to the teaching of dance. I can do that from rote, so while my mouth is blabbing on and on about the freedom of the body and the artist's expressiveness being like the flame of a candle set by the sea, two-thirds of the committee smiles these toothy smiles. The other third raises her lip so her upper gums show.

Finally, upper gum-lady, department chair, Dr. Jessie Garant ("please call me Ms. Garant, not Dr. Garant") asks if there is anything else I would like to tell them about my goals for their dance team?

My goals for their dance team include the girls not bothering me in the middle of the night crying over some idiot college romance and not losing their cell phones and going ballistic during college trips, and to please remember they are adults so their mommies shouldn't call me when they don't get a solo. I stuff that answer and let them know that I believe any group of girls under my tutelage absolutely blossoms and that a mere state championship would be the least of our goals, because the national championship can be achieved, never mind that my illness right before nationals last semester prevented a championship at Port

Townsend State. They nod and look sympathetic, and I expect them to pull the contract out and let me sign on the dotted line and then I can get the hell out of here. They ask me to wait outside for a moment.

A moment turns into five minutes. When I lean against the door I hear fierce whispering, but catch none of it. Nothing has ever happened the way I expected it to, so I am shocked when it finally does. Ms. Garant calls me in, says the vote was 2-1, puts a contract in front of me after asking if she should include *Quintanilla* on the pay roll form, and I sign on the dotted line. She points out that I have agreed to a security camera in the dance studio throughout my probationary period, one she can monitor from her office and that Veronica will be in charge of setting up each practice session.

"No problem," I agree. It sounds like a good safety measure for me to escape charges of being overly harsh with the dear girls.

I am quite giddy with relief. Veronica cuts her eyes at me and says she has to run to catch her next class. Ms. Garant unloads the campus tour and department introductions onto David, which I definitely prefer.

He walks with a hitch, saying he needs knee surgery after all the years of dance. He is taller than he appeared when we were all seated. He has flashing green eyes, but maybe those are contact lenses. Anyway, we walk across the campus, which is mostly concrete. I wish I had my tennies in a tote because these heels are killing my feet

Dave is chatty, filling me in about the growth of the college and the dance department, alluding confidentially that he expects to be the next department chair when Madame retires.

"What about housing?" I ask to break up the monologue.

"Unlimited! Condo or an apartment out near Mira Mesa or in Escondido for a third of the cost near the beach. All that fog and overpriced property, who needs it anyway?" He peels his sunglasses out of his pocket as if he just remembered it's sunny out and he needs to look cool.

I ignore the question about the beach because losing the trailer is one more new heartbreak this week. "How about Hillcrest?" That's where Chloris and Eric live.

Dave looks at me, his mouth open a trifle too far, and his profile no longer looks handsome. "It's expensive and über-trendy, especially with the gay community. You're thinking Hillcrest?"

"Maybe. My friends live near there."

"There's always a roommate," he suggests, raising his eyebrows as if I might tell him more about me than came out in the interview. "And the college will pay your moving expenses. Go to the personnel office and get the relocation forms."

"I don't have much time to decide," I hedge. "Plus, I've got other appointments today, so I better run. Where do I report for my first day of class?"

Dave lets me know that I'll get a packet from personnel with all pertinent information, including the appointment for a physical and a drug test. Drug test? I hadn't thought of that, but it's as good a way as any to stay on the straight and narrow, the concrete as Phillip said. Sand into concrete, just add water.

I can hit my mom up for first and last month's rent. My mind is running through a thousand details. There's always darling Uncle Bill, who could come through with a cheap rental or freebie somewhere.

That's about as likely as my having a heart-to-heart with my mom. First, we'd have to find her heart.

I swing into the trailer park with plans to call my mom and see if maybe she can find a word of praise for the fact that I am once again employed, which will be the best time to ask for my little cash advance. I know my job news will make her day. I'll call from Grandpa Joe's phone, or maybe I won't because seeing that number might give her a heart attack like some séance deal, voices from the dead. With her yoga junk ongoing, who knows what weird stuff she's into on the side?

Simon's hanging out in front of his trailer. I'm exhilarated enough to tell him thanks for coming to the funeral so I wave as I park the car and hop-skip on over there.

"Hi Simon," I say with what I think is convincing enthusiasm. I don't even wrinkle my nose from the stench of his cigar. Before I can get another word out, his face gets red and he looks like he's going to keel over in front of me.

"Don't you hold anything sacred?" he asks me. "Joe's barely in the ground."

"Huh?"

"That moving van. It came about an hour ago. I swear they took everything in there. Why'd you have to take his stuff away so fast? He said there were things he wanted me to have for old-times' sake, like some movies."

"What?" My heart rate zooms, and I trot away from him to the sliding doors of the trailer, which gape open.

The place is stripped. Not a picture, not a chair, not a bed. The telephone and telephone table, *nada.* Grandpa's closet is empty. Yet the patio furniture and the Buddha sit unmolested on the deck.

Everybody says Uncle Bill is a cold-hearted eel, but this is ridiculous. I call Mitch to ask what he knows, but I can't reach him. Art, no answer. Grandpa's Rolodex phone list has evaporated. My cell is in my little business purse, so I impulsively hit my mom's number.

All I get is her voice mail. I call the school directly and tell Dorrie it's an emergency. It is an emergency, isn't it? Dorrie can't get through to my mom's classroom, so they send some lucky soul up there— her classroom is about a quarter of a mile up a hill from the office. I can picture my mom's annoyance to be interrupted in the middle of teaching Yeats or Keats or whatever she considers the most important thing in life today because she would jump back in without missing a beat even though her dad just died.

I'm on hold for like twenty minutes.

"What is it?" she asks, without even a hello.

"Did you know Uncle Bill was going to empty the trailer today?" I'm mad and getting frenzied.

"Why would he do that?"

"He said the lawyers want the trailer sold. I came home, and it's empty. Simon saw a crew strip everything out of here." My voice echoes in the void. I look at the empty walls. Grandpa's quilt is gone.

My mom sounds like she's hyperventilating. She gives me Uncle Bill's number for his cell and suggests I ask him directly because she has to get back to class. I forgot to tell her about my job.

I ring through to Uncle Bill. I'm amazed he picks up because of the way I exited our last conversation. He's probably surrounded by big wigs at a four-star restaurant lunch and doesn't want to look bad in front of his buddies. The district has weird priorities when it comes to principals and lunch versus kids and books.

"Suzann," he greets me, "what can I do for you?"

"Well, you could tell me where my stuff is for starters."

"Your stuff?"

"Look, the moving van you ordered got here and all my stuff was taken along with Grandpa Joe's. I know you want me out of here. Still, this is pretty crappy."

"What moving van? Slow down. What are you talking about?" He finally sounds somewhat concerned instead of just putting on a show. He says he'll call me back.

While I wait, I wander through the three rooms. The crew missed taking the pots and pans out of the cupboard. A wet towel and Grandpa Joe's pajamas that I wore last night are piled in a sodden heap in the corner of the bathroom where the shower leaks. The medicine cabinet is empty.

Bill calls back, and he zeroes in as if I'm on the witness stand on the Perry Mason reruns Grandpa watched.

"I didn't ask for a moving van. No one else has keys to that property except Mitch, and we both know he would go through things slowly. The photo albums and all that."

"What happened then?"

"I'm sure you know what I think."

"I do?"

"Don't play dumb. You're angry and you're broke and you're about to be homeless. Just tell me who you hired and let me see if I can get some of the stuff back. Did you think insurance would cover your 'loss'?" My Uncle Bill sure knows how to turn on the charm.

I walk to the window and breathe to clear my head. "We should call the cops."

"The cops?" His tone shifts to genuine surprise.

"Simon saw the van. He can describe it. We'll never see Grandpa's stuff again." My throat is tight, but I choke out, "Where am I supposed to sleep and what am I supposed to wear?"

He agrees this is serious, and he'll call someone he knows in the I.B. police department.

In the midst of all this, I've forgotten to tell Uncle Bill that I have a job. Somehow, work equates to worth in our family.

I don't have much more than damp pj's, a towel, this dressy outfit, and a set of pots to piss in.

It's probably the Cisneros boys involved in the Great Furniture Raid. Simon said the driver was Hispanic, with two flabby white guys, each with a bad leg, doing all the loading. The driver sounds like Gil. I have nothing left to lose, well, except my life, but whatever. I toss my blazer on the bed, keeping on my camisole, skirt, and heels. I zoom away to the Cisneros' house, where Gil and Sal Junior are out front, no surprise there.

Maybe I should talk to their dad because Sal Senior is the best friend my grandpa had here in town except Simon. But Gil says his dad's not home. "What's up, Chica? You only come around here when you think we got something you need."

That's basically true, but I'm mad and shrug it off.

I stand up straighter and try to look tough. "Who stripped my Grandpa's trailer?"

Hoots of laughter. Sal Junior, who's swilling cerveza, snuffs beer froth up his nose he's laughing so hard.

"What?"

"My grandpa's trailer. There's nothing left in it, and I need my stuff back, and his too."

"Dude, we wouldn't do that." They both shake their heads vigorously. "No way."

"You wouldn't?."

"Over there." Gil leans his head to the left. "Those dudes who hang here sometimes, those white boys who think they are cool-io, they like to fuck with people, you know? Oh, 'scuse me. We ain't supposed to toss F-bombs at white girls. Except that one who was with you. She's a hot mama."

"Why would they do that to their own family unless somebody told them there would be drug money to gain?" I feel my pulse racing with the insult of it all. And of course, there's Mel, who has introduced herself into my family. Why didn't I hear MEL being screamed from the empty trailer? "Got me there, chica. But check back with us. We hear stuff. What's the big deal about the old man's crap anyway?" He tosses his empty beer bottle towards a trash can.

I don't want to go into what's the big deal. But I play the nostalgia card, which isn't a fake. I leave them looking serious. They promise to help me if they hear anything in the neighborhood.

Mitch is sitting on the porch when I get back to the trailer. He has seen the damage and if a man ever looked like a zombie, it's Mitch.

"I didn't do it," I toss out for openers.

"I know you didn't. Bill called me to check on things." Mitch's chin quivers. He didn't cry in front of us at the funeral, but this seems to be the last straw.

"You can stay with Winona for the next couple of weeks if you want. She has room."

I'd rather go stay in the Tijuana jail than stay with Aunt Winona, but I thank Mitch for the offer and tell him I'll get back to him. He touches the Buddha, waves with the slightest motion of his wrist and tromps over to Simon's.

I try to reach Eric and Chloris by phone. I leave messages and even consider driving out to the hospice, which would be really rude when I think about the work they do. My problems diminish if I remember to weigh them against other people's. Grandpa Joe always said if we all put our troubles into a circle and walked around them, we'd pick up our own instead of someone else's.

I drive by Winona's apartment to see if I could stand it. In the plus column, it's only five blocks from the beach and around the corner from Uncle Mitch and Aunt Kaye. In the minus column, it's around the corner from Uncle Mitch, Aunt Kaye and their injured, probably Oxy-addicted sons and Mel, which means the proximity might undercut my abstinence plan, staying away from Mel, staying away from drugs.

The building is painted tonsil pink. It has a wooden green palm tree motif going on around the front and this tiki-thatched roof portico. In the '50s it was the luxury hot spot in Imperial Beach, totally Hawaiian. There are eight apartments, four up and four down. Winona is on the ground floor because she wouldn't climb a flight of stairs ever.

Poochie greets me at the door with his little doggy grin and his tail wagging furiously, his fur all shaggy where Winona has been petting it against its natural flow while she watches a religious telethon. Her house smells like dog, which is fine with me, but also like burned oatmeal layered with gardenia. I'm practically gagging while she shows me the how the couch pulls out into a bed and reminds me that she likes to watch her nightly preacher on cable from 11 to midnight and she hopes the late hour won't bother me. My first class is Thursday at 8 a.m., and I have to get up at 5 and she hopes the midnight preacher won't bother me?

I am thinking of borrowing a sleeping bag and bunking in my office at the dance department when Eric rings back. My Brady Bunch ring tone bounces off the walls of Winona's studio apartment, and I step outside onto the front porch stairs to see what Eric can suggest.

Poochie scoots past me in a blur of blond fur and heads towards the street. I'm trying to talk to Eric and chasing after Poochie in my stilettos. I sign off with Eric and kick my shoes off just as Poochie makes it out the opened gate. Winona is screaming in her nasal voice, "Poochie, Poochie!" from her doorway without stepping foot outside.

The dog smells freedom or females or both. He takes off like a squirt of butterscotch syrup and dashes down the sidewalk. He veers across the street at the corner near the bus stop. A city bus rolls to a stop in a cloud of carbonous smoke. Two of the women who are waiting on the bench have pulled their legs up as if Poochie has rabies. He streaks by, barely three inches from the bus's tires.

Having missed the bus, or vice versa, the dog is frolicking down the busiest street in town, and I am not at my fastest in my stocking feet. I'm yelling, "Here Poochie, here Poochie" to his disappearing fluff. He's headed through a bougainvillea bush, still flaming with magenta flowers. He emerges on the other side covered in blossoms like confetti at a New Year's party.

Three little kids look up from their circle on the sidewalk across from the Cisneros' neighbor's house. Popsicle juice trails from the kids' mouths down their arms. They've been throwing pebbles from the gravel driveway at the yard sign that boasts "Royal Day Care for Your Prince or Princess."

"Grab him if you can," I holler. "He's named Poochie."

They laugh harder and chase around in a mad dash. Poochie stops running away to play tag with the kids. He sits and puts his paws up, and the littlest girl throws him a piece of red popsicle. Poochie slurps up the treat, and I grab his bratty ass.

"You are a bad, bad dog, Poochie."

The tallest of the kids points at me. He's wearing a battered Mickey Mouse hat with a single ear still attached, grimy blue-jean cut-offs, no shirt, no shoes. "That's a stupid name, lady."

"He's not my dog."

"We say something stinky is *poochie*. Does that dog stink?" The kid scratches what looks like a ringworm patch next to his belly button.

"Well, no, but let's just say his behavior stinks." I laugh too now that the danger is over. Out of the corner of my eye, I glimpse what looks like Grandpa Joe's chair in the garage.

"Hey kid. I'll buy that chair from you," I tell him to see what he'll say.

"It's not ours. That man who lives down there dropped it off. He was with a skinny girl. He says he's selling it at a swap meet."

I go check; the bed, the table, the recliner and love seat, all that stuff is definitely Grandpa's.

"What does the man look like?"

"I know the man's name. It's Mike, and mine is Michelle," says the littlest girl, her brown eyes lustrous with pride. "He was with a toothpick girl. Her hair is my color, only shorter." She is chewing on the ends of her braids, and then adds, "His parents are nice. They live over there." She points toward my Uncle Mitch's.

"Thanks, sweetie." Mystery solved but not the problem. My cousins are involved. Mel is involved. We have the weirdest family ever. Do I tell Mitch or just borrow a truck to remove Grandpa's stuff? How do I keep myself free of Mel's sticky web?

Poochie has finished his popsicle, and I tuck him under my arm, dog hair floating through my camisole's armhole into my bra. The hair itches like mad.

I walk on back to the pink pagoda, and Winona almost faints seeing the red on the fur near Poochie's mouth.

"Calm down, Winona. It's not blood, it's from a popsicle."

"Oh, my baby," she oozes. She looks skyward, saying, "I thank Thee Father for Thy loving care of my darling, Poochie."

I'm so glad that good old God saved the dog.

Winona scolds me and soothes poor little Poochie, who appears quite saucy and proud. I ignore the end of her speech, walk away to call Eric back, to explain my housing problems and finally remember to tell him, "Guess what, I'm employed!"

"Zoozle, you're the bomb!"

"Yeah, awesome. But I'm still homeless as soon as Bill makes a move on the trailer."

Eric doesn't offer immediate answers. He says he has to work. He'll see if Chloris can come over on the weekend. I ask Winona if I can borrow an outfit, and she tosses me a disgusting yellow t-shirt printed with "I'm Saved, Are YOU?" and oversized flip flops. I can wear these with Grandpa's pj bottoms. Chloris won't care how I'm dressed, and together, we'll hatch a plan.

CHAPTER 14: JOLENE

Coming back to school was about the sixth hardest thing I've ever done. The worst was burying my husband and the second worst was Daddy's death. All the rest relate to Suzann and her increasingly repellant behavior. I won't think about it, especially after her hysterical phone call yesterday.

It's been three days now, and I am back into my morning routine. I open my classroom door in the dark, since class begins at 7 and I get here at 5:50 to see that every thing is ready, my notes are on the podium, and the pages are marked in my textbook. The door squeaks open as it always has, no matter the kind notes I've left to the custodians, who actually like me because I don't let the kids eat in the room EVER.

My desk is still covered with three stacks of papers to grade, each over a foot high. I knew Jim wouldn't grade anything, but I wish he could have just tossed a stack or two. The kids have been grousing about this assignment or that one and wanting to know when I'll update their grades on the web site.

Soon, I tell them, soon. Bill emailed the staff as I asked him to, so of course there was an email to me too, saying "Please do not contact Mrs. Zimmerman about the loss of our father. She would prefer to keep this a private matter as she is still grieving." He hasn't thought that I will receive this email in his "all staff" quick memo. And it seems to imply that people can offer him all the condolences they want.

Today, as the others this week, is planned as an easy day back. Phillip confirmed that he and Jacques will be here by third period. That means I only have to survive the three morning classes and then he and Jacques will entertain the exuberant ninth graders both before and after lunch, and tomorrow I can make them write an essay about careers with animals. The computer lab is all set up. My mantra for today is one day at a time.

At 6:45 the first of the seniors wanders in, mumbles "How can you smile at this hour?" and puts her head down on the desk. Kristin works late; I don't know why she forces herself to take the early class.

Ten minutes later the warning bell rings, and the rest of the class saunters in. Some are friendly, some are half asleep, some look at the agenda on the television power point and comment rudely on the art work or the color scheme. Never let them see you sweat, I think, since I know a few mean well and a few are trying to get a rise out of me. It's their daily duty to torture the teacher.

We begin by going over a pre-AP exam prep quiz, arguing out the answers. It makes no sense to me to reduce poetry to scantron multiple choice, but Bill wants the seniors in AP everything, and AP Lit has a wide open curriculum. That's the only reason I'm teaching it given the pain and suffering AP anything adds to a teacher's life.

The kids get full credit for the quiz whether they miss one or all ten, but that only makes the discussion more vehement. They're so sick of being graded on everything, not being graded is a chance to show their stuff.

We are looking at Stephen Spender's "What I Expected." I lead them into thinking about how often our expectations are undercut by reality.

"Yeah, like AP Lit," tosses in Mr. Cool, Aden Fleeker.

"Shut up, Aden. I like AP Lit. And Mrs. Zimmerman," Matt, teacher's pet wannabe, offers. "This poem is amazing. But I don't get the question about the ambiguity of the word *struggles*."

"Anyone?" I ask.

No answers. No hands. Everyone looks down.

"Bueller? Bueller?" I ask, trying to make them laugh. They are too cool to laugh. "Well, who can define *ambiguity* then?"

Matt can.

"So how can a word like *struggles* be ambiguous?"

"Maybe they all feel differently about what they are doing?" Thao rarely talks in class. I smile to encourage her.

"What kinds of feelings would those be?"

Hands shoot up, and answers bounce off the walls. We are back in synch. We move from Spender to the essay in the works, rough drafts due in a week. The class resumes moaning and reminds me that they have UC essays due in the month of November, plus Halloween and Homecoming soon. I counter with the calendar I have prepared that shows the second week of November with NO HOMEWORK so that they can write their essays for UC.

"God, Mrs. Z, you think of everything," moans Aden.

"I try to," I tell him. I don't mention that at school I don't think about my dad or my daughter or the moment Phillip is going to walk in with Jacques. But my cheeks flush.

"Get out your pre-writing papers and your outlines and use the remaining ten minutes to go over your ideas. I'll be right at my desk if you need any help."

They look at me, shove their books in their backpacks, check their cell phones, and put their heads down, with the exception of Matt and Thao. I check my email and input attendance.

Two more periods, and Phillip will be here. A blip of adrenaline hits my heart. Both AP classes after the first one pass even more pleasantly with smaller enrollments and kids not half asleep.

It's brunch. I run to the bathroom, return to knosh on a bagel, and take a gulp of water. My phone rings. Today, I didn't unplug it to let my voice mail handle all the annoying parent calls not to mention the office looking for someone to cover for this malingerer or that one, waiting for this very phone call. Phillip is on his way up with Jacques, escorted by the career advisor, Ms. Polonsey.

I check the mirror in my teacher's closet and accept that this is how I look — better than on the other days Phillip has seen me, certainly. This is the first time he hasn't had to see me in crisis mode. I smile.

Standing at my classroom door, I can see Phillip and Jacques walking with a small group of students. Jacques is in his Guardian Angels vest, and Phillip has on his tweed. My heart goes zippety blip. "Welcome to my world, Phillip! Hello, dear Jacques." Everybody looks a little anxious.

"Can we come to your class, teacher?" a long-haired string bean of a kid asks me. I don't know him.

"Not today. Ask your teacher to contact Ms. Polonsey."

"Crap, we have a test next hour." He wanders off.

Phillip and Jacques come into my room, which seems too small with the desks crowded so close together and the big dog and the extra adults. I have Phillip and Jacques move to the far corner behind my desk to help with the element of surprise though it's a tight squeeze for them. Phillip puts his finger to his lips and shakes his head at Jacques, "No barking." Jacques sighs, and lies down as much out of sight as a 150-pound dog can be in a corner behind a desk.

"May I stay?" Ms. Polonsey asks. She is an efficient person, and I'm glad she's in my corner.

"Thanks. You can help me with proximity control. We'll make sure they're polite."

"Why wouldn't they be?" asks the very innocent Phillip. Did he really go to that Career Day at San Clemente? I am assuming those kids are the same as these.

"It's their nature," I reply, as the bell rings. Minutes tick away. When there are about thirty seconds to the tardy bell, the class rushes in en masse, tripping over one another, tossing backpacks into chairs, acting like ninth graders. The aptly named Celeste Bratkowsky enters after the bell, and I hand her a fifth detention for the quarter.

"Hello. As you can see on the screen," I tap the power point, "after the quiz on your reading, we will have a guest speaker." Mr. McKillop nods to them, and a little buzz breaks out along with smiles.

"Cool, no work, dude." Celeste pulls out her cell phone, which I pick up and put into my pocket. She begins sneezing, not dainty glamour girl sneezes, but huge snorts. She laughs with the class.

I give them a short quiz, and we go over the answers so they'll have knowledge of results.

"Now, you have been researching careers, and here is a man who can tell you about some careers that you may never have thought of. And he brought along his co-worker, Jacques."

Mr. McKillop walks out from behind the desk. Jacques takes his place next to his master. Some of the kids stand up for a better look.

"Can we pet him?

"What's his name again?"

"Does he bite?"

"Did his mom have breast cancer?"

"Is he a fag with that pink vest or what?"

Mr. McKillop smiles and holds his hands up to quell the mini-riot. I give them the look, which works. Phillip begins, "Now class, let me tell you about the work Frère Jacques and I do. Then I'll answer some questions. Then if Mrs. Zimmerman says it's okay, we'll go outside and let Jacques show you some of his skills."

There's loud applause, and Jacques barks, adding to the chaos. Celeste sneezes again and again and reaches into her backpack.

"I have to take some allergy meds, Mrs. Zimmerman." Mrs. Polonsey ushers Celeste to the nurse's office.

Mr. McKillop provides a brief overview of the Newfoundland retriever breed. He has a power point show with maps and even a brief video of the famous Newfie, Josh, who won Best in Show at Westminster. The kids are mesmerized. Celeste returns to class with a dramatic sigh and blowing of her nose. She scoops the tissue box off my desk.

"Can we see him do his skills?" asks Celeste. I am worried that she has something contrary up her sleeve, but outside is always good medicine. We exit to the quad. Phillip and Jacques provide a good show of retrieval, Frisbee, and even a quick *how to* of rescue techniques though there's no water. We could have gone down to the pool. That's more than these kids need, and more than I can handle thinking of the black night when Jacques saved Suzann.

The class ends with a crowd around Jacques that disperses as they run for the lunch lines. Phillip has taken off his tweed jacket and wipes his face with his pocket handkerchief, and turns to me. "How many more classes?" We walk back to my classroom.

"One after lunch if you can stay. I packed a picnic for us." I open my teacher's closet and get out a wicker basket with fruit, cheese, crackers, and iced tea. For Jacques, I have a water bowl and a dog treat. Phillip grins.

"You think of everything, Jolene."

"I think I think too much. I'd like to be less organized and less obsessive."

"Mmmm, Zoozle called it something else."

"I'm sure she did. What else did you do in San Diego?"

"Wait. Let's talk about Zoozle."

"Suzann."

"That too."

"Not here, not now, Phillip. Let's enjoy lunch. It's too short for psychoanalysis."

"One of many interesting challenges you create."

"I bet you'd find out my secrets."

"I bet I'd like to try."

"Dinner? My house? So Jacques has a place to be comfy?"

"Draw me a map. Jacques and I can present this next class, go rest up, and I'll see you at six?" He leans forward as if to kiss me, but I back off. Not at school. Can't. Won't.

The bell rings. We clean up our cracker crumbs. The kids rush in before the tardy bell, having heard the tales of Jacques the Great from the previous class. Once everyone is seated and begins the quiz, I note two extra kids that I have to counsel quietly to go to their own classes.

Mr. McKillop handles the post-lunch crowd with aplomb. Once they're out the door, my school day is finished. He looks around the room, opens my closet door, brushes his hair out of his eyes, adjusts his cap just so, and then sweeps it across his heart.

"To a delightful evening, Jolene. I will see you at six. Come on, Jacques."

Jacques looks at him with his ears up. Jacques walks over and sits in front of me. I hug him tightly and give him a kiss on the snout.

"I should be so lucky," says Phillip. And out the door they go.

CHAPTER 15: ZOOZLE

The easterly Santa Ana winds have roared into San Diego. From the beach cities to the mountains, the county is baking in an oven-dry heat. The winds can hit during any season, but they feel truly cruel in the fall. Kids are back in school, sweating in their desks, and the whole city is in a bad temper, particularly me. The wind sets off my negative ions. Everything I touch sparks with electric shocks. I can't even pet Poochie in the static.

I have been making do at Winona's. Her apartment is crowded and stuffy, and I get claustrophobic even when the t.v. isn't blaring, which is between midnight and 5 a.m. when I leave for Puente Rojo. I'll stay here for a few weeks, at least until I get a paycheck and I can move somewhere else. It's only Poochie I'll miss. He has taken to sleeping on his back on my couch bed, his bottom teeth peeking out from his little black lips.

I have nothing to wear but my grandpa's flannel pj bottoms and the ugly t-shirt from Winona, one of her baggy jumpers, and my dressy skirt outfit. My mom offered to drive down with a few of her extra sweater-and-jeans ensembles. She has her outfits planned for the whole year so what seems like a self-sacrificing gesture is expedient for her. She never wears the same thing twice in a semester. I can see her clothing chart on her closet door with the X's through each day, like a prisoner in a cell.

The scent of her Anne Klein perfume permeates her clothes. The scent connects to memories and sends me to a very dark place.

Chloris said she knows some cool second-hand shops downtown. We would go to the big swap meet at the old Sports Arena, but she has to work Saturday, and I have today free before I work on my manual for the dance team. If crabby Chris is working, then I can hang out at Eric's and use his computer after I shop with Chloris.

I sit on Winona's porch and run to the curb when Chloris pulls up in a prehistoric Buick, but she insists it is only polite to say hello to Winona. She greets Poochie and Winona with such enthusiasm that Winona almost doesn't let us out the door again. We make a rush for the car, laughing, as Winona waves Poochie's paw.

"Say bye bye," she says to Poochie.

Chloris pumps down her window and cranks up the radio, and reggae rhythms pulse as she eases away from the curb. Chloris dances her hand out the window.

"Dance with me," she urges, and soon my hand is dancing out the right-hand window, the wind tearing my hair into wild ripples. The car has wings, one long, elegant, and brown, one short, scarred, and white.

Our first stop is the hospital's thrift store. There's a sale going on and I can buy t-shirts for a quarter. I have fifteen dollars to spend. My goal is fourteen acceptable, not-too-dorky shirts. If I can find a couple of pairs of sweats, I'm set for Puente Rojo and the new boss, Ms. Garant. I received my school warm-ups, which help the wardrobe.

We're shopping away, laughing at the ridiculous sayings and horrible colors. "Surf Minnesota" with a row of cows and surfboard is the worst. I find a few sports logo shirts, volleyball, gymnastics, and the local Padres and my old Seattle Mariners. Capris range from elephantine to my size.

I hold up a shirt that makes me laugh and yell, "Hey, Chloris. This one's right for you! See —'Sistah for Sale.'"

Her mouth droops. "Not funny," she replies. She turns her back on me.

God, I'm stupid. I wish I'd think rather than blurt. I look for something to buy for her.

Chloris can't find any blue jeans that are both long enough in the legs and small in enough in the waist to fit her. I've thought her legs a dancer's dream. Calling my legs stumpy would be a compliment. Every advantage has a disadvantage. Chloris hums with joy over a little denim purse, but shakes her head at high price and puts it back.

We get checked out, having spent a total of $8.75. Chloris walks with her head down into a blast of wind, heading towards the car. I tell her I'll be right there, go back and grab the denim purse, and wait behind a man with a stiff ponytail at the counter. I can smell vomit and urine. I move further back from him. Despite the Santa Ana heat, he's wearing a long black trench coat. He's arguing about the price of a pair of red high top tennis shoes. He says they had a sale dot on them. The clerk disagrees. I just want to get out of there and surprise Chloris with the purse.

As the clerk tosses the shoes into the returns pile, the man stomps through the side exit towards the parking lot. I pay and put my shoulder into the front door against the wind.

Outside, a weird growling sound and a scream pierce the
noontime buzz.

The trench coat man, tall and wiry, is yelling. He is no more than
ten feet away from Chloris, moving towards her in a shuffling gait. I
don't see a weapon. He's waving his hands, agitated. She backs away.

"She cut off my lover's cock!" he yells.

Other people in the parking lot look, but make no move to help.
I drop the denim purse and run. Chloris is talking calmly, "It's okay now.
I didn't hurt your lover."

Her assailant is Chris, as in Eric's Chris. Until this moment, I
hadn't seen his face or recognized his voice or anything other than his
loathsome appearance and smell.

"You cut his fucking cock off." He reaches for her shoulder as if
he's going to throw her to the ground. She is still soothing and fearless
as she keeps her distance, but he lunges and grabs her.

I sprint and jump him from behind. The first thing that hits me
is the noxious odor, almost enough to make me faint. But I hang on.

He's so startled, he drops his arm from Chloris and lets my
weight pull us both to the ground backwards. We're wrestling in the
middle of the parking lot; he straddles me. He scratches my face with a
filthy fingernail and bites at my neck with sharp, yellowed teeth. His
gums are bleeding. Chloris keeps making a grab for his legs and curbs the
left one by bending it up at the knee.

"*Fadlan I kaalmee!*" she yells to the small group of astonished
bystanders. "Help, please, call for help!" From my position under him, all
I can do is push back with all my strength and snatch at his flailing arms
as I flip my head left and right to keep out of gnashing range. Chloris

lands a kick near his kidneys. He erupts with a loud yell and goes somewhat limp.

I roll out from under him and drag his hands above his head. He's still yelling for the now-larger crowd, "She cut my lover's cock off." He's thrashing around again, powered by drugs and mania.

Two cops and a fire truck plus EMT's arrive and take over containment. I am shaking and breathing hard, so Chloris and I sit down on the hot blacktop. The EMT's check us for wounds. We hug one another. They ask if we want to go to the hospital. Chloris and I both say no and sign waivers. The police ask for our preliminary statements, a few witnesses give their names, and the cops whisk Chris away in a patrol car. It's over in a few minutes that have stretched into a blur. Was it ten seconds or ten minutes that Chris held me down on that burning asphalt, and I fought for my life?

"What in the world? Was that really Chris?"

Chloris is shaking, but she nods. "Are you okay?"

"Are you?" I shrug, but put out a hand to keep her from standing up. I can feel my knees quivering, and I need to sit a few more minutes. Someone in the crowd brings us each a Coke, offers to stay, but we say thanks and wave him off. A woman brings over the denim purse. I look at it as if I'm not sure what it is. "For you, Chloris."

She pats my hand. "*Mahadsanid, kumaan helin.*"

She seems lost in a distant place, and I put my arm around her shoulders. Her eyes refocus on me. She has bandages on her hands and knees. The scratch on my cheek prickles where the EMT's put the antiseptic. A scrape on my elbow stings.

"What will happen now – to Chris?" I ask.

"Seventy-two-hour hold, unless we press charges, and he'll be released. Chris has cracked before. C'mon. We can rest at my house— it's around the block. I'll call Eric. Poor Eric." Chloris stands, pulls me up, and we place our packages into her car. She hits the ignition, and we both wince at the radio's blaring volume. She twists the off button, and it comes off in her hand. She shakes her head and sighs.

Several blocks south, we pull into the driveway of a blue bungalow. Planters overflow with gerbera daisies. A pepper tree waves its spidery leaves in the wind. On the porch in a rocker, a gaunt and grizzled woman sways. Her head jerks up and down, a book on her lap on top of a loose-stitched shawl.

"Auntie. Wake up. I'm home, and I brought *kumaan helin.*" Chloris touches her aunt's cheek.

Her aunt looks at me with rheumy eyes and extends a veiny hand towards me. "*Soodhawoow,*" she says in a whisper, and I answer "Soowoo," my best attempt at Somali.

Chloris introduces me and identifies her aunt as Chandrace, though everyone calls her Auntie.

Indoors, the main room is furnished with two hip-slung couches and a small chrome kitchen table with matching chairs, an ancient white stove and small refrigerator beyond them. Bookcases extend floor to ceiling and each is packed with books, hardbacks, paperbacks, children's books, and newspapers. The house is cooler than the outdoors. No windows are open.

Chloris stoops to enter the low doorway of the bathroom, and we splash cold water on our faces. There's barely room in there for the two of us. Auntie has come to watch us from the doorway. Chloris fibs that we fell in the park. Stepping back into the living room, I note the number of locks on the doors and windows.

"I will fix you squash soup," Auntie offers.

"Not today." Chloris leads me, with Auntie following, into the next room where there is a double bed. It looks too short for Chloris's long body. She takes a moment to hang her new purse in a closet filled with the bright colors of her work clothes. She puts her hands on her aunt's frail shoulders. "We must go to Zoozle's house where her own auntie is waiting for us. She'll come again another time." I notice the formality of their speech with one another, a foreigner's English.

Auntie raises her thinning eyebrows at me, and I agree that I will visit again. Chloris urges me out the front door with a hand under my elbow.

"Her vision has been failing in the last few months. She can't read all day the way she used to. If we stayed, she would ask so many questions, and I don't like to lie to her and I don't want to worry her either. Besides, my aunt would want to tell you stories." We drive away and catch the freeway south.

"What kind of stories?" I am thinking of Grandpa Joe, how much I would like to hear his stories again, how arrogant and impatient I was too often.

"Of our homeland. Of our travels here and my mama. Auntie can go on for hours. She is an educated woman, unusual in Somalia. That's why we left."

"I'd be interested, Chloris."

"Another day. Today has been enough. Are you sure you're okay?"

"Could we walk a bit? I feel all tight inside. Do you have time?" We have arrived near Winona's, and I can't face that whole scene right now.

"Yes, let's. Walking is peaceful."

Even though I'd like to be close to my job and my friends out in Hillcrest, I can't afford it and there's nobody to room with. I can see that Auntie needs Chloris home with her. They are devoted to one another in a way rare among families, it seems, except maybe Mitch and Grandpa Joe. It's a relief to be walking around the neighborhoods, remembering favorite places Grandma Janie and Grandpa Joe took me to. Lots of things have changed with McMansions looming where two or three old homes once stood, condos edging up to most of the beachfront and a wide artsy plaza in what used to be a dirt lot. Grandpa Joe liked to buy ice cream treats at the cement-floored old market on First Street. Thinking of those days, I rub my ribs where I used to balance on the store's freezer, trying to reach my Fudgesicle, not letting Grandpa choose it for me. I thought I could find the biggest one.

My chest feels tight with longing, the moments that flitted by without my full attention. Grandpa Joe's smiling face hovers in my memory as we walk. I try to remember that today is the only sure thing I've got and feel the sun on my shoulders, the wind in my hair. I have let my hair grow out so I could cut the split ends. I'm ready to look like a grown up.

Chloris and I stop in front of a for-rent sign at a house a block from the beach. The house sits back from the street and looks really old with a sweet wooden porch and green shutters. A flyer says the house was built in 1926. That date seems incomprehensible to me. My great-grandparents' home was built in the thirties, so I guess people did live here even sooner than that.

Knocking on the door brings no answer. Chloris calls the number on the flyer. She announces the rental fee the agent quotes her, and I shake my head. I can't pay $1000 a month in rent, even if my mom helps me out for a few months. Chloris leaves my name and number just in case they need a tenant more than they need rent at that rate.

"I guess I have to wait it out and stay with Winona," I lament and grimace at the image of the tight quarters and Winona's wide mouth.

"Something will turn up."

"Before I lose my mind?" But then I think of Eric's situation with Chris and realize I have another blurt against me.

"Your family has been good to you, Zoozle. You underestimate them too much." Chloris has stopped walking and is gazing at the setting sun.

"I know. I've been awful. I've only been respectful to Mitch. And Phillip."

As Chloris and I continue our loop through the streets, we're not very hopeful, but the weather is wonderful now that the wind has died down. The crepe myrtles are blooming in tufts of lollipop colors. If I ever wrote a children's ballet, it would be filled with crepe myrtles in bloom. Dance costumes in purple and pink along with initial choreography pop into my mind. Little kids would love it. A college team would roll their eyes. They are so cynical so young these days. No sweetness and light for them.

"I liked that house back there," Chloris says at last. "My house with Auntie has that same littleness, not so, what are the words? pushy and proud. Just a house to make a space for yourself."

"Me too." We have walked across Seacoast and have started up the pier. It's low tide, and the waves are breaking at the far end of the pier with a subdued soughing. There are a few fishermen, some moms with babies in strollers, two men on a bench, their old bodies hunched into question marks as they monitor the sea. I should bring Simon here. He used to come with Grandpa Joe, Simon with his walker, Joe on his personal scooter. On the pier one day, Grandpa Joe saw a lady with a scooter like his and he called to her, "Race ya!" I bet that lady hadn't laughed that hard in years. I know that I hadn't when he phoned to tell me that story.

Grandpa fought the idea of the scooter at first. My mom suggested it, but never got around to doing something about it, and I puzzle about how she let something so important slip her organized mind. I'm proud that I did the paperwork last New Year's after our Christmas phone call. He regained a lot of mobility to places he had given up on visiting, like Grandma Janie's gravesite. He'd point to her marker and say, "And that's mine, right there next to her, honey." He didn't sound sad.

We've reached the end of the pier. "The water reminds me of the ocean near my homeland," Chloris swallows hard. "I don't come out to the sea often enough."

"Do you miss Somalia?"

"No. Yes. I miss my family, my older sisters, my parents who are gone now. My father was a good man, an educated man. My mother was from the countryside. She believed in too much tradition for the world as it is today. Auntie brought me here before they could marry me to someone I did not choose."

"How could anyone do that?"

"It's a matter of honor in the old country. Women are property, first of their fathers and brothers, then of their husbands. A woman's honor is more important than her life. If I had stayed, I would have had no audience to speak to about my life, my choices. But I would have had children. I think I would have liked to have children."

I start to assure her she can still bear children when I remember she is nearing forty. Probably, Chloris doesn't have the money for all the medical procedures pregnancy would entail at this point in her life. "You could adopt a child. You'll find someone to marry one day."

"He would not want me." Chloris stops and presses her lips so tightly shut that they change hue. She allows herself to go on. "My Auntie wanted to take me on a trip, but my mother said no. She said she needed my help with my sisters' little ones. When Auntie traveled to Paris one summer, my mother used her absence to hold my pre-puberty rites. My father died long before. My older brothers insisted. Do you know of these rites?"

"No." I know a few dances from Africa, some musical instruments, but nothing of Somali pre-puberty rites.

"It's called female circumcision."

"What?"

"They cut away those female parts that give sexual pleasure. Then a man is sure his wife will stay chaste. A man does not want to worry about another man's *doobbadillaasco*. It means to uncork one's rutting froth. You understand?" Chloris's eyes reflect shame and pain and regret.

I stretch up and hold her tightly. People around us look twice.

"God, Chloris, did you go to a hospital?"

"No, we had no doctors or hospitals. A village woman did this, with an old rough knife and not very clean water. I was sick for many weeks. When Auntie returned, she knew without asking. I was thin and barely able to walk. Auntie hired a car and guards, and we drove away in the night. I owe my life to my Auntie. She feels so guilty for not taking me to Paris with her."

Chloris, whose smile wakes up the hospice corridors, who dances her hand in the wind, who wriggles her toes in the grass of the eucalyptus grove, who sleeps in a small bed next to her Auntie has much more in her life to make her an angry druggie than I do. But she isn't.

"Do you hate your mother, Chloris? Sometimes, I think I hate mine."

"No. My mother was not at fault. She followed the ways of her people. And my brothers, who had education, they should have stood up for me. But they liked to think I would always have my honor." She smiles a small smile. "My brothers were once my heroes. No more. I met your mother at the hospice, Zoozle. She worries about you. The time will come when you can talk to her and find your love for her again." Chloris doesn't know how deep the betrayal was to me. I wish I had a bigger heart and a thinner wall of reserve. I consider telling her my life story, but not today, though she would be sympathetic and consoling. She has let down a barrier of her own, a façade I never knew existed in her.

The sun is starting its glissade into the sea in a sweep of colors that remind me of Chloris. I hold her hand, and we watch, a companionable, trusting silence between us.

"I lost much, Zoozle. But not everything. Please remember that." Chloris releases my hand and leans on the rail of the pier, as if she might dive into the small swells below. "Beauty makes each day worth living. Beauty and laughter and love."

She sounds like Grandpa Joe. His advice left me feeling smaller in my calamities and larger in my humanity. I can learn a lot if only I will listen. So would my mom.

We are quiet in the car on the drive to Winona's. Our last energy is as depleted as a wave's once it breaks. Will I be able to forget about Chris, the crazy man, his smell? But then I think about Eric and remind Chloris we didn't call him.

She dismisses the reminder with a wave. "He's at work. I'll see him there and explain. He may be relieved; Chris has been away almost a week."

"A week? Nobody told me." Anger hits hard.

"You had enough to worry about. Your grandpa. Your family. Your job."

"I feel so bad."

"We all do. I try with Eric. He has to see that Chris cannot be saved until Chris chooses to help himself."

"Another few months in Port Townsend, I could have been like Chris. I was out of control. Penny and Grandpa Joe, Mr. McKillop, you and Eric saved me."

Chloris says nothing else until we arrive at her car.

She gets in and reaches out the open window, squeezes my hand, bandages smelling of tape and antiseptic. "You are saving you, Zooz."

CHAPTER 16: JOLENE

Phillip and Jacques are gone. I straighten my desk, lock my classroom door, and run to the office for tomorrow morning's copies. Mornings are better if I don't have to wait in line while Mrs. Gruel prints out a hundred class sets of *Moby Dick*. And who knows how late I might be tomorrow morning getting out the door? Things look tantalizing with Phillip, maybe, I hope, I think. I don't know what I think.

The copy machine ratchets into gear, and once I input my originals, I can wait while it copies and collates though I'd never trust it to staple. I grit my teeth thinking of the times I've waited while a twenty-something in shorts and a t-shirt gets the whole machine screwed up because he just couldn't manage to actually staple things himself. The Old Guard is well aware that the machine inevitably goes haywire when asked to staple.

The flow of copies sets a rhythm, and I staple while it works its work, I mine. There I go again, paraphrasing Tennyson. Tomorrow's lesson on dramatic monologues, re-teaching Mr. Dowd's doubtful renditions, may go better than today's on Spender, but the ninth graders are going to panic at the essay assignment. We could have a graded discussion about careers and Jacques. No. I stop myself. Why would I change the calendar because I'm feeling lazy especially now when I have the kids trained to count on the class calendars? All I have to do with the essay is hand it out and stare sternly until they write.

My thoughts drift off to tonight's menu, when the PA squawks, "Mrs. Zimmerman. Report to the Principal's Office." I hate that word, *report*, as if we are privates in Uncle Bill's army. I've reminded him to ask the secretaries not to use *report*. The word demeans the teachers. Bill is a good principal most of the time, but he doesn't get it on this issue.

The phone is a step away from the copy machine, and I call his secretary. "Dorrie, this is Jolene. Why was I paged?"

She hesitates. "It's the Bratkowskys. They said you had a dog in class, and Celeste is allergic. They're not happy."

"Are they here?"

"No — they talked to Bill on the phone."

"I'll drop by and explain."

I pick up my papers, all collated but the rest of the stapling will have to wait. Bill's office is a shrine to himself. Every wall carries photos with Bill front and center. He thinks he's a god at school and a god of our family. His wife and Dorrie, half the school employees. People treat him that way. He's sitting at his desk, pretending to write email, but probably checking job promotion possibilities in districts near and far.

Leaning into the office, I try to avoid sitting down in "the chair" directly in front of him. Once started, he never shuts up. "Hey, brother of mine. Don't sweat the Bratkowskys. Celeste brought a permission slip. Mrs. Polonsey took it with her when she brought her to the nurse's office. Do you want me to go get it?"

"Why don't I see your visitor on the Master Calendar? I could have had the newspaper here to give us good coverage! Can't have enough of that these days."

The quest for PR never ends with Mr. Bill. "Look, I've only been back to school a couple days. Your door was closed this morning when I arrived. Mr. Dowd had the kids get signed permission slips, and I checked them. Do you want Celeste's? Do you want me to call the Bratkowskys? I'm in a little bit of a bind this afternoon. I have an appointment in an hour." This is sort of true since I have an appointment at the grocery store, with my vacuum cleaner, and my linen closet.

"I think they want to deal directly with the head honcho. I'll call them back and tell them about the permission slip. Make sure there's a copy in my box in the morning, would you?" He sighs as if he carries the weight of the world. "How are your classes going? Did the AP classes lose any ground that will cost us test scores?" He thumps his pen against a stack of documents from the State of California.

"Everything is extraordinarily fine. Mr. Dowd did a great job. We're on track."

"That's what I like to hear," he says, reaching for his ringing phone. He listens for a moment, waves me out. I am free.

I throw my copies into my faculty mail box rather than hiking to my classroom and run to my car, leaving a voicemail for Mrs. Polonsey about Celeste. Then, I'm off to the grocery store to buy flowers, fresh bread and produce and white wine. Last month's book club dish, Chicken Fricassee (one served, one frozen), with its olives, raisins, and tomatoes, should impress Phillip. My hopes soar.

At home, I put the wine in the 'fridge, pull the main dish from the freezer and put it on the stove in my largest pot. I set the table with festive plates that match my flowers and table runner. A quick vacuum over the living room rug, a dash with the sheets, switching from every day white-on-white dots to zebra stripes, and I'm ready for a quick shower and fix up. The clock says 5:30, by the time I'm dressed in a shimmery gold top and red pants.

Phillip arrives at the stroke of six. He carries a bouquet of violets, which he presents with a sweeping bow. Jacques puts his paw up to shake, and I begin to giggle like a schoolgirl.

"Welcome to my home, gentlemen!" I grin.

"What smells so divine, Jolene?"

"It's a secret."

Phillip and Jacques follow me into the kitchen. Phillip lifts the lid from the boiling fricassee and waves the aroma towards his nostrils. Jacques pushes out the back screen door, having found its access to the deck. He sniffs the peach tree for squirrels.

"White wine?" I tilt the bottle out of the cooler. Glasses await on the counter.

"I think water, Jolene. I'm very strict about AA. Weren't you there when I talked to Zoozle about AA?" He frowns. "I guess you weren't. Anyway, today's a new day. Please pour yourself a glass if you like."

The wine can wait. I am intoxicated enough with Phillip.

We switch to club soda and sit on the deck. A timer goes off. "Time for dinner!" I serve our plates from the kitchen. Phillip has slipped his violets into my table bouquet where the purple adds scent and vividness to the white daisies. The violets match my mood, intensely vivid.

Phillip praises my cooking. We make small talk about my teaching and his work with Guardian Angels. I realize he's scheduled to begin his trip back to Washington tomorrow morning, and my stomach tightens with apprehension.

"Let me clear these dishes," Phillip offers. "I'm an old hand in the kitchen."

"No, please, let me. Come sit at the counter while I clean up. It's quick, and the kitchen is a little unorthodox."

"Like your daughter?"

"No, like me."

"Jolene, I have never seen you make one unorthodox move since I met you. Now Zoozle. . . "

"I don't want to talk about Suzann."

"I know you don't. But you should."

"I've done it all, everything you can think of and then some. She is an adult stuck in this immature, impetuous, rebellious teenager mode, who leans on her mom way too often. I told her I had had enough on that trip to Washington. Her choice to live at Grandpa Joe's was absolutely the right compromise for both of us. Or would have been. I can't help what the lawyers decided about the trailer. I'm glad she's got a job. She can work the rest out by herself."

"No, she can't. She needs you."

"Phillip, please, could we let this go? I was really looking forward to being here with you tonight and forgetting I'm a mom for awhile." I smile with what I hope is an inviting, sex kittenish look.

"One last word, and then I'll stop on this subject, Jolene. Zoozle feels cut off and unloved. I'm not saying it's your fault. I'm providing you with some information that she has not." He jingles his keys, and Jacques comes running.

"Phillip, don't go yet. I made sure I don't have homework. Stay and let's just be for a bit, okay? I'll deal with Suzann, I will." I come around the counter and place my hand on his shoulder. "Let's sit in the living room. Do you want to watch a movie?"

"Let's dance." Phillip picks up the remote to the television and finds a music station. "Save the Last Dance for Me" by Michael Bublé is playing, and Phillip sways me into a cha cha. He's a very good dancer. I feel awkward and stiff. I remember when my daddy danced with me. He always said, "Relax, Joleney, honey, follow me." A slower song follows, "Alone," and Phillip draws me smoothly, tightly into his arms. Jacques settles himself into a corner, head on paws. He'll snooze this one out.

Phillip and I slow dance, and then the charade of dancing ends, and we lean into one another. His kiss is tentative. He tips my chin up. His eyes sparkle. "I like that. Could you kiss me again?" I do. I start to lead him back towards my bedroom, but he stops.

"This isn't a race, Jolene. Let's go slow. More dancing?"

I feel rebuffed though I know he's right. I push away feelings of humiliation.

"I thought you'd like it, that I could surprise you."

"Well, yes indeed. How do I say this?" Phillip pulls me onto the sectional sofa, into the corner. "I may not be ready."

"What? I thought men were always ready,"

"And you know that how. . . ?"

I am mortified. I haven't been with a man since Mark died. First I was busy with Suzann, and then when she left for college, I threw myself into my career. Men seemed like so much trouble.

"Because that's how so many of the books I've read portray things, except maybe *Jane Eyre*."

Phillip laughs. "I'm more of a Jane Eyre kind of man. The stranger in the night and all that."

"You're no stranger, and I'm a grown woman, not some innocent little governess."

"Let's call it mutual respect and a mutual decision."

"I haven't voted yet." I edge over to the middle of the couch and pull my afghan from the corner. I wish I could throw it over my head and disappear.

"Jolene, we're good together. We're friends. I admire your intellect. You amaze me. You're beautiful. Do you promise you won't get skittish on me if I tell you a secret?"

I see his caressing gaze. He is the kind of man I've dreamed of, suave and kind and good, serving a purpose each day of his life. Best of all, he knows me with all my mothering faults, and he likes me anyway. He likes my daughter.

"I'm ready for anything, Phillip."

He begins to walk around the room and settles by Jacques' side, petting the dog's long hair, lost in thought.

"My wife, Ariel, died after our twentieth wedding anniversary. She had lymphoma. It was a long, slow diminishing, and we fought that fight together. After she died, I'm ashamed to say, I went quite wild, picking up women at bars, at casinos, at work. That went on for about a year. I woke up in Reno one Sunday morning, married to someone I had met in a slot machine tournament on Thursday evening. What a mistake. We agreed to annul the whole thing."

Phillip moves from Jacques to take a place next to me. He pulls the afghan into his lap and spreads it across the two of us.

"Since that year of stupidity, some three years ago, I have been celibate."

"But Phillip, that's a good thing." I hesitate. "Would you believe I haven't been to bed with anyone since Mark's death, no one? More than twenty years."

"I guess it's true, what I've heard about vibrators."

"Oh my God, you are a dirty old man!"

"Sex is not dirty. Needs are not dirty. Where did you get such an idea?"

"My mother. Over a college break, she caught Mark and me before we were married in bed at her house. It was only Daddy who kept her from tar and feathering us. Mother never did talk directly to me about it though I still have the letter she wrote me, asking me not to bring Mark home again. I worked it out with her, but somehow, she never warmed up to him. I think that moment was the biggest disappointment in her life."

"Lucky woman if that's the worst thing that ever happened to her."

"I miss her. I miss Daddy. Right now though, it's a relief not to need to explain Suzann's actions to my mother. Daddy understood that people aren't perfect."

"Here we are, back to Suzann. Is it time now?"

"No."

"When?"

"We'll know."

"Is it time for another kiss?" Phillip plants a smacking kiss on my cheek before I can answer.

The clock chimes. It's time for a bedtime kiss. I wish I could keep Phillip here, to hold me, sex or no sex.

"Do you believe in bundling, like the Swedes?"

"Who wouldn't? I don't have a change of clothes with me for morning."

"You can wear a robe from the guest room in the morning and do a load of laundry if you like. I have to warn you though. I'll be up and in a rush and you'll have to take care of yourself, and promise to call me later at school."

"I can do that and better."

"What could be better?"

"You'll see when you get home from school tomorrow."

"You're staying?"

"You could convince me." He kisses me.

"Tease." I walk towards the bedroom, dropping my blouse in the hallway, my sheer bra feeling flimsily sexy. I hope he'll relieve me of it.

"Calypso." He follows, unbuttoning his shirt.

"James Bond." I scramble up on the bed, flipping the covers down, revealing the zebra-print sheets. I slip my slacks off, stand in front of him with my back turned. He unhooks my bra. I am left in my Hanes no-line panties and nothing else.

"Not Lothario?" He slips out of his pants, leaving his boxers on.

We fall on the bed, kissing and touching and he whispers in my ear, "Just bundling, you promised."

After a moment, I whisper, "Rochester, the mystery man."

He chuckles. "Yes, Miss Eyre." He wraps his long body along me; we fit perfectly. I'm surprised at how much I want him, how much he fills the well of grief Daddy's death opened in me for all that I've missed in life.

I trail my fingers lower. He starts to catch my hand and then allows me to explore. There's no erection, and I'm disappointed. He kisses my neck. We spoon our bodies and bundle to sleep. Some Lothario.

—

CHAPTER 17: ZOOZLE

First day at work, and I'm already in hot water. I arrive to a pile of messages in my box and a parent camping outside my office door at 5:45 a.m. Thank God he is a skinny guy with glasses, like some engineering nerd lost in the art department. Seeing him sitting there by the office with his legs straight out in front of him, all I want is to finish my coffee and get into the dance studio to warm up before the girls arrive.

Instead, Mr. Luster starts yammering about how his daughter, Lacey, was going to be the next "it girl" for dance and had just missed a spot in the Kansas City Ballet Corps (yeah, right, I think) and now she's not on the Puente Rojo Junior College Dance Team? I wish I could say what I'm thinking: Mr. Luster, I don't know your daughter from Adam, make that Eve, and you'll need to back off for a couple weeks while I sort through the tryout tapes. Maybe I will have some good news for you (and maybe I won't). Instead, I offer, "I'll look into it, sir."

He's raising Cain about his friends on the Board of Supervisors and his private endowment of additional mirrors for the dance studio. Honest to God, these new helicopter parents are nuts. Dog walker sounds better by the minute.

So I come running into the studio, and there are my girls sitting on the exercise mat, most with cell phones out. One is stretching at the barre, and fourteen more are lazing about in various states of early waking, some propped back to back. They are probably texting one another because who else would they know awake at this hour except the ones who work as baristas?

Veronica from the interview looks up at me and then at her teammates. She projects a hard edge to her, long blond hair and too much make up. Her dance practice outfit is a skimpy halter top with a pair of men's basketball shorts resting at the edge of her hip bones, the hems drooping well past her knees.

I'll get to know them all quickly enough, but the old saying about first impressions sweeps through me. Mom strikes again.

I stand in front of them and hope they'll all look up without my resorting to the whistle around my neck. The brunette at the barre walks quietly to the mat and seats herself with athletic grace in what would be the front row if they would all sit up instead of being flopped there like so many tuna tossed on a fishing trawler.

"Good morning, ladies. I am Ms. Zimmerman, your new coach." I hope those words sound authoritative. I'm not much for authority myself, but there's no way to run a dance program without it. Professionally, my mom's influence on me comes in handy.

"First, each of you will introduce yourselves to me. Before we begin, you need to take those cell phones and Ipods and put them into your backpacks or lockers."

The outcry is spontaneous.

"Dahlia let us wear them on our belts."

"No way."

"What'd she say?"

"Bitch."

I repeat the instructions, with a louder, stronger emphasis. "You have two minutes to put your electronic devices where they need to be and return to this mat. Anything longer will count as a tardy. We'll talk about consequences shortly."

There's much grumbling and shuffling. They return and plunk themselves on the mat.

"Sit up, ladies. Straight and tall. I have a manual ready to distribute when our session is over today. Read it tonight and be ready to discuss my policies tomorrow."

A hand goes up. "Does that mean we get to vote on things we disagree with?" asks a Latina in a proper leotard, tie-dyed chartreuse though it may be. She has acne scars below her scapula.

"No voting, but discussion. Let's get started with names, please. You are?"

"Amy Shaw."

Besides Veronica, the girl who makes the biggest impression, the one who looks like an ally is Sandy Griffin. Sandy smiles and nods as I speak. The other dozen flash by. I have brought my digital camera to take pictures so that I can remember who's who, another idea that produces squeals as if I had stepped into a nest of vixen.

"Ladies, let's begin with the routine you used at the opening ceremony of the semester, the one you performed for camp last summer. Veronica, come forward and set the count. I want to see the first minute only."

Within thirty seconds I can see where we stand. Several of the girls are not well trained in basics, their movements sloppier than those on the first session of *Dancing with the Stars*. Carla is overweight by at least twenty pounds. Sandy is a star as is Veronica. I thank Veronica and tell them all to stay put, spaced across the mat. We will be choosing music for the fall revue.

An excited buzz breaks out. Suggestions ricochet around the room. Ms. Garant arrives at the height of the bedlam, giving me a look that says she's not sure she has made the right hiring decision and nodding toward the security camera/VCR set up. "It's working like a charm," she says.

She wanders over to the CD player and puts a CD in, something classical. The girls watch her, smirking. Who dances to that stuff anymore? She claps her hands and tells them that I will lead them in barre exercises. She instructs me to drop by her office between classes.

Despite this bit of negativity, the girls and I stretch for half an hour. I ask them to divide into two groups of eight and seven, put on Michael Jackson's "They Don't Really Care About Us" in a loop, hoping they're familiar with it, but haven't danced to it before. I ask them to compose a small-group dance for presentation in three class days. Sandy leads one group, Veronica the other. I wander by each group at intervals, correcting posture and complimenting footwork. Veronica choreographs some nifty turns and then adds NFL cheerleader grinds that I nix. When she thinks I've turned away, she sticks her tongue out. Before class ends, the girls reassemble on the mat, and I provide each with a handbook called *Zimmerman's Zeitgeist*.

"Isn't that the name of a beer?" asks Carla.

"Don't be a dork," Sandy shushes her.

I thought the title was catchy and intellectually challenging, but most of them are staring at me with eyes narrowed. Veronica seems to

- 171 -

get it. To soften the edge of rebellion that I feel growing as they flip through the pages, I ask them to think of a competitive slogan for our season. We'll put it on our practice t-shirts and on a banner in the practice studio. The response is positive, lots of chatter and a few goodbye smiles. Thus ends session one with the girls.

I'm not too sweaty so I go directly into Ms Garant's office, but she's on the phone and waves me away, mouthing "Tomorrow." She's not smiling although it could just be her Botox problem.

Dave is in the hallway so I confide in him. He's not too hopeful, but he has a class and can't explain much more than that Jessie likes to go over rule books and policies before they're distributed. And Dave tells me Ms. Garant has already heard from Mr. Luster once this morning. As far as Dave knows, Dahlia's tryout decisions are final, but he does suggest I look at Lacey Luster's tape, to be on the safe side. I sit cross-legged on the floor of my office where Lacey's tape is tossed with about 100 other tapes in a box marked DUDS. The tapes are labeled but not alphabetized, and I'm starving. There's no VCR in my office, and I don't want to go to the department lounge where I might run into more people. I consider running after Dave Inman, but he was already late. Eric's house is the closest. I wonder if Chris is home after treatment?

I stroll down the hall and Ms. Garant's door is open, and she's missing as I peek in. The VCR is just sitting there begging for me to use it. Popping the tape in, I hover over the screen and watch as Lacey executes the try-out routine. Her smile is a winner, and her steps are fundamentally strong. I compare her to the others and decide that she would rate at the top of the class. I'm pleased that I can solve this thing with Mr. Luster, even though he's a pain and not the kind of man I like giving in to.

I reach in to stop the VCR, and Jessie's voice barks from the hallway, "Is this your office, Ms. Zimmerman?"

Feeling like a thief, I blush from head to toe and show her the tape. "I wanted to check on this for Mr. Luster. I think Dahlia made a mistake." I'm shaking, I'm so nervous.

Jessie is standing there with her hands on her hips.

She points to a chair across from her desk. "Sit." She arranges herself behind her desk.

"And what makes you think an experienced teacher like Dahlia made a mistake? We don't want teachers here who give in to every parent's whim, Ms. Zimmerman."

I shake my head. "The team needs more fundamentals. Lacey has them. I think she could help us."

"Interesting. Now then, I received your references from Port Townsend." She points to a pile of faxes on the corner of her desk.

Why do I have a knot in my stomach when I know Bert would give me good marks?

"No one doubts your talent. No one doubts your motivational ability. What's in question it seems is your decision making. Any comment?"

"I had a lot going on last summer. All that's behind me, I assure you."

"They want you back."

"I'm happier here."

Jessie cracks a smile, truly almost literally cracks with the face lift or dermal injections or whatever it is she tried.

"I will call Mr. Luster. And please remember that I will have an eye on you, Ms. Zimmerman. Need I remind you of your classroom camera? Conduct your classes with more authority and discipline and please stick to the classics for now. I don't care what the girls beg for. Our Puente Rojo audiences do not want to sit through sleaze."

"Yes, ma'am." I can breathe again. It's not that I love these girls or have any allegiance to this program. I have the Zimmerman illness called work ethic. Without work I've felt defeated and small.

Day one on the job has been torture, but it's an exquisite torture that I've missed. On my way UP! Yes!

Down the hallway, I glimpse a student on those wheelie tennis shoes, rolling across the end. She returns in another fly-by in a moment, and there's something familiar in the swing of her hair.

Mel. Down is the only direction I connect with Mel. Could I duck back into my office? She has turned the corner and she's almost on me, and besides the custodial staff at the college is unfortunately efficient. Dahlia's name is off the door; mine is on. Mr. Luster didn't have to look past the directory and neither would Mel. I can hunker down inside, but she'll show up again tomorrow.

She's already rolling down the hall with her arms wide open. This was once my best friend. Now not. She would lead me places I can be too willing to go.

"Hey, Zoozle-Woozle-Shamoozle! Who doesn't answer the phone anymore?" She slides to a stop and wobbles, and I catch her to keep her from crashing into the frosted glass part of my office door.

"How'd you get here?" I open the door and pull her into my office. I leave the lights off.

"Your mama got her ways!" She grins with impish delight.

"Did you take the trolley? Did Mike drive you?"

"In what? He's not working. I hitched. Cost me a favor, but you know those college boys. De-li-ci-ous."

"Shut up. You didn't? Don't you remember you said no more of that?"

"Nope. Don't remember. Was that back when we were friends?"

I skip an answer. "What are you doing here?"

"Looking for you. Since I see your car and you and that new friend of yours, the black one. Your Aunt Kaye was talking to Winona on the phone. I heard about this gig. Thought I'd visit! Aren't you glad to see me?"

"No."

"Real enthusiasm there, Zooz. Tell me how you really feel." She brays her donkey's laugh.

"This is my first day. Plus, I have zero cash." I sort of push her away, and she flops into the desk's swivel chair.

"What the heck. We can get some *cashe*." She uses a long *a* in *cash*, an old joke that used to make me laugh. She pulls a bag of something powdery out of her jeans.

"You need to leave."

"You need a life." She flings the chair in circles and across the floor towards the window. Cute behavior if you're three years old. She's twenty-eight.

"That's exactly what I'm trying to do, Mel, get a life." I grab the back of the chair and turn her to face me.

"Look Miss High and Mighty, I was all you had for a long time."

"And I'm supposed to be grateful? Remember this?" I lift my sleeve, thrust my scar in her face.

"But in between, it was good times."

"How do you know? We were never sober enough to remember much. I went bankrupt. I lost a job. I lost Javier."

"Don't be bitter," she says.

"I'm past bitter."

"Never mind then. Drop me off at the beach, okay? I'll walk back to Mike's."

"Not unless you dump the drugs."

"Why would I do that?" Her cheeks flare red. I stare her down. I'm not driving anywhere with drugs in the car.

A knock at the door stops our conversation.

"Miss Zimmerman, it's me, Lacey Luster. And Veronica."

"Hold on," I yell, "I'm on the phone." I glance at the outside window. There's no way to get Mel out of here through it. "Mel, just sit there, okay? Say hi and no more," I urge her in a whisper.

I open the door to Lacey with Veronica all right, along with Lacey's father standing there, his glasses all steamed up.

"Ms. Zimmerman, you've met my father," Lacey says with a beaming smile. "We so wanted to thank you for reviewing my tape. I'm so excited, and I'm so sorry I missed the first practice. Veronica said I could pick up the handbook and stuff from you."

Mr. Luster walks into the office a little further. He's appraising Mel head to foot. Veronica stays in the doorway.

"Uh, this is Melody Cookson. She's visiting for a few days."

"How's it going? I love this area! I'm really pleased to meet you!" Mel is shouting, and I give her a look I learned from my mom.

Mr. Luster coughs. I'm fumbling past Mel into my file cabinet where I swear I put the extra copies of *Zimmerman's Zeitgeist*. Mel rolls the desk chair again, and Lacey is waving to someone in the hallway.

"Hi, Mr. Inman. Thank you, too. My dad and I dropped by to check in with Ms. Zimmerman. I can tell this is going to be the greatest!" Lacey won't stop burbling.

Dave takes it all in: Mel swirling, Mr. Luster's frowning, my harried searching. He says only, "Good. Welcome to the team." I can't read his expression: understanding or concerned? As he turns to leave, I push Mel, feigning playfulness, to move so that I can get into my desk drawer.

Mel jumps up, pulling my desk drawer out in one motion. The drawer empties on the floor, a chaos of envelopes, pens, cd's, and paper clips. Change and dollar bills scatter from corner to corner. "Oops," she giggles.

Mr. Luster harrumphs like the world has ended and asks, "Could we get the manual, please?" He shoves his hands into his pockets. He's rocking toe to heel.

Lacey steps in front of her father. "I'm so sorry, Ms. Zimmerman. I can come back tomorrow or pick it up at morning practice. I wanted to be totally ready for the quiz is all." How could Dahlia have skipped this candidate? She seems an advisor's dream.

Mel is on her hands and knees scooping up the junk from my desk drawer. Her low cut jeans dip below her butt crack and the reefer leaf tattoo above her tailbone is on full display. Mr. Luster's intake of breath is audible in the suffocating office. He is sweating.

"Mel, could you wait outside, please? It's a little crowded in here," I urge. She walks towards the door. I can see her with her head leaned towards Veronica's. They're talking and nodding. Mel hands Veronica something, probably her phone number. Mel loves to make connections.

I have finally managed to locate my manuals on the same shelf as the box of tapes clearly marked DUDS. I grab the box and shift it so that the label isn't toward the two happy Lusters and pick up the manual to get Lacey and father out of the office.

After they exit, Mel returns. She has given Veronica, Lacey, and Mr. Luster her favorite regal queen's wave, followed by a single digit to their backs. She tosses the baggie on my desk, inhales, and tucks her pocket flat into her jeans. "Your mama getting flabby eating at your Aunt Kaye's. Here. You take care of this. Then can I have a ride, pretty please?" She has turned away to gaze out the window. I wonder what she's plotting.

"Let's go flush it." I gather my things, lock my office door. Mel retracts her wheelies and walks like a normal person with me down the hallway to the faculty restroom.

I empty the powder into the nearest toilet so that she can see that's exactly what I've done. I toss the baggie into the waste can. That's what I'm thinking, what a waste. Mel isn't stupid, she used to be pretty, she had a good job in finance, and now she's a junkie and a whore, and I can't help her. Back when, I followed her lead until I woke up in Puget Sound with Jacques pulling me to safety. It's time to be free of her. One more ride. Yeah, she knows where I work, which is creepy, but I'm clean. I can call campus security if I need to. Have I sold out? Or simply bought into life?

We don't talk on the drive. As she asked, I drop her at the pier. She skates off, carefree and goofy. The surfer group ogles her, and she sails towards them in a mad rush that ends with her on her butt in their midst. Mel's donkey's bray burst out. I am not responsible for her. Poochie wags me home at the apartment when I get back. Better yet, Winona's at a church choir practice. I cuddle on the couch with the dog, wishing for some balance, for some semblance of a normal life with a normal family, normal friends. Is there such a thing as normal?.

CHAPTER 18: JOLENE

The wind howls through the open screen door, and the bedroom window slams shut. Jacques barks. Phillip awakens with a grumble and a shake of his head. He sits straight up in bed, looking lost. I return to the bedroom from the bathroom, rushing. I slept too late, slept too well, wish I didn't have school today when the Santa Anas will make the kids as skittish as race horses at Del Mar's opening race and make me more on edge than I would be anyway with all these new thoughts swirling through my mind about this man, last evening, what's next.

"Are you the cat that swallowed the canary?" asks Phillip.

"Am I smiling? This weather makes me a little crazy. I guess I'm happy."

"I've heard about these winds and watched the wild fires on news." He reaches out to touch my hand and a spark flies between us. We both pull back and laugh. "No such worries in the Northwest. Let's plan a visit."

"Let's!" I kiss the top of his head. "I have to get out the door now. You and Jacques have a good day. Can't wait for tonight!" If I don't leave now, I won't leave at all. Discipline and duty kicking in, I make myself leave.

At school, there's a note in my box to call the Bratkowskys, immediately. Would they really want me to call them at 6:15 in the morning? No email is listed, but with Celeste, I know that we have certainly had prior communication.

My lessons are ready, so after signing in I hurry up the hill to scan a few sets of homework or quizzes. The paper mound is shrinking slowly. I sit down at my desk, appraise the paper stacks, and randomly choose a set. But then I remember to check for the Bratkowskys' email, and there are twenty other messages. I email the Bratkowskys that I will call them at brunch, which assures the call has to be short so that they can't launch into fifteen additional issues. A red-flagged email pops up just as I'm about to sign out:

"Coverage for Ms. Mary Nagel this afternoon. You will supervise the cheerleaders. Please confirm."

We have to cover when we're tagged. I've gotten out of five prior assignments, and there's no getting out of this one. Besides, the cheer team runs itself and shouldn't be a big deal. I can grade some papers even if I did want to leave early to get home for Phillip's evening surprise.

School is school; a few surly students, a lot of energy in AP for their group projects on Victorian poets and poetry, making recipes from their poetic images and biographical details. The laughter of my students raises my spirits from the lows of the looming phone call to the Bratkowskys and the extra duty assignment this afternoon.

The ninth graders whine their way through their essays, saying "teacher" every five seconds until they actually begin writing and then they are silent, pens, papers, dictionaries, thoughts flying. Every time the door opens, leaves blow in, and I have to put an additional paperweight on papers on my desk.

At brunch, I call the Bratkowskys, but get their voice mail. Huzzah! Mission accomplished. I assure them that Celeste is improving as they can see on our web portal with a reminder that the allergy incident goes back to a permission slip as they already talked to Bill about.

I lunch alone. The one class after lunch is harder to settle than my morning ninth graders and more than one kid pleads for more time on the essay. I collect them anyway and tell the class we will finish up Monday after the vocabulary quiz or that they can come in at lunch Monday, which I know they'll never remember to do and works into my plan for a lunch with Phillip if he stays.

What should be my final bell rings, sending me scurrying to the gym, my book bag stuffed with easy-to-score quizzes.

Twenty girls and one guy are already practicing. Thao waves at me and comes over.

"Are you covering for Mary?"

"I'm covering for Ms. Nagel," I respond, not liking her use of a teacher's first name.

"She said somebody would be here for her today. She had to take her cat to the vet." Thao giggles behind her hand. "I think she's really going to have coffee with that cute new track coach, Mr. Molson."

I'm steamed.

"Girls and gentleman, I will call roll and then your captain," I look at the lesson plan, "Yara, will lead you through stretches and your practice. Yara, if you would please?"

Yara is not present. Yara often arrives late at practice I am informed.

"Who would like to lead today until Yara arrives?" I ask, trying not to sound as helpless as I feel.

"We can stretch on our own. She'll get here, Mrs. Zimmerman," says the guy, Ben Somebody.

"Fine." I sit on a bleacher and watch their lithe frames as they bend into impossible postures. Each is wearing a green leotard and baggy warm up socks in gold, except Ben is in his gym shorts. For my dance lessons, the whole two years, Mother refused to buy me a leotard. She said it was a waste of money, and at my first dancing lesson I made the mistake of wearing a dress. When we did tumbling, my underpants showed, and I was the laughing stock of the dance class, especially since I couldn't do a cartwheel. For future lessons I wore pedal pushers. My dance teacher, Ms. Giancone, kept asking when I would get my leotard, and I kept telling her pretty soon, even though I knew Mother would never give in on something so insignificant. The other moms watched the dance lessons. Mother never came to watch a recital, much less a practice.

All these thoughts pulse through me as I grade quizzes with the answer key to one side. I can score five at a time, keep an eye on the cheerleaders, and think about my childhood. I am a miracle of multitasking, of keeping busy.

So by what right is my daughter such a mess? I bought her a leotard of every color. I went to all of her recitals and dress rehearsals. Not wanting to look like a stage mom, I held myself aloof from the vampire moms over-correcting every step. I didn't attend her private sessions either. She said she loved to dance. Wasn't that enough? I quit dance after two years. I didn't like the way Ms. Giancone laughed because I was too stocky and talked about my strong buttocks to a visiting teacher. I went home and told Mother that Ms. Giancone said a dirty word to me: "Buttocks." Mother and grandmother laughed so hard, but I felt as if they were laughing at me. My mother was glad I quit dance. She didn't ever have to buy me that leotard and she said she didn't want me to grow up to be some chorus girl. Me? I don't exactly have the legs for the Rockettes.

Yara runs in and turns the Ipod station on with some horrendous rap and hip hop. The team forms lines and cranking out some moves that look robotic to me. I try to concentrate on my grading. The music stops and starts, stops and starts. Yara blows her whistle for about the 100th time. My head is beginning to ache. The gym is at least ninety degrees. We can't open the doors because they blow shut again and half an oak tree's worth of leaves already mounded at the door sill.

With twenty more minutes to endure, Mrs. Polonsey slips into the gym, says "Sorry" and hands me a message. URGENT it says. Bill has set up a meeting with the Bratkowskys directly after this class finishes and I've earned my sub credit.

Will this day never end? I turn to Thao at the Ipod player and think, I guess today I face the music too.

CHAPTER 19: ZOOZLE

Veronica is waiting outside the studio when I arrive. "You didn't leave the door unlocked. How can we warm up if you do stuff like that?" she pouts.

"Sorry. I forgot to tell the custodian he needs to unlock before 6 a.m." Thank God it's Friday, and Monday, no school for fall break, which is our district's way of handling the Jewish High Holy Days.

"Dahlia never forgot." Veronica flounces to the corner VCR and switches out the tape. "Doesn't this tape monitor give you the creeps, Ms. Zimmerman? Dahlia wouldn't have allowed it." She sets the previous day's tape aside, along the wall next to her crammed duffel bag. She delivers tapes to Ms. Garant after practice even though Ms. Garant can monitor our sessions from her office feed.

It is creepy, but what can I say? I signed the release, and I think it might work in my favor if the girls get out of line with me; Ms. Durant probably thinks these barracudas are toothless.

Veronica begins her stretches, and I do too. Sandy joins us. Lacey arrives in a whirl of backpack, papers, and CDs falling to the floor, in other words, a grand entrance that makes us all look up.

"Hi everybody, isn't it so beautiful this morning?" She doesn't wait for an answer. "Coach, can I speak to the class about our second fund raiser and a volunteer day and the Chancellor's Dinner?"

"Choose two of the three, Lacey. We have to practice as well as talk, right?"

"Oh, goodness, of course. I'm just so excited. Let's deal with the fundraiser and the volunteer day since all the campus organizations owe about a million hours and we haven't done one yet.

Veronica sighs. "Yeah, Dahlia made sure we did some in the summer before we had papers and performances and all the crap that comes with school."

"Language, please, Ms. Slattery."

"*Crap* isn't okay? How about *bs?*"

"How about *stuff?*"

The rest of the team has straggled in. They begin stretching on the mat, no cell phones in sight though several hold their manuals under their noses as they stretch. I count this as a victory.

"Good morning, ladies. Before our quiz on the *Zeitgeist*, Lacey has a few words. Let's hear it for Lacey."

I applaud, and several girls sneak their manuals open, which I walk around and remove. If looks could kill, I'd be dead.

Lacey stands in front of them, her feet in ballet's fifth position, her back straight, except that her hands are filled with flyers rather than held above her head.

"Okay, let's go with the good news first. Sandy said that we made over $500 at the car wash two weeks ago, which means we can afford new leotards for the Chancellor's dinner performance and then maybe get the department to pay for scarves or skirts." A loud cheer goes up. I glance at the security camera. Does Ms. Garant consider this undisciplined?

Lacey turns to me. "Is it too soon to order the color, or could we go with burnt orange?"

"No way."

"Puke orange?"

"Like when we vomit screwdrivers?"

I intervene. "Let's think about the color until Tuesday—we don't have to finalize the choreography— but we agree on the mood, right? So I'll price out this style and cost and have the purchase order ready once we agree on a color."

"That's a very good idea, Ms. Zimmerman," agrees Sandy and heads bob in agreement. I wipe some sweat off on a towel. "Let's get going then."

Lacey touches my shoulder. "Could I have thirty seconds for the volunteer pitch?"

"Thirty seconds, I'm counting."

"There's a river walk clean up at the Tijuana Estuary."

Groans break out along with protests in unison about sewage, rats, and touching trash.

"It's a three-day weekend," moans Veronica. "We're going to the Lake Powell."

"Wait, come on. It's a Sunday. All the frats will be there and the Surfriders Association, and if you're in a sorority and stay an extra hour, you get credit for both the dance team and your sorority. Plus, if you love the beach the way I do, you know it's important to clean up the riverbed before the winter rains. Here are the flyers."

She hands them out, including one for me.

"Thank you, Lacey. Ladies, please fold your flyers for later. After the quiz, you can take a five minute break to put things away, stretch while I scan the quizzes. Then we'll practice, ending early to talk about the *Zeitgeist*. Here's a ten-question true/false quiz. You have five minutes from when the last quiz is distributed. Please separate yourselves sufficiently to prevent wandering eyes. If you must stare into space to recall an answer, please stare at the ceiling or your own paper." Half of this speech comes from my observation of my mom's classes back when I was considering teaching secondary school until I realized I was attempting to finish my incarnation as her clone.

I set the timer and walk around to assess the girls' attitudes. Three are clearly playing a guessing game, including Veronica. The other twelve are concentrating as if their lives are being threatened by the dance police. I glance at Lacey's flyer and wonder if I'm required to attend if the girls do. I'll ask Dave rather than Ms. Garant, since there's no need to sound more naïve than I am about policies. If Eric or Lordman or Chloris will come, it could be fun.

The timer goes off. I collect papers, dismiss the girls, "Five-minute break—stretches required if you weren't stretching before" and go to the department office to score the quizzes. Most go through without the beep that signals a wrong answer though one beeps steadily. I pull it from the machine and see red tics by every answer and a total score of zero. Who's the genius? Lacey. Oh holy crap, I can picture Daddy Luster now.

The girls have stretched. Practice breaks into our "They Don't Care About Us" groups, and I am encouraged at some new steps. Veronica's group invites me to join in. We laugh as I step backwards instead of forward for the hand clap.

We are sweaty and ready for a cool down. The team takes their places. I take a deep breath.

"I am happy to say that almost everyone passed the quiz." Lacey hangs her head. "If you didn't pass, as you know if you studied the manual, you can take another quiz tomorrow after practice. But you will have half a strike."

"Who can tell me what earns a full strike?"

"Skipping practice without phoning Coach, missing a performance without a doctor's note, academic probation" recites Sandy.

"Penalty for two strikes?"

"Benched and a conference with Ms. Zimmerman and Ms. Garant."

"Penalty for three strikes?"

"Off the team until the end of the semester as long as Ms. Garant agrees."

"Parental involvement in these decisions?"

"None. We are all eighteen."

"Discussion?"

"Did I get a half-strike for swearing before we discussed the rules?" Veronica repositions her hair clip.

"No."

"What if we have an IEP for dyslexia and need our tutor when we take quizzes?" Lacey.

"We'll discuss it. Could you come in early tomorrow?"

She agrees, and the all-call buzzes the end of class. As I walk back to my office, Ms. Garant appears in the hallway, crooking her finger at me to enter her office.

"Good morning," she says with that skeletal grin. "Much better, today, dear."

I'm relieved for at least two seconds.

"But of course you could have controlled their language, been aware of Lacey's IEP from the file on your desk, and made sure the car wash money was appropriately deposited. You shouldn't have that money more than a few days, or have you not read the faculty handbook? Her eyebrows would arch if they could move.

"I'll get it deposited today. Associated Student Body or Department of Dance, Ms. Garant?"

"The Department, Ms. Zimmerman. We are not under the purview of the students. This is considered an academic endeavor though associated with extracurriculars. We have standards. Speaking of standards, I reviewed your *Zeitgeist* manual. I will recommend it to the spirit squad advisor. Mr. Luna is struggling with discipline issues. Coed squads require such finesse." She shakes her head over the woes of life at junior college, and I wonder why she's here instead of the University. "By the way, you have a strike by my accounting for yesterday's need for my assistance with discipline. Try to remember to choose calm music for your opening stretches."

"Yes, ma'am," I pretend to agree though I think she's completely whacked out. Second day with a group of fifteen young women, and I'm supposed to be capable of Harry Potter wizardry?

"That is all, Ms. Zimmerman, except that I hope you have a good turnout at the River Rally Clean Up. Make sure the girls wear their dance team sweatshirts."

Once Ms. Garant has minced away to her office, I pick up Lacey's file to read tonight and grab the envelope from my desk drawer. I count the bills into piles, and count again. Then again. Lacey said

$500. We have $182. I dive under the desk, scoot around on the floor inch by inch, check behind the file cabinets, sweep my hands back into the corners of the desk drawers. Reaching behind the computer's CPU on the floor and whisking dust from under the printer, I find one more bill along with notebook paper and dust bunnies. It's a hundie. So now we have $282, but where's the rest?

The scramble in the office the first day: Mel, Mr. Luster, Lacey, Veronica. There's only one person on my list of suspects. That money will be long gone, and I have to find $218 in the next twenty-four hours. Mom? Winona? Eric? Chloris? Uncle Bill? That's a big no on all fronts. Mitch? Mr. McKillop? Could I hock a couple of items from Grandpa Joe's things in the garage if Norm and Mike haven't gotten there yet?

Placing the money into a new envelope, I log in and Google "egg donation" and "cash for blood." Those are old stand bys from back when.

Whatever I decide, the clock is ticking. God, I hate pressure. I'll go home and take a nap with Poochie.

CHAPTER 20: JOLENE

Dashing to Bill's office, the wind blows my hair into a duck tail, but all I want is out of here so I don't stop to brush it. The Bratkowskys are already seated. Mr. Bratkowsky stands when I enter. Why doesn't his daughter have his manners?

Bill nods me towards a seat and makes the introductions.

"Now, Mrs. Zimmerman," he acts as if I'm one of his drones, "the Bratkowskys are quite concerned about Celeste's progress in your class. They feel that you are not doing all you can to enhance her learning experience. Is that correct?" He eyeballs them.

They fidget. Mr. Bratkowsky speaks after taking out a note card. "We made a list of a few questions, Mrs. Zimmerman, the first one being how Celeste was allowed to be endangered by the presence of a dog in your classroom?"

I look to Bill for support. He sits there, mind obviously elsewhere, probably on a promotion or being named a California Distinguished School or an American Blue Ribbon School, so I answer. "Mr. Franklin has the signed permission slip. I'm sure he went over that with you yesterday on the phone?"

Bill pulls the paper and copies from a file. He hands one to the Bratkowskys. They study it.

"Anyone can see this is Celeste's writing," Mr. Bratkowsky grumbles. "Since it's a matter of health, I would hope there would be more accountability from the school."

"I had a sub for a number of days, Mr. Bratkowsky. Didn't Celeste mention my absence during my father's illness?"

"No, she did not, and I stand by my assertion that the school should be more accountable." He takes his wife's hand, a united front. His wife does not look up.

Bill smiles his winning politician's smile. "How can we clarify this situation, Mr. Bratkowsky? As we spoke of yesterday, Celeste did return to class after the nurse gave her the allergy medicine. What exactly do you expect us to do except to promise this kind of thing will not happen again? If the drug dogs are on campus, I will personally be sure that Celeste is not in the room when they search. I will remind all of her teachers to double-check signatures on her homework sheets."

I sit still. I do not want to further antagonize these people. Celeste has something in her insouciance that reminds me of Suzann, that devil-may-care mouthiness.

"As you can see from the web site, Celeste's grades have improved recently," I offer.

"I noticed three zeroes," Mrs. Bratkowsky states tremulously. Her husband looks at her aghast.

"Three zeroes? There must be an error in your bookkeeping, Mrs. Zimmerman. I personally check Celeste's homework and her backpack every morning."

It's now or next week to break the bad news. "A zero can mean an assignment not turned in, an assignment that arrives after the tardy bell, or an assignment that has been copied." Both parents allow their jaws to drop.

"That's quite harsh, Mrs. Zimmerman," says Mrs. Bratkowsky.

Bill regards me as if he thinks I should bargain. He's flipping through Celeste's file. He pulls out another folder, this one with my class standards.

"Here are Mrs. Zimmerman's standards, and here is her standard on tardies and late homework. Both are clearly spelled out for you. You signed them as required."

Mr. Bratkowsky shakes his head, but his wife nods. "I signed. We get six of those to read and sign the first day of school. How could anyone remember all the rules, especially ninth graders?"

"I give the students and their parents two weeks to read, sign, and discuss my policies with me," I say, my head about to explode.

Bill drums his fingers on the desk. "Just a reminder, Mrs. Zimmerman, teachers have standards and procedures while schools have policies. Nevertheless, I tell you what. Mrs. Zimmerman and I will discuss each of these zeroes, and we will choose one Celeste can make up to assist her growth as a student and your new understanding of the class *procedures*. How's that for the spirit of compromise?"

I don't like Bill's interference in my class, his attitude, or giving credence to a squeaking wheel, but I also don't want to be here until midnight. "That's a very good idea. I will give Celeste a special assignment and a new due date, and I will email a copy to you. Will that work?"

The Bratkowskys believe it will work. I get to go home, free at last. And I have in mind the make-up assignment from hell.

Singing loudly to a Jimmy Buffett CD, I'm thumping my steering wheel as I inch through residual after-school traffic, the students in their new cars, hot trucks, even Hummers, the teachers in their old family sedans. Students honk their horns to get my attention, and I'm chagrined to have been caught so completely and unguardedly giddy. I have a session with Antonio, my trainer, who asks me what I'm smiling about as I swing a kettle bell up above my head and down past my knees. I shake my head, "Just happy," I tell him. The training goes well, I shower and shampoo, and put on shorts and a white cotton blouse that I tie into a halter. I smile into the locker room's misty mirror.

Phillip's car is in my driveway. I hear Jacques' joyful woof at the door.

As I walk in, Phillip stands before me, smelling of citrus, dressed in a new robe. He picks a plush white robe off the dining room chair, saying, "Get comfortable, my sweet," untying my improvised blouse. I slip the robe on. Jacques checks in with me and then discretely chooses to explore the deck. He's a gentleman too.

Wine glasses center the table, with a cheeseboard and grapes.

"Wine?" I ask, surprised but hoping for the little zip I get from one glass.

"Sparkling apple cider," says Phillip. "You'd be amazed how much the fizz resembles champagne!" He clicks his glass to mine, sips, traces my pudgy fingers. The music he has chosen, a jazz trio, fills the quiet between us. He leads me to the couch and pulls me to rest against him.

"Relax. Breathe. Take some time to let the school day go away." He rubs my temples and strokes my hair across the top of my head. I fall asleep.

When I awaken, Phillip has switched from music to a news commentary. "Phillip, I'm so sorry. It was a long day."

He smiles and puts a finger to his lips and pulls me to my feet. He sweeps his arm towards the table, which is set with two place settings. He brings out a Caesar salad with shrimp. We dine and grin. Chocolate meringues add a final, sweet touch. He leans forward until neither of us can wait another second. We kiss.

I try to get my bearings, to prevent moving too quickly. I'm worried about the other night, the night he obviously could not perform.

As if he has read my mind, he pulls a blue pill from his robe's pocket. "I filled this prescription today. I've had it for some time, but never thought I'd be using it." He's not the least embarrassed.

"Oh my!" I giggle.

He eases me to my feet, setting our glasses back on the table, slipping my robe from my shoulders. I had thought I would worry about my flabby arms that are not cooperating with my conditioning program and my pooching tummy. I don't.

He's not looking at those flaws, long arms around me, stroking my breasts. He kisses my ears, propelling me towards the bedroom.

Soon, we are naked, exploring, amazed, and then we are spent. We curl into one another, warm and fulfilled.

"I gave up on men years ago. Should I say thank you?"

"Just don't give up on me, Jolene."

I roll out of bed, grab our robes, and toss him what I think is his. It's comically short on his lanky body so we switch. "How about some time in the hot tub?" I'm not sure if he's going to spend the night, and I want him to.

We put the bubbles on high, and with the noise of the pump and our own hypnotic state, there's no reason to talk. After three cycles, Phillip yawns. "I'm turning into a prune in all this water."

"Then let's go to bed." He follows me in, we straighten the bed from its fracas-frazzled condition, doff our robes, and I set the alarm.

He calls Jacques, who looks at me, looks at Phillip, and circles on our robes, pawing at them, on Phillip's side of the bed.

Phillip's long arms enfold me. We both sigh, and then Jacques exhales, a huge, deep, whoosh of air. We fall asleep with contentment between us.

CHAPTER 21: ZOOZLE

I never got that nap with Poochie. After spending a couple hours on the Internet and on the phone, I learned a few sad facts of life that should be taught in high school or college instead of algebra or trig. The egg donation would work to provide some cash but not fast enough for Ms. Garant's rules. I'm going to do it anyway. The catch is the length of time it takes for the application, the screening, and the match, plus my own cycle, which is not exactly cooperative. I can see myself with an extra ten grand, living the life.

Since the blood bank will give me fifty bucks for an immediate donation to the cause, thank God I am drug-free, hep free, and healthy. I've got it down to needing $168. I can round that up to $175, claim urgent car repair, and see if Mom or Winona will come through. I pull a hair and brush an end across my cheeks, sort of like giving myself butterfly kisses.

Ms. Garant is off my back about the deposit for a few days. I've agreed to host a parents' night dinner next Friday and you know I'll push donations to the program, so I told her I would get all the accounting done at once. That gives me some breathing room. In the same email to our dance parents, I also suggested participation in today's River Rally.

Winona isn't coming, not even to sit under an umbrella. I thought I could get Chloris and Eric to keep me company, but they work early, and we'll be done by afternoon. Eric said Chris isn't home yet from his latest hospitalization, which is a huge relief. Lordman said he'd be there. I hope he's not hitting on the girls on the team because that would be beyond embarrassing.

It's foggy this morning, the Santa Ana having blown itself out. I put on tennis shoes, my dance team parka and dance team sweats. The Estuary has a decent parking lot since it's a National Seashore. When I arrive, a dozen cars are lined up.

To my surprise, I see Ms. Garant standing with Veronica, Lacey, Sandy, and Carly. Some surfers are listening to a guy on a bullhorn. A group of volunteers is standing around a table handing out plastic gloves and big trash bags. Yuppie parents with little kids in tow are actually putting their efforts where their mouths are for once.

Barking dogs get my attention before I join my team. A beagle is facing off in fun, and his opponent is Jacques! My mom is holding Phillip's arm and tugging on Jacques' leash. I consider avoiding them, but can't resist Jacques.

Mom sees me and waves, so I rush in that direction, and hope she can read gotta-go body language. I do need to have a word with the team before we begin the river work.

Mom pats my arm. "Good morning! We got your email and thought, "'Why not?'"

"That's good, Mom. Hi, Phillip." Phillip is wearing a colorful straw sombrero, which he sweeps across his chest. It makes me laugh, and I drop to my knees to embrace Jacques.

A mom and a dad follow a delighted, rosy-cheeked toddler in a battery-powered Barbie-mobile as their greyhound strains at his leash.

My mom points the couple out, "So the dog gets exercise, and the kid gets fat."

"I didn't hear them ask for your advice."

"I was just making conversation, Suzann."

"God, Mom. Like you're such an expert on raising perfect kids. See ya." I trot off, but Phillip catches up to me.

"You're going to try with your mom, aren't you?" He hasn't looked so annoyed with me before..

"Yes, I should," I say, thinking car repair that I supposedly require and soon. "Hey, Mom. Sorry to be so grumpy!" I call back to her. She rewards me by blowing a kiss. The needed patch is applied.

I join the team. Ms. Garant stops talking and defers to me. I tell the team, "Thanks for being here. Let's get going. First step will be gloves and water bottles and trash sacks. Do you want to do this as a race in teams?"

Sandy squeals yes, and the rest of them zing her with furious scowls.

"I'll take that as a *no* to the race." We go over to the tables to pick up our supplies. Handing out gloves is Lordman.

"Hi, good lookin'" he says to me, or I assume he means me, not all of us.

Veronica makes a rude noise behind me and scoots past to pick up the rest of her supplies. She pulls Lacey with her. They are talking to someone way down the line, somebody handing out maps with highlighted areas to cover.

"I'm almost done, Zooz." Lordman hands his stack of gloves to the women working with him, telling them "Changing duty stations." He gives me a dazzling smile. "Zooz, let's clean the world together." He has a dimple on his right cheek that I haven't noticed before.

"That sounds like a noble goal, Gaylord." He kills me.

We step on down the line. The team has already fanned out across the river's bank with a few surfers tagging along, some of the parents and their kids. The Barbie-mobile has been left behind. I can hear its rattling battery.

In the kid's car Mel is circling the parking lot. She swings the car into a parking place and bounds after a group walking upriver. First, I think good because I won't have to talk to her. Second, I think crap because she's going to spend time near my team, which I don't want in the worst way. She has already reached them and has paired off with Veronica and Lacey. She couldn't have chosen Sandy and Carla or anyone normal, could she?

I decide to not let that ruin my day as Lordman has unfolded our maps. We are assigned to a box of terrain back from the river bank. I hope there aren't snakes. I know there aren't snakes. Whenever I'm in any brushy area, I worry about snakes. Lordman will keep me safe. Maybe.

We work silently for about ten minutes. He exclaims over every bit of debris, "It's shoes, it's toy trucks, it's bread wrappers. God, it's condoms, don't people have a clue?"

He's wrinkling his nose and holding things at arm's length before he drops them into his bag. He finds it all quite amusing. I'm working along, wondering how anyone can enjoy this. My mind wanders to the riverbank and to my girls over there with Mel. I won't think about it.

Lordman's bag is already full. Mine isn't, so he puts his load down and comes to help me.

"You found bigger stuff — it's not a fair comparison," I moan.

"It's not a race. We'll work together. Isn't it pretty here? Did you see the pelicans?" Gaylord stops and breathes deeply.

"Pelicans?" I haven't noticed any bird except pigeons since I left Washington, I think.

"Way over there, across the river on the Mexican side of the fence." He points.

"I see them! Are they illegals if they fly over?"

"We'll have to ask the Park Service. Isn't that sad?"

"There's too much that makes me sad. I can't be sad." I go back to picking up trash.

"Maybe you need someone to share with? Maybe then you wouldn't be sad?" Lordman has come up behind me and rests his chin on my shoulder.

"Maybe." I lean back into him. Usually, I'd bolt as if prodded by an electric current. With Lordman, I'm comfortable.

He pulls me to face him. "You've got some secrets, don't you?"

I look down. I'm not ready for this.

"Never mind," he says. "Step by step."

"That's what Phillip tells me. And my AA meetings, and my shrink, and my mom." That's a confession right there. I hope he understands.

"Phillip, the guy with the big dog? Introduce us later, would you? I love dogs. I don't have one because my mom thinks they're too much trouble. God, my mom."

"Ditto," I say as I see my mom and Phillip and Jacques way down at the river's mouth. "There I go again. Phillip thinks I could try harder with my mom."

"If you remind me, I'll remind you, okay, deal?" Lordman laughs. His trash bag has ripped. We carry my bag to the refuse pile and return to take an end each for his bag. It's heavy enough to make us grunt as we drag it away.

Mel is sitting on a curb between Lacey and Veronica. I doubt they've filled a single bag among the three of them. I don't want to sound like a control freak in front of Lordman and let it go. Mel is Mel. She's not going to ruin my day.

Lordman suggests lunch at the pier. I check to be sure all my girls have clocked in. Sandy's still out putting in extra hours. Mom and Phillip are not in our general vicinity.

Lordman takes me by the hand. He leads me to the beach side of the estuary and the restaurant on the pier. We order fish tacos. He pays.

"Hey, I don't have to sing for my supper, do I?" I ask.

"How about a dance?"

"Where? Here?"

"No, downtown. Let's hit the Gaslight District tonight."

"Really?" God, that would be fun. I haven't been out in a million years. Out and sober, what a concept.

"Yes, really."

"I don't have dancing clothes."

"I bet you can find something to wear. It's San Diego, not New York. Eightish? Dancing, light dinner? We can walk to Tante Tango from my place. I'll draw you a map. You can meet my mom and then we can compare. Live a little, Zooz."

About that he is certainly right.

Aunt Kaye is excited that I'm going out and has loaned me a blue-and-green tie-dyed dress with skinny shoulder straps. She has a jacket for it too that I won't wear. Her daughter gave the dress to her for her thirtieth birthday, back when Grandma Janie and Grandpa Joe and Uncle Mitch and Aunt Kaye went dancing every Saturday night. The seventies' vibe is back, and the dress looks really cute even if I have to wear it with my black stilettos.

Outfit ready, I ready the bathtub. I am sandy and dirty and swampy. All of this disappears into clouds of vanilla-scented bubble bath. Four small candles light the bathroom, adding to the spa feeling. Poochie comes in to check on me at intervals and acts as if he's going to jump in with me.

"No, Poochie," I order. "Down, buddy. Wet dog I don't need."

Winona is out preparing for Sunday night services, and I have the apartment to myself, blessedly free of background preaching, praying, and television noise. I envision Lordman on the dance floor with me. He doesn't have a dancer's body. The times he's broken into routines, he's been light footed and most of all, irrepressible and joyful. That's the secret of dancing. You have to drop your ego on the first beat of the music and move as the sound goes through your feet and heart.

I like what I see in the mirror for the first time in a long time. I have gained a little weight in the right places, my eyes are shining and so is my hair. I have to decide what to tell Lordman about my arm scar, but why not tell the truth? It's easier. It's easier with everyone except my mom. Mom. I make the money-request phone call, happy to leave the message on her machine when she doesn't pick up.

The directions to Lordman's are easy, and I make it there in under twenty minutes. He said I could park behind his PT, and he's right, my VW fits right in. His fifth-floor condo is in Little Italy. He answers the buzzer. I take the elevator up, straightening my dress and fluffing my hair.

He is waiting at the opened door of #510, reaches out, and twirls me as I enter.

"Smooth maneuver, Hoover," I laugh, with one of Grandpa Joe's favorite sayings. "You look fabuloso!" Lordman is dressed in khaki pants and a long-sleeved blue-on-blue striped shirt. We sort of match, which is nice.

"Likewise, my tropical flower," he whispers into my ear, then yells, "Mom, she's here!"

A tall woman with a dowager's hump walks into the room, leaning on a cane. "Hello, dear."

"I'm pleased to meet you, Mrs. Blanchard." I put out my hand to shake. Her nails are manicured, and I'm reminded again of my raggedy nails, another little habit I have yet to conquer.

"Call me Sharon, please."

"Zoozle."

"I beg your pardon?"

Lordman jumps in to explain the morph from Suzann into Zoozle and has me sit on the sofa. I'd rather get going, but suffer through the introductions.

Sharon embarks on a tale of her last cruise from Seattle to Vancouver to Alaska once I mention UDubb. She's about to pull her photo album from below the glass coffee table, when Gaylord shakes his head. "Mom, we need to get going or we'll be in line half the night to get into Tante Tango. Remember when we went there with your cousins?"

"What a night that was! I wore my red velvet dress. I have a picture around here somewhere. Wait, here it is." She uses the picture as a bookmark in a coffee table book about Alaska.

In the picture Sharon was younger and prettier and slimmer, and the red velvet dress fit her, no humped back, no cane. Time does a number on bodies, that's for sure. I never noticed Grandpa Joe's aging because he was so young at heart, his laughter so constant, he just never seemed old. And then he died.

"Beautiful, Mrs. Blanchard, so beautiful."

"Here, Mom, take a picture of us, and then we've got to go." Lordman hands her a digital camera.

"Thank you, son," she says as she clicks at least five shots without warning. One of them might turn out to be okay. "Have fun, kids. What time are you coming home, Gaylord?"

"Mom. No curfew. Not for the past fifteen years."

"Of course. See you in the morning. Nice meeting you, Suzzle."

"Zoozle, Mom." Lordman picks up his coat and propels me to the door.

"Bye now," I wave. "We'll dedicate the first dance to you and your red velvet dress!" Sharon swoons back to the couch.

We walk the city's streets. Lordman points out the U.S. Grant Hotel, which looks like a temple to the city's past. As we approach the Gas Lamp District, crowds and noise increase.

There are lines for every restaurant and music bar, especially at Croce's and Belo and the W Hotel's entrance. Tante Tango is busy. We wait ten minutes, people watching and trying to decide who's there for the tapas and who will actually dance. A tall Latina greets us and insists that we show identification. Lordman and I laugh. I'm used to it, but he's almost thirty.

We're given the choice of sitting at the bar or at one of the tiny tables. We look at one another and nod simultaneously towards the tables. If we sit at the bar and hop down to dance, we're likely to be replaced. That's what I'm thinking.

A trio composed of a guitar player, a drummer, and a singer. The singer is arranging their music at the far side of the restaurant. The singer and drummer are wearing tuxes. The guitar player is a woman in an orange flamenco dress with piles of ruffles. I tug at the hem of my short dress, and Lordman whispers, "You look beautiful. Relax."

We order five small plates to share with sparkling water to drink. He does not suggest wine or hard liquor, and I'm grateful.

As the plates arrive, we split the bites. I prefer the spinach artichoke dip with veggies. Lordman takes over the platter of tiny lamb chops. He thinks they're divine; I think only of baby lambs and nursery rhymes and fuzzy creatures. No lamb for me.

There's a general buzz in the room. Most of the clientele appears to be in their twenties. Several older couples occupy a booth overlooking the street scene.

"They'll be the ballroom experts," Lordman points out.

"Maybe we'll learn new moves," I counter.

"Let's show 'em what we've got," he says and offers his arm to escort me to the dance floor. I'm used to dancing with tall men, so it is a surprise that his short stature, short arms, make my initial stance effortless. "International or American?" I ask.

"Fourth of July and apple pie." The trio launches into "Red Petticoats" and Gaylord and I dance as if we've been partnered for years. I like the feeling of the close embrace until the contact in the pelvis feels too intimate for who we are as a couple. "It's a dance," he reminds me as he reacts to the tension in my hips. He begins a corte as we promenade to the left. He throws in a contra check, a four-step change, and an oversway. I'm still in synch with him, and my heart rate is up. The music ends, the audience applauds, and we grin and applaud one another. We return to our table, waiting to see what other couples dance. Three couples stand up for the next number. Gaylord and I watch a moment, confident in our dancing..

We take the floor again. The Latina from the door is now dancing with the drummer. They throw in some moves from Argentine tango, and I ask Lordman, "Can we match that?" He leads me into outside swivels and a set of foot taps. I trip, Gaylord catches me before I fall, and we concede that we are outmatched. After the dance we bow to the other couple. They are gracious in victory. The woman hands me a card for her dancing studio.

"I'd love to have my own studio, Lordman, but I'd teach little kids. I'd get them into ballroom and ethnic dances, more than ballet and tap."

"Explain ethnic."

"Indian, Japanese, even Eskimo, known as Aleut."

"Aleut?"

"It was my area of expertise in grad school. Didn't I tell you about performing "The Copulating Caribou" for my dance team last spring? It didn't go over very well with the admin at Port Townsend." Gaylord laughs and hugs me. "I went too far pushing the envelope. I'd like to see American kids embrace the world. Don't you think we're too self-centered?"

"I know I am." He hangs his head.

"What?" I lift his chin.

"It means I worry about me, where I'm going, what am I doing, what is the meaning of my life?"

"God, Lordman, I would have sworn you knew all that. You seem confident enough."

"My mom's favorite game is charades. I get a lot of practice." He blows air through his lips, cheeks puffed out.

"Mine too."

"I pledge to you I will never be a fake around you unless I am at work." We hook fingers and shake.

"What's your pledge to me, Zoozle?"

"I pledge to you, um, I pledge to you. . . ." I can't think of an appropriate pledge to Lordman.

"How about that you will trust me?" He leans closer.

"I do trust you. I like that. Lordman, I accept that you will not be a fake, and I pledge to you that you have earned my trust." I back away from a kiss.

"What a night! Let's stroll to the bay—it's all downhill so take off those heels!" We walk to the Embarcadero. Lights reflect off the harbor in long streams. Gaylord holds my hand and squeezes it as we pass couples with dogs, couples with shopping bags, couples with eyes for only one another. We stop to look through a metered telescope. We can't get the focus right and lose our quarter. This makes us laugh. Where my mom would be stomping around to demand a refund or find the 1-800 number to get her money back, Lordman sees the humor. In front of the old sailing ship, *The Star of India*, he pulls me close. He kisses me, soft and sweet. I don't step away. He points at the ship. "That's the past, anchored safely in port, a tourist attraction. Let's live for each day and all the future holds, huh, Zooz?"

I embrace him and kiss him again, still soft and sweet, no pushing tongues or roving hands.

I didn't know it was in me to feel this safe, this hopeful, and this cherished. I wonder if the scar tissue of fear Francis left in on my heart and mind is like those stairs of sand Phillip talked about, the ones you can learn from and climb up and over.

CHAPTER 22: JOLENE

My first thought upon waking is "I hate my job." My second is that today's not a school day, which gives me permission to pull the blanket up and keep my eyes closed. The blanket doesn't budge because Phillip has pulled it to his side of the bed.

I curl my body against his. He's warm and snoring and doesn't react. In ten minutes, I've stayed still as long as I can manage, and I grab my robe from the floor, and sneak out of bed, trying not to disturb my sleeping prince. Jacques pads after me into the kitchen. I don't know if I should feed him. A box of dog treats is by Phillip's briefcase on the counter.

"You'll have to settle for this for now," I say, tossing Jacques two. He takes them into the living room, where he settles on the couch afghan with his treat.

I want to impress Phillip with my domestic side. My cookbooks are yellow and stained on their covers. It's been a long time since I cared much about a meal that I prepared. Coffee percolating, I consider adding a shot of whisky or tequila. I'm not sure I really want to live alcohol-free for life. What if he caught me drinking? What would he say? I check my answering machine and see the red message light blinking. How soon do I want to listen to this? Do I want to with Phillip in the house? I know it's something with Suzann.

I add cream to my coffee and flip through the pages of my brunch book. Even though it's almost fall, my heart pulses as if it's spring, and I choose a spring menu: bacon, scrambled eggs and carrot-biscuits. Humming, "Someone to Watch Over Me," I chop carrots, hoping the soft noises and homey scent of bacon sizzling will awaken Phillip a little at a time instead of his being clobbered with an alarm's buzz or my roaming hands. I guess men like to be awakened with someone fondling their penis, but I haven't read the pamphlet on Viagra, and I don't want to embarrass him.

The biscuits are proving more problematic than I thought they would. The dough is sticky and hard to roll. Frustrated, I add more flour to the board. The dough remains unworkable. Now the bacon is frying too fast. I toss the biscuit dough into the trash and rummage in the 'fridge for a tube of biscuits that I can top with carrot shreddies. I'm not good at most things that matter, like cooking and homemaking, raising children, and the Kama Sutra.

Jacques wanders down the hall, and I hear the low murmur of Phillip's voice. Phillip comes in to sit at the table, his eyes sleepy.

"When did you get up?"

"Maybe forty-five minutes ago? I'm such a morning person."

He opens his briefcase and brings out a pill container. "May I?" he asks. I look to see if one of the pills is blue. It is.

"How about just vitamins and breakfast, and then we'll see?" Once I'm in cooking mode, I'm really not ready to hop back into bed, new romance or not. Another shower, my dry skin, honestly, do men ever think about anything else besides sex? I thought Phillip appeared divinely different.

Phillip swallows his vitamins, and nothing else, I hope. "Ah! I love mornings! Maybe a cup of coffee now?"

Does he think I'm his servant? "Be my guest," I offer as I put the last of the bacon on paper towels and begin to stir the eggs. The oven dings with the pre-heating timer, and I push the biscuits in.

"Phillip, I didn't feed Jacques."

"He's okay. Did he go out?"

"He did." Why are we so awkward this morning? This morning should be paradisiacal. I've pictured it a hundred times.

Seated at the table, Phillip glances at the counter. He goes back to his briefcase and pulls out a green leather journal with cream-colored paper. He begins writing. I feel ignored and secondary, but I don't want to interrupt his thoughts. I busy myself arranging a smaller bouquet, pulling the flowers that have drooped and going out front to cut daisies and pick up the morning paper. Phillip is still writing when I return even though the timer on the oven is buzzing. Something is burning. "The biscuits, Phillip. The timer. Honestly." Hot pad on hands, I rescue the biscuits from a black death.

He puts his pen down. "Sorry. I get lost in my thoughts when I journal. Zoozle too."

Here we go again. "She journals?"

"She's been sharing some of it with me by phone now and then. I think Dr. Stockton is using this dialectical journal to help her make sense of her choices." He flips a few pages back in his journal. "I've mentioned her a few times in mine. And you." He sort of blushes.

"That's nice to know, about me, I mean. Suzann, well, I'm glad she's confiding in someone. The two of us have a hard time saying what we need to without exploding."

"Yes, you do. Maybe you should journal too, Jolene?"

"I say let's eat and leave the shrink talk for later today."

Phillip helps himself from the dishes in the kitchen, which I appreciate. He doles out a serving for me, too much food. I wish I could eat like a man, but I can't.

Jacques' nails drum against the flooring, and he's at our side drooling. "One bite," says Phillip, tossing a piece of bacon into the air. Jacques nabs it, reaching up with his chunky neck, not moving a paw. Phillip pronounces the meal delicious, tells me to stay put. He cleans up the kitchen, whistling a tune I don't recognize. He folds the dish towel over his arm and brings the coffee pot to the table, "More, Madame?"

We focus on the paper, the morning awkwardness seemingly past. He chuckles at an editorial cartoon about the state budget, which he shares with me. I don't agree with the politics and offer a token, "Ha!"

Phillip feeds Jacques in his own dish from a bag of kibble he has brought with him, putting his journal carefully back into his briefcase. "Shower time for me. Join me?"

I decline. "I showered this morning once. Maybe tonight after our spa." He turns abruptly. The bathroom door locks with a click. I look at his briefcase, as if his journal is calling my name. Dare I?

The shower is still running as I close the journal. I've read maybe ten entries. Phillip seems as smitten with me as I am with him, but he has all kinds of remarks about my daughter — her growth, her secrets, her need of me. Well, why doesn't he just come out and share this with me?

Or maybe he's been trying and I've been avoiding.

The pipes rattle as the shower turns off. I close the journal, return it to the briefcase, and press play on the answering machine.

There's a message from Suzann, asking for money to tide her over until pay day. We've had this talk before. Does Phillip know about this phone call? Is that why he's been secretive? Is he going to give her the money that he knows I won't? He should know enough about co-dependency not to fall for this.

Am I going to lose a chance for my own life because my daughter had a grip on this man before I even met him?

I rush to the bedroom, dress in workout clothes. When Phillip comes out of the shower, I'm tying my running shoes and tell him I'll be back in half an hour. I need exercise after the big breakfast. Disappointed, he wipes his eyes with the corner of the towel around his waist, revealing the beginnings of a hard-on. I'm not enticed. I kiss him and run. I see him watching me from the front window. I wave. He waves and turns away.

CHAPTER 23: ZOOZLE

Winona is shaking my shoulder. Poochie is barking. The air in the apartment prickles my sinuses.

"Honey, you were screaming in your sleep," Winona says. Her hair is up in a net, and that's enough to make me scream right there. Poochie scoots up, licks my face, and sits panting on my pillow.

Anxiety spreads heartburn from my stomach to my throat. Winona sits on the bed, and the bed springs whine. I lean into her soft body. "I was dreaming. I was in a narrow room with sliding screen doors. A man put his horrible scarred face into mine and tried to make me hold a snake. He ordered me to dance."

Winona says, "Hush now. You're okay. You're okay."

I'm not okay, and I need to tell the rest while I remember it. "Mel sat on a couch, eating chocolates. I wanted some. She wouldn't share." I think I understand the connection with that part, but I don't want to offer my insights to Winona. So I finish what I remember, "Grandpa Joe was there. He wanted to help me. We went to a big indoor room to play volleyball. Grandpa Joe could only play from his hospital bed, but he did play, and he made us laugh. As I was touching his cheek, the skin became colder and colder. That's when I screamed."

Winona lifts her hands in praise, "'In thy father's house, there are many mansions. If it were not so, I would have told you so. I go to prepare one for you.'" She opens her eyes. "Praise the Lord! I was wrong about Joe. He found his way to Jesus at the end."

"Sure, Aunt Winona. I'll bet that's why I dreamed all that stuff, especially about the volleyball game." I sniff the air again. "What's that smell?"

"I don't smell anything." She wanders back to bed.

The clock says 4:30 a.m. I get off the sofa bed and step into the kitchen to brew a pot of coffee to clear my brain. As it perks, the coffee's heavy scent ignites me into action. I pour a cup and walk out front to make sure the gate is closed. I latch the gate before Poochie zooms out the front door.

He trots around, roots near the lemon tree, pees, and returns with a rag doll in his mouth. He lays the doll at my feet. I am absorbed in coffee haze, and I lazily toss the doll into the air,catching it one-handed.. Poochie barks, saying, "Let's play." I set the cup next to me, and a heavy, petroleum scent clings to my fingers.

The doll is a Raggedy Ann. It has been soaked in something. I walk further from the doorstep, still holding the doll, and Poochie follows.

Under the lemon tree, a pile of twigs smolders. Someone has tried to start a fire. I leave everything as is and hurry back inside, my nerves jangled.

Is this random? This street alone has enough teen vandals to stock a neighborhood in the entire white ghetto my mother lives in. Or is it more shit from Mel? Now what do I do?

I examine the doll. Under her dress her heart has been crossed out with black marking pen. I turn the doll over. A marijuana leaf is penned on her flat butt.

Damn, stupid Mel. I don't have time to fool around with cops and firemen and investigations and phone calls. I can't be late for work. I leave a note for Winona, "*A little vandalism out front. Everything okay. Home afternoon. Z.*"

I rush off to work, having thrown on sweats. My car is especially balky, but it gets me to Puente Rojo. I trot straight to the studio. Today the girls are presenting their routines and voting on their choice for the upcoming Chancellor's Dinner. All I need is my whistle, which I keep in my gym bag.

Veronica is already there, warming up at the barre. She looks intent and ignores me. The rest of the team straggles in, but Lacey is not among them. She runs in before roll call as the girls take their places on the mat.

Lacey stands next to me, and I look at her with my eyebrows raised.

She pulls a paper out of her shorts and hands it to me. "This was on your office door last night, Ms. Zimmerman. I stopped by even though it was a holiday to ask a question about my make-up quiz. The door was locked, and this was on there, and I thought you should see it. I haven't shown Ms. Garant, but the team should see her as soon as possible."

The paper is a photo of Mel's bare flat ass, with her distinctive tattoo. There is an arm flopped across her butt, my arm, with my distinctive scar. A web address is listed at the bottom, which mentions Big Daddy and girls.

"I made copies of this, Ms. Zimmerman," Lacey tells me. She hands copies out to the team. "We don't know much about you, and your personal life is not our business, but I went to the web site listed, and there's a lot more shots of you, and it names the Puente Rojo Dance Team. I'm sure none of us want to be associated with a porn queen."

The team is screaming and laughing and their phones are out. Only Sandy looks sad. She shows me the web site on her phone, shuts it off, and cries in the corner.

What I'd give to never have met Lacey Luster. What I'd give never to have met Mel or Big Daddy.

What I find it in me to do is walk out and sit down outside Ms. Garant's office. If anybody is going to report this, it's going to be me. If I'm in the trouble I think I am, it's time to get things straight with my mom. I've done the rehab, done the suicide attempt, done the worst, and I'm ready to choose something new, something best for me.

I pull out my cell, scroll through the names. I choose my mom's home phone. She answers on the third ring.

"Mom, I need your help. I need you now."

"It's a school day, Suzann."

"I need you now."

"Are you in a hospital again? What could possibly be so important?"

"No, Mom. I need YOU. Things are out of control here. Could you take today off and meet me at Winona's, please?"

"Hold on."

I can hear her talking to someone in the same room.

"Phillip here. What's going on, Zoozle?"

"I can't tell you over the phone. Could you please come with my mom to Winona's?"

"We'll be there. Give us ninety minutes."

"That should be enough."

The team is standing at the far end of the hall. They are huddled around Lacey Luster. Sandy is crying. Veronica is laughing. I am numb.

Lights flood Ms. Garant's office. She has come in through her back door. I knock, and she calls out, "Enter" in her normal peremptory tone.

"Why, Ms. Zimmerman. I was going to stop by practice this morning. The Chancellor's Dinner is less than a week away. I need to time the number to be performed along with my introduction of you. You don't mind, do you? Are the girls ready?" She has opened her purse and is patting at her hair.

"I have some bad news, Ms. Garant."

"Did someone die? Are you having family problems? You don't look good, dear." She purses her lips to the extent possible for her.

"It's worse than that." I hand her the photo sheet. "I was mixed up with some strange people in Washington. They've resurfaced. They're harassing me, and now they've put it on the web and they mention Puente Rojo."

She studies the print, looks at me, and stares out the window. She picks up a copy of my *Zimmerman's Zeitgeist* and waves it at me. "Your own policy, Ms. Zimmerman. You had two strikes if I include the lateness of your car wash deposit even though we've worked that out. Still, Lacey was asking about the purchase order for the Chancellor's dinner presentation, which has not yet reached me. Did you think you could drop by the mall to pick up fifteen scarves in the color Lacey showed me? Now, these posters constitute a third strike. The college has a morals clause which you signed off on as you know. What is your choice? Resign now, let me place you on leave, go through with an investigation?"

"What choice do I really have? Resignation. Now."

"I had high hopes for you, Suzann. We can't let this taint our team, however. People have enough notions about cheerleaders and dance teams, as if they personally make 'Girls Gone Wild' tapes and sell them." She hands me a form.

I sign it and hand it back. "There's nothing in my office that I want."

It takes everything I've got to talk to my team. "I have resigned. Ms. Garant will handle things for the time being. I'm sorry things turned out this way. We were going places." The girls' circle tightens. Sandy comes forward to shake my hand.

"Goodbye, Ms. Zimmerman. I liked you."

I leave to meet my mom and Phillip at Winona's. It's time to confront the past because I am ready to live a future. A job is a job. I can replace it. I can't replace me. I can't replace these true friends, who trust me and love me. My mom owes me more, and if I open up to her that might be the key to her locked up heart. She's different now with Phillip in her life. I am confident in my decision, ready for full disclosure.

Plus, there's Lordman. He gives me hope.

JOLENE: CHAPTER 24

This is not how a Tuesday after a long weekend should go.

I'm about to kiss Phillip goodbye for the day, when the phone rings. Unless it's Bill telling me my classroom has been vandalized, it has to be Suzann.

It's Suzann. She has a crisis. Again. I protest, trying to insist that she can weather this storm, she's an adult, but Phillip wants the phone.

He turns to sit on the edge of the bed, pulling sheets over him, listening intently. I hear the cadence of Suzann on high gear through the phone, which sets off memories of dozens of other calls like this, the worst having come in July from the hospital on Whidbey Island. Or was it the time before that when she was fired in June? Or the time before when she nodded off at the wheel and nearly killed us both?

Jacques whines and paws lightly at the bedroom door. I go outside with him to the deck to settle my nerves.

I try my breathing exercises, standing in a crane position on a towel from the spa. The deck is wet with dew. The sun is rising, and I try "Apollo" as my calming chant, envisioning the god in his carriage as he streaks the sky with the colors of Eos. It's the Romans who called her Aurora. I am calmer, but nervous about Suzann's call when I come back in.

Phillip has slipped his pants on. "We need to get moving, Jolene. Suzann's calling for help."

"I talked to her first, remember? I have to be at school today. A certain percentage of teachers call in sick after a long holiday, mostly the young ones. I don't want to be associated with that kind of sloth. Besides, there won't even be any subs." I lift my chin. I do not want to go to her.

"You really should be with your daughter today." He snags my sweater's belt and pulls me back to him, not for a kiss, but a lecture.

"Phillip, I think I know my own daughter."

"I'm not sure you do. Trust me. Try to call your sub and let's get out there to Suzann. It must be pretty important."

"What is important to Suzann is most often a trifle to normal people. She's a grown up. I want her to act like it." Should I go over the meth addict's penchant for manipulation with Phillip? Why did she have to call today, this morning? Things were going well enough for me for once.

He reaches out to put both hands on my shoulders. "I'm not sure she can, grow up, I mean. There's something holding her back. Let's go this time. If I'm wrong, I won't interfere again."

Here I am in that too-familiar spot, torn between duty and daughter. If Phillip weren't here, I wouldn't question myself, but he is here, and I do trust him. What does he see in Suzann that I don't see?

I grab the phone and call Jim Dowd. He is awake, happy to work again today. He loves my classes because they behave. I record the absence with the district's sub page on the computer, and email a lesson for my classes. I claim personal necessity, sweating the fine print that such absences are supposed to be cleared by Principal Bill, especially if connected to a holiday. My hands leave wet marks on the key board.

"Better take my car, unless you want to leave Jacques at my house?" I say, wrestling with my coat. Phillip holds the coat and helps me to slip it on smoothly.

We pile into my car. Phillip rubs his forehead with his long, elegant fingers. I wish he were massaging my neck. Stress has me all wound up already..

As I turn the ignition, I try to have one last word, "Before we get there, I want you to know that I don't think this helps Suzann."

Phillip nods. "I know. I heard you before." He is quiet a moment. "There was something in her voice that sounded desperate."

"She's always desperate. She's a master of deceit, Phillip. I want to believe she's in recovery, but she's given me no good reason to trust her, other than that she's working again."

"Suzann sparkles, haven't you noticed? She has new friends and a good outlook. If she says she's in trouble, shouldn't you be there?"

"I've had too many years of being there." The anger chokes me., A tension headache builds in my temples. I love this man or I might anyway, I love my daughter within reasonable limits, but I don't love being pushed around. "You didn't have children. Dogs are easier."

Phillip laughs tightly.

"Children or dogs, it's a lifetime commitment, not an at-your-leisure thing."

"Leisure? Come on, Phillip. You've seen my daughter pull my strings and punch my buttons. When she's around, my adrenalin is so high in stress-mode, I practically fly, like Eurydice following Orpheus except we're going straight back to the infernal regions, not up to the light."

"Helen and Hermione?" he challenges.

"Got me. . .who's Hermione?"

"Helen's daughter, deserted by Helen for Paris when the daughter was three."

"Are you saying I deserted my daughter? That I put myself first and foremost and that I'm like the archetype of a legendary slut?" I'm about to pull over to the side of the road, open the door, and strand one tall man and one large black dog. I'm so mad my vision blurs with tears.

"No, Jolene. Ease up. I'm saying I see a very beautiful woman who is being torn by twin desires. I'm saying there's a lot of rebuilding to do. Didn't Helen return to her home when the Trojan War was over?"

"I see. And you think that the war can be over?"

"Yes, maybe you can end the war, call a truce this morning. That's what I heard in Suzann's voice."

"I'll drink to that," I say, pulling into a drive through Starbuck's. "What's your pleasure?"

Phillip grins a mischievous grin, saying, "I'll take a tall macchiato with whipped cream and a caramel drizzle, for the time being."

Ordering the same for both of us, I add blueberry oat bars. I hand the cups and bag to Phillip. I should have gotten something for Suzann and Winona, but I'm too late with the thought.

I pull the car into a spot in front of Winona's. It's so early, we don't want to knock. Phillip and I sit on the porch in front of her apartment, sipping our coffee, scattering oat crumbs on our laps. If we weren't on a rescue mission, I would feel quite contented in the morning air with this lovely man, these aromatic scents of coffee, citrus trees, and sweets.

Within ten minutes, the door lock rattles, and Winona yips as she opens the door for Poochie.

"Jolene, goodness, you gave me heart palpitations." Winona's frowzy hair sticks out of a hair net.

"We didn't want to wake you. We're meeting Suzann here. Winona, remember Phillip? And Jacques?"

Winona shields her eyes against the morning sun as she watches Poochie scramble across the yard, pawing at Jacques. "Oh my word." She tugs at her hair net. "Hello, Paul."

"Phillip," I remind her as we walk inside.

We make small talk about the dogs and the weather. We look up at the sound of the VW's distinctive engine.

Suzann parks at the curb and slams the car door.

CHAPTER 25: ZOOZLE

It's only on the drive home that I process what has happened. It's not just about a job. People believe in me. I have told Mel she's out of my life, and though I worry about what will become of her, I am proud of me.

And there's something else: Phillip was at my mom's at six in the morning on a school day. It makes me smile for her for a millisecond even though her own heart is still hammered into something small and tight against me. Today I can start to loosen her hold on the fake world she has woven for me to live in.

As I turn the corner, the apartment house seems smaller than it used to seem. I notice how the bushes haven't been trimmed and the fencing is broken in places. I hear Jacques barking inside. I wish I were a dog.

I straighten my shoulders and walk in.

"We're here," Mom says from the kitchen table for no reason.

"Thank you. I'm glad." I fend off Jacques' wet muzzle.

Mom looks at Phillip, who nods and offers her his arm, and we walk into the living room together.

"Mom, this is hard to say, so just let me talk and then I'll answer your questions, okay?"

"Maybe we should wait and call Penny or your new counselor, Dr. Stockton, to come down." She's always looking for a way out of talking with me.

"Jolene, I am here with you. We don't need Penny or Dr. Stockton. We need Zoozle to trust our love for her. Unconditionally." Phillip looks at me, and his clear eyes hold nothing but confidence.

I edge into the living room and slip into a chair opposite Mom and Phillip, who sit on the edge of the couch. I kick off my flip-flops and pull my legs up under me. Winona has disappeared into the bedroom without our asking for privacy. Miracles do happen. I can hear her praying for one now.

I pick at the frayed hem of my jeans. I know my tired eyes tell the same old story. But I have a new chapter that Mom never anticipated and surely doesn't want to hear.

Phillip begins, "Your daughter invited us to be with her. None of us can go forward until we take this step." He waves his arms as if he were conducting a symphony. We sit close in proximity but caverns of anxiety, secrets, and fear yawn between us.

I nod to Phillip, grateful and anxious to finally be about to release this pain. I go to my cupboard and retrieve my journal.

"Go ahead now, Zoozle," Phillip urges.

"Mom, you made fun of me when I pulled my hair. You acted like it was a big joke with Grandma Janie. You didn't think even once that maybe I needed help." I stop, breathe, go on. "You never once would rub my feet after practice. 'Too busy' you said, 'go soak in the tub.' Don't you see how much I needed your attention?"

Mom glances at Phillip. This-was-the-emergency skepticism is written all over her face. She picks up her jacket and eyes the door.

"See how she is?" my defensive sarcasm returns.

Phillip nods "Yes, Zoozle, these are incidents in your life that you never forgot. These things meant so much to you except that your mother didn't understand how much. Go on now."

"You didn't stop Uncle Bill from selling the trailer, and it's like you were hoping I'd go far away again, get out of your way." I break down into wrenching sobs.

Phillip intervenes. "Jolene, do you see that Zoozle has felt cut off from you for a long time? We talked after Joe's funeral. Since then she has shared her journal of memories with me. We wanted to bring you in now because it's you that she needs."

I listen and look at Phillip with something between adoration and apprehension. I sit again on the chair across from them, delaying, ripping another long thread from my jeans hem. "Mom. I went to Penny to find out what's wrong with me. Why can't I have a normal relationship with men? Why did I treat Javier that way? He loved me." I hesitate and reach out for Phillip. He makes a rolling motion with his other hand.

"I didn't feel safe with Javier, or with any man, except Uncle Mitch and Grandpa Joe." I stop. I stretch my neck to both sides.

"I was sexually abused. By Francis." I stop and cover my eyes.

My mom grasps the edges of the couch, and her coat falls to the floor. We both seem to be remembering Francis's long hands, his angular body, his face a blur of pock marks from old acne. "No, you couldn't have been," she answers. "Moms have the intuition to know things like that."

Phillip is holding Mom with his arm around her shoulders. He seems to be keeping her from running.

"You didn't know. You didn't see me or look at me, except when I was practicing or performing on stage. I was molested, Mom. From when I was ten to when I was thirteen. You liked Francis. You delivered me to him. You thought he was the best coach for me. You even increased my private lessons with him. The only reason it stopped was that you thought I was dancing badly like I was going through a phase and needed new motivation, a new teacher. As if it was all teen rebelliousness. I couldn't tell you the reason. You made me feel that everything was always my fault, that I was the bad one."

"Oh, Jesus. Where was I?"

"Outside the studio or off on errands. Remember how you never watched lessons? So you wouldn't be the 'stage mom' type? And Francis told you I concentrated better when you weren't nearby. He praised you for not hovering around, not interfering like other moms." Mom lifts her eyebrows a notch. Her shoulders stay hunched and forlorn.

"Did he. . . rape you?" She can hardly say the word and stays fused to the couch. She doesn't reach out for me.

"No, but he put his hands all over me. It was disgusting. I felt like his filthy handprints must show on me after every lesson. Remember how I always yelled, 'Don't stare at me?'' even when it was just you or Grandmother? I knew everyone was staring at me. For years only a performance or leading a class has offered a safe place. Up there on stage, no one can touch me wrong."

"I don't believe this," Mom appeals to Phillip. "If this happened, I would have known."

Phillip's lips turn down in simple sadness. "Jolene, you can not know what your child does not tell you. Remember being that age?

Think of her age then. Zoozle's exploration would be exciting as well as disturbing to her. You were distanced with adult concerns, job, and finances. Zoozle was seeking solace from your busy life and her father's death in her own way."

"This makes me sick if it's true. I need time to think. I'll talk to Francis, I'll talk to the other moms, I'll call the police. Are you sure, Suzann, that this happened? That it's not one of your nightmares?" She's reaching for her purse on the floor.

"Remember when I came home from school that day and Lynnie's mom called to tell you we had seen a naked man in the car in the shortcut home? That he was jerking off?"

"I remember." My mom's voice sounds unfamiliar, too nasal. She had been mad because I was not supposed to be in the alley in the first place. And the adults never reported the incident to the police. They pretended it was best that we girls just forget about it.

"That's what Francis did. Only he said I had to touch him." A shiver convulses me. "I wish I could have told you. It would have stopped so much sooner. I kept putting my face up close to yours when you were grading papers, and you'd say, 'You're in my space.'" I reach for a tissue, but Phillip hands me his handkerchief, with its fresh shaving cream scent. "I didn't know how to get your attention. And I was afraid of your mocking me, like with my hair pulling."

The room falls quiet. Winona is still murmuring in her room. Jacques and Poochie are back outside barking in the yard.

"Mom, I can live better. Penny said so a long time ago. But I have more to tell you." I look at my mom again, and I dare her to show me that she cares.

Phillip says, "Think of lighting a little candle in the darkness." His loving presence re-energizes the room. My mom pulls me from the floor where I have collapsed into a fetal ball. Mom hugs me tightly, and Phillip's long arms surround us both.

I slip away. "I lost another job. Look."

I give them the paper with the photos.

"What is this, Suzann? What have you done?" My mom starts to crumple the paper, but Phillip takes it. His hands are shaking.

"Somebody put these up at Puente Rojo, probably Mel. A team member, Lacey, found one of these online, made copies, and distributed them. Ms. Garant asked me to step down. See the web site listed? That was the last straw because it names Puente Rojo and the dance team." I put my head into my knees.

"This is unacceptable." My mother grabs her purse as if to leave. Phillip gets up, stands between her and the door.

"Yes, Jolene. This is unacceptable. That your daughter has been victimized and that she acted out and that she almost killed herself and just when she's got herself moving again, she is sabotaged by someone she trusted. That's what is unacceptable. You and I are not going to join the list of deserters."

I look at Phillip with awe, feeling his love, and seeking Mom's. My mom still won't talk.

"I have no job. I have no money. But I have my life, Mom. I'm changing everything. I'm going to need your help, yours and Phillip's. Chloris and Eric and Gaylord, well, a lot of people have helped me see that I'm not alone."

"So what's next, Suzann? Are you going to move home again?" she asks in a voice I don't like. Phillip walks into the kitchen to refill his coffee cup.

"We need to talk to Uncle Mitch. We need him to get Mel and Mike out of his house. They're dangerous. They're the ones who stole Grandpa's stuff. I found it in a garage over by Sal's. Look, here's Grandpa's quilt." I go to pull it from my pile of bedding in the corner to give it to Mom, but she springs past me and runs outside. Before I react and run to the still-open apartment door, my stupid mom in her stupid car is escaping, practically taking the corner on two wheels. I don't know where she's going. God, she's a coward. I never have thought of her as a coward before.

Phillip follows me to the door. He's shaking his head and clenching his fists. But then his long arms encircle me, and he's saying, "It's okay, it's okay." I want to believe Phillip. At least I know that Phillip believes me.

CHAPTER 26: JOLENE

I am driving north on Interstate 5, with no reason except escape. I am hoping if they decide to follow, Phillip will assume I'm going home or to school. Suzann will go to the beach.

The I Street exit is coming up, and I take it, thinking perhaps I can double back and spend time walking at the mall. Instead, I continue on to Glen of Peace and wind my way along the narrow roads. I park and cross step down the steep hill to Daddy's grave alongside Mother's.

The grass is slick, and my shoes slip, making me more nervous and wary. Rain clouds scurry in from the sea towards the mountains. When I turn northwest, Point Loma shines in a pool of sunshine the distance.

Graves are dotted with bright flowers; Mother's has some new roses because Art comes by so often. Daddy's smells of earth. Debris has been raked away. Time has stopped with him gone. My entire world has changed, and I'm stuck again, because I can't name the start of all this changing. Seattle trip? Hospice? Meeting Phillip? I have always judged time by Suzann, Suzann, Suzann.

Wind scatters leaves across the path. I take off my jacket and let myself feel the cold. Compared to the numbness of my heart, the cold is good. Placing my jacket under me, I sit at the foot of both graves, reaching to crumble a clod of dirt into fine, sticky granules.

"Daddy, did you know?" I ask. "You couldn't have because you would have killed that man. What is wrong with me? I'm so ashamed.

Suzann was in pain, using drugs, cutting herself, jumping off a ferry, rather than trusting me."

In front of Phillip and Suzann, I kept my mask on. I don't really doubt her story. Enough other mothers had warned me about Francis, but I simply refused to see, to ask, to bother, because Suzann was performing well, and all that status and recognition made me feel like the great mom of moms. Until she quit performing well, and then I chose a new coach. I am not great. I am nothing.

A cloud passes over the sun, and I can't take the cold much longer. My knees ache. My heart aches.

"I have to go now, Daddy. I love you too, Mama. We just could never talk, could we? And now I talk and listen to everyone except Suzann. What happened to us?"

I look across the park at a family that has arrived graveside. They are holding hands, all of them. Our family never held hands, our family never hugged, our family never said "I love you" until it was too late to matter. Is that true? Can it be too late?

Can it be too late or is there always time for forgiveness? I kneel again by Daddy's grave and say what is in my heart, "Daddy, please help me heal my daughter. Please show me the way to live in the light of love. Please let me forgive those who have hurt us and changed us."

As I walk to the car, I picture the little girl I once was, the little girl charged with acting like an adult, acting as little mama to Art, the little girl ignored and placed behind Bill's shining star.

I sit in the car, trying to remember. Am I competing with Suzann the way I competed with Bill? Should I call Penny?

What did Phillip say? "She was comforting herself." How often did I comfort myself? How often did I act out, cutting my hair with pinking shears, acting promiscuously as a teen, but not sexually functioning with Mark as freely as a wife should and relieved to be free of the sexual obligations of marriage when he died? Not finding a man to love after Mark died, no one until Phillip, and that truly a wild, hunger to replace the empty spot of my love for Daddy. Daddy never hurt me; Daddy never neglected me. My mother taught me by example to keep children at a distance and in their place, the old seen but not heard technique.

Does Bill know more than he tells me? Can I help Suzann move on if I wallow in guilt and shame?

How could Phillip love me, train wreck that I am?

CHAPTER 27: ZOOZLE

Phillip releases me from the huddled embrace as he sees that my mother is not coming back, not this minute anyway. Poochie and Jacques leap out the door and sniff my purse.

I lift my purse and toss Phillip the smelly Raggedy Ann doll. Jacques and Poochie bark with joy, for they have no worries and expect a game.

"Look at it, under the clothes," I say. "You'll see why we have to go to Mitch's."

Phillip examines the doll. He discovers the crossed out heart and the tattoo on her back where her butt should be.

"That's Mel's mark, isn't it?" Phillip asks.

I firm my mouth. "Yes."

"Let's get moving then," Phillip suggests.

"Wait for me," Winona calls out from the bedroom where she has stopped praying and started easedropping, when?

"Winona, I would appreciate more of your prayers," Phillip calls to her. I follow him as he looks into the bedroom. "Suzann's car is too small, and Mitch is going to be embarrassed enough. Could you stay behind this once?" He gives her a little bow, and she practically kisses his feet.

"Yes, yes, yes. I know just the verses in Job. Come, Poochie, let us read the Lord's word about adventures. No that's not right. What is the word, Poochie?" She waits. Poochie cocks his head. "Adversity, yes, that right, adversity.' Winona closes her door and opens it one small crack.

Phillip calls Jacques, I get out my car keys, stuffing the doll into my gym bag, Grandpa's quilt across my arm. Phillip holds my door open and comes around to get in front with me.

I park in front of Mitch's house, and my hands begin to tremble. Phillip puts his large hand over mine.

"All will be well," he says. He has his phone in his other hand and keeps trying Mom's number.

We knock on the door though of course we don't have to do that. Jacques barks a hearty bark. Kaye answers the door in her housecoat, rubs her eyes, but doesn't open the screen.

"Mitch," Kaye calls out, "Suzann is here with Phillip." To us, she asks, "Where's Jolene?"

I shrug. Phillip silently checks his phone for a message.

Mitch arrives at the door with an ambiguous smile. "I'm glad to see you, I think."

"We need to talk," I tell him. "It's about Mel and Mike and Norm."

"When is it not about them?" He waves us in. "Every day I curse the war that took away Linc and injured the twins. Well, never mind the saga. What now?"

I pull the doll out. "This was left in Winona's yard, Mitch. There was a fire. And I've had other problems. It all goes back to Grandpa's trailer. Look," I push the quilt forward, "here's Grandpa Joe's quilt that I found in a garage down the street with his other stuff. People say that

Mike and Norm were involved with Mel in what happened at the trailer. It's gone beyond mischief and teasing to threats."

I stop. I don't want to talk about my lost job and the pictures, but I have to get this across to Mitch. "It's gotten really bad. They even followed me to work."

Mitch and Kaye look baffled. Or it might be hurt.

"Let me bring them out. We'll get to the bottom of this." Mitch walks with that slow step of his towards the back wing of the house. We follow.

He knocks on a bedroom door for propriety's sake. No one answers.

Mitch opens the door. The room smells heavy with dope and beer and sweaty clothes. Phillip looks over my shoulder as Jacques gallops in and jumps on the bed. His feet have mud on the toenails. He woofs ecstatically, pawing at the bed clothes.

From under the pillow, a dark head emerges, "What the fuck?" Mel mumbles as she slides a sheet over her head to escape Jacques.

Mike yanks the pillow from her and wraps a quilt around himself. "Do you mind?" he says to the room at large.

"You know what? I do mind," Mitch answers in a strong voice. "You two put some clothes on. Norm, get out to the living room." Phillip hesitates at the bedroom, then orders Jacques to desist and follow us.

"Let's make some coffee," Phillip suggests.

Kaye begins preparations for breakfast. "We might as well eat." She gets out the Bisquik and a big bowl while I search for a coffee. Phillip and Mitch sit at the table. A shower turns on in the back bathroom. Norm emerges with bedhead, hairy chest shirtless, a pair of shorts drooping at his hip line.

Mitch chooses a shirt from one of five piles of unfolded laundry, and flings it to Norm. Mel and Mike come out dressed, clean if not bright eyed.

"Nothing like a family reunion to make your day," Mel laughs. Mike says nothing. He pours himself coffee and ignores the rest of us.

"This is serious, Melody." I sound sort of like my mom. I shake my head, not wanting to believe my own ears. In the living room, I retrieve the doll, and drop it in Mel's lap, "Nice work, idiot."

Mel looks at the doll. "God, Zoozle-Schamoozle-Woozle. It was a joke. It was all a joke. Don't you laugh anymore? Your mama like to laugh, you know?"

"Shut up! I have a mother. Only she's not here right now." I realize how stupid this sounds and turn around to make sure Phillip is near me. "This isn't funny. Guess what? As if you didn't know it would happen, those posters at school cost me another job."

"What posters? We didn't do any poster stuff. Besides, I learned once that all press is good press. Didn't you learn that in one of your fucking Ph.D. classes. Or does the PH stand for PHONY?" Mel scratches scabs between her toes. "Listen, Zooz. Big Daddy said he's got work for us. We can go back to Washington. Why do you want to work for the establishment anyway, turn all Betty Crocker on me?"

I sit on the floor in front of Mel, glance around, bouncing my gaze between Mitch and Phillip, the door, the kitchen, Mel's toes.

Aunt Kaye flips pancakes. Phillip and Mitch are silent, holding back. Mitch seems to have receded into his shell. Mel's foot is wiggling up and down, heel to toe. "I told you, Mel. I told you when Grandpa Joe died. I told you on the ferry. I have a life to live, and it's not with you, and it's not with drugs. I should have you arrested." Phillip takes my arm.

Mitch stands up. "Now, that's the way to the light, but let's not go into legal issues. What good would it do to put the kids in jail and tear the family apart?"

Phillip lets go of me. He stands at the window, lifting the bamboo blinds. "Zoozle said Joe's things are down the street. Mike and Norm, is that true?"

Norm itches his scalp, but Mike answers, "Yeah, so what? It's worth $500 tops."

Phillip pulls five one hundred dollar bills out of his billfold. "Here's your money. Now you're going to help me put the stuff on a truck and help me unload it into a storage shed. Do you know that things like pictures and Grandpa's clothing are worth more than either of you can earn in a lifetime?"

"Phillip, that's overly generous. I'll pay you back. We'll only agree to this loan on one condition," Mitch looks at the twins. "You boys are going to use that money for a deposit on an apartment. You are adults, and you are through leeching your lives off us. No more laundry duty for your mom; no more freebies for you and your pack of friends coming out of this kitchen unless Kaye invites you.

Kaye flips the last of the pancakes. "Can we eat these at least?"

Mel rapidly texts someone. "Guess I'll be hitting the road, guys. Cool while it lasted." She turns the door knob.

Mike pulls her t-shirt sleeve back, but then he leads her out the door. They argue in the front yard. Mel twists away and walks barefoot, west, toward the beach.

"I'll be right back," I yell as I backpedal towards the gate. Mel and I need some last words together.

"No, don't go," Kaye begins, but Phillip puts his finger to his lips.

"Trust her," he says. Those welcome words are the last I hear before I take off running. Why doesn't my mother say good stuff like that?

CHAPTER 28: JOLENE

For now, I know what I need to do, to face, to be. I start the car and hurry back to Mitch's. Suzann's car is still there, and though I am afraid, I am also determined.

Before I open the gate, Phillip is in front of me with an umbrella. Rain began on the drive back. I want to rush into his arms, but his stance is aloof. He doesn't reach for me.

"It's good you're back," he says neutrally.

"I know. I'm sorry I panicked."

"It's not always about you, Jolene."

"I understand. I need to talk to Suzann."

"She's not here."

"Where did she go?" I can picture her driving into Baja or walking off the pier. Lately, I have a very strong panic reflex.

"She'll be back. Have some faith in her."

"I want to."

"Let's go in. We can sort out things between us later." Phillip's posture eases. He puts his hand out to me.

"What do you mean?" I don't really want to know, but then again, I have to know. I've made a mess of something that could have been good.

"That we've moved a little faster than we should have, and that I want some time to think — you need some personal time too. Let's deal with your family here first, okay?"

Phillip turns and leads me into the living room. We wait without talking. We are not the same couple that went to bed so contented last night.

CHAPTER 29: ZOOZLE

Mel walked out barefoot into the rain, and I grab a pair of purple Crocs from Aunt Kaye's garden box. I race down the street, practically bowling over Winona chugging up the sidewalk, Bible in one hand, umbrella and Poochie's leash in the other. She is slowed by her girth and Poochie's interest in every tree, shrub, and lawn. Our collision results in an oomph from both of us, and then I'm long gone. She flaps like a wet, worried bird, "Come back here!"

"Soon," I yell.

I catch up to Mel. I fall into step next to her. She doesn't look at me and pulls away when I make an effort to slow her down.

"Mel, here, take these." I offer the Crocs.

She stops and slips them on, doesn't look at me and walks faster.

The wet streets are quiet. Our feet are in synch. She shoves me from the side. "Go away, give up, I hate you," she says, but her voice is low, and in a glance, I see tear tracks.

"It's not hate, Mel." I want to stop and talk, but she's still moving forward. She doesn't look as she crosses Third Street. No cars are coming.

"Fine. You made your choice." Her voice is shaky.

"I did. I'm glad." Grandpa Joe's nearness as I look west towards the pier tugs me towards a good place.

"So why are you here, huh?" Mel snaps me out of my daydream.

"You needed shoes." I take a chance and add, "And hope."

"Who needs your fuckin' fake hope, la princessa, Suzann? You are one big fake."

"No, this is the real me," I protest, and I nudge her, "Who needs hope? You."

"Thanks for thinking for me. 'If I only had a brain,'" she fake-sings, hanging her arms like a scarecrow.

"Hey, it's been a long time since you used your brain."

"Just shut up and leave me alone." She takes off running. She doesn't have half of my speed, and I catch her without even breathing hard. Within a block she is leaning over, holding her knees. You'd think she had run a 5K.

"Mel, you're going to do what you want to do. You always have. When you get as low as you can stand, I'll help you through rehab. No more attending meetings and breaking the promises with a bottle or a joint or a pill in your pocket. Call me. Just say the word."

"Which word? Yeah, sure, Zooz. Friend? Fun? Oh, how about help? I've heard that before."

"You haven't heard it when I was clean." I inhale the salty air, and the raindrops make me feel renewed.

"The fucking difference between using and not using for Queen of Sheba You is a lot different than it is for regular me. You've got a family. I've got Big Daddy." Mel sits on the curb, splashing her toes in the street's run-off.

I sit next to her, not worried about the rain on my shoulders or the cold water on my pants. I stretch my arm around her shoulders. She is very thin. "Think. Remember our last AA meeting? The ferry? That was about feeling there's no way out."

"Well, I'm not there yet," Mel mumbles, "And I don't plan to be there any time soon, thanks anyway."

"When you get there, call me. When you're ready for real rehab." I pull her to face me and lean in to hug her.

"Your mom hates me." She says this into my shoulder. The rain makes her skin smell fresh and soapy, like the Mel I met a long time ago. Her drugged out, ratty scent is gone, and maybe today she will let things start over in a good way for her.

I pat her back in a circle with Grandpa Joe's gesture that I remember from my childhood of skinned knees and aching feet. "My mom has issues. You didn't see her at Mitch's supporting me today, did you? She did what I do, run away. My family is not so perfect, is it?"

Mel pushes back and away, splashing her feet into the gutter's running water. We are both drenched. "You have new friends."

"They've struggled too. They know how to help. They won't shut you out." I say this with full confidence.

"Big Daddy will send me a plane ticket."

"Yes, I'm sure he will. If anything changes before or after you get on that plane, you call me."

We're at the beach. Mel can turn left and walk towards Border Field or she can go right, towards Kinko's and ask Big Daddy for her ticket. She stands still.

"I didn't do the posters. Blame me all you want for lots of other stuff. I didn't do the posters." She is miming her scarecrow again "Bye, Zooz. I'll call from the land of Oz, maybe. Oh, and check with your girls on the dance team about the posters."

"My dance team? Huh? Mel. Call me. Don't wait too long." Leaving her there is hard. Nothing works until the time is right. I know it, I've lived it, I accept it. I walk back to Kaye and Mitch's.

Ten minutes later, my mom's car is out front, and I'm standing in Kaye and Mitch's living room. Before Mom can respond to my "Well, look who's here," Winona begins babbling.

"Praise the Lord, kind Jesus, a message has come to us from the Heavens." She has her Bible on her lap. Phillip and my mom are seated at the table with Kaye and Mitch across from them. Each head is down, and everyone is zoomed in, squinting at a small paper, no bigger than a note card, flat in the center of the table.

"Suz, um, Zoozle, Winona found this in her Bible." Mom holds up the paper.

"We think it's a clue," says Phillip. "We can't read it. Winona was going to read Job, but thought of your grandma's favorite, about Jabez from Chronicles. And it seems as if it brought us something to show Uncle Bill."

"Really?"

"Tell us what you think it says." Phillip hands it to me.

If I am honest, as I assess the page, I would swear in a court of law it is from the notebook Grandpa Joe and I kept his plans in. The note has a scrawl that doesn't look like my grandpa's handwriting. The writing is tentative and light. All I can make out is the letter *T* and the number *four*. There's something after that, but what? Is it a numeral eight?

"I don't know. T48. Is it a code or a locker?"

Mitch takes the scrap. He turns it around and upside down. "This is from Joe, I just know it."

Winona stops praising God and wanders over. "Joe gave me this that last day. I put it into my Bible and didn't think of it again. He didn't say what it meant, or if he did, I can't remember what it was he said. I'll pray on that. Excuse me."

Mom is already on the phone. She has called school and gotten through to Bill.

"Yes, I know it's a school day. Yes, I know the principal's meeting starts at 11 a.m." She listens another minute. "Yes, I know I have to have personal leave approved by you in advance. So dock my pay! Jim Dowd has my classes, and I bet they survive one more day without me. What I am telling you is that we have something important down here at Mitch and Kaye's. For once, could we put family first?" She nods and hangs up the phone. "Bill will try to be here in a hour, so he says."

Phillip takes his turn reassessing the paper. "We can take it to a handwriting expert. Where's the phone book?"

Mitch unstacks a set of DVDs and library books, finds the phone book, and says, "Keep my marker in. I need to rent a truck for Norm and Mike and a storage locker too." Norm looks up from the couch where he has settled his wide man-boy body to play a video game.

"God, Dad, today?"

"We can start tomorrow at 5 in the morning if you prefer." Mitch sounds like a new man.

Mom and I clean up Kaye's kitchen. The skillets and the dishes are put away, the sink is scrubbed, and we help Kaye fold the laundry in the baskets in the other room. Winona has toweled off Poochie's paws and Jacques' too. Mom gets out a mop and begins work on the living room floor, Phillip picking up his big feet as Mom mops under them. Jacques jumps up on the couch and burrows next to Phillip.

"I'll turn the heat up," says Mitch.

"No, look, the sun is out," I say, opening the blind.

We gather at the window, a small group, known as a family.

Mom can't stand sitting around. "Let's play some cards until Bill arrives," she suggests. Winona's mouth opens, clamps closed as she reaches for her Bible. "Not poker or anything like that Winona. How about Crazy 8's?"

Kaye locates a deck of cards and even Mitch and Phillip sit cross legged on the braided rug. Mom smiles as if someone has told her a joke that she just got. She seems to be enjoying the game, a first that I know of, since everything in our lives has been a competition to this point.

We play, and take turns looking out the window, waiting for Uncle Bill. After an hour, Mom calls him and gets his voice mail. Dorrie says he left for the principals' meeting. Those can last for twelve hours. We won't be seeing Uncle Bill today, and we toss in our cards, make ready to leave.

I'm looking at the score pad where Mom has written columns, K, M, P, J, and S, forgetting Zoozle, which I don't let annoy me for once. I stare at the S. I stare at the cards I've been dealt. I have an 8, but now it doesn't matter. Then it hits me, and I drop my cards and run for the scrap of paper sitting on the table.

"Look, maybe it's an S, not an 8." Everybody jumps up to join me. "T4S. What are T4s, Mitch? Phillip? Are they airplanes? Or cars?

Maybe tax forms? Was Grandpa Joe trying to tell us about some hidden stocks, do you think?" I twist my hair and begin to pull. Mom reaches up and eases my hand into hers, away from my scalp.

What if it means "Trailer for Suzanne? Am I reading too much into this?" Mitch asks.

Phillip smiles. "I think we have something here."

Mom smiles. She hugs me, she hugs Phillip. "Come here, Jacques." He gets his hug too. But there's a false note that the finale won't be all smooth sailing. Which one of us is she going to leave behind, me or Phillip?

CHAPTER 30: JOLENE

I am driving to Bill's. Traffic is crawling, and I wouldn't do it every day as he does, but there's a time-to-prestige ratio he has all figured out.

He knows I am coming, no dinner invitation extended, and a one-hour window because he has another appointment, probably to lessen the possibility that I might overstay my welcome.

Bill's no-show at Mitch's is not a surprise, though I am anxious to see his reaction to our news. He has never put family first and never will. I shouldn't cast blame. Phillip helped me retrieve Bill's voice mail from my cell and then patiently gave me a lesson. Zoozle can't make fun of me anymore about my inadequate phone skills. I'm learning something new every day.

My feelings for Phillip hurt more now because I know he's right. There's too much going on around me for me to give him my whole heart I think for a moment of an e.e. cummings' sonnet, "Heart Exchange." How can I exchange this pieced-together heart for a whole one? I need to settle things within myself and within my relationship with Suzann. I see her not as a victim of her own stupid choices, but as a new and victorious Sisyphus. She has spent her adult life conquering the rolling ball and the mountain, starting over and over with little emotional support from me. It was easier to write a check than to listen.

This time there will be no backsliding because I'm there behind her. I have held her back with my view of the world as it pertains to me, me, me. If I continue to look at the world in a new way, if I am there for her, she will heal.

Phillip treated me well when I got to Mitch's, but it was as if he saw through me for the first time. Before this morning, it was one death and three new lives, I would never have expected such good to accompany such heartache, like a miraculous ending in Shakespeare's, *The Winter's Tale*, one I used to mock as desperate-deadline writing. Now I see that this is not going to be a fairy tale romance, for as my mother always told me, there's no such thing. Phillip has left for home up north. He promised to keep in touch, but I don't think he means physical touch, not until things are more balanced.

Right now, I tell myself, I am making progress. I am moving ahead. I am seeing my daughter as a person, not an extension of myself, and I am learning more about my issues than I let myself be open to since Mother caught me in bed with Mark all those years ago. It was as if once she opened my bedroom door and saw us, my door to sexuality's pleasures closed, until that desperate night with Phillip. Even then I was covering grief with lust.

The exit to Bill's appears sooner than I expected with all this day dreaming distracting me. I maneuver into the right lane, getting little cooperation from weary, grid-locked drivers. Once on Bill's street I expect to park behind his Camaro, but his driveway gate is closed. Parking across someone's driveway gets you a ticket this county. Parking within blocks of any beach is an issue in our coastal cities, Cardiff being the worst of all. I try honking. No answer. I know Bill's number by heart, but Bill doesn't answer his cell or his home phone. I circle the block several times, profaning his name as my search radius widens.

Eventually, I reach the market's lot. I run in for a Chapstick and a pack of pocket tissues, which should qualify me as a customer, allowing me to leave my car there without a ticket.

Walking is good exercise, and I've been off my routine since Daddy's death and getting to know Phillip and going back to the classroom and hearing the truth of my daughter's mental illness, and my role, my central role in that, and all those other things that have become my life.

By the time I get to the sidewalk to Bill's front door, I am out of breath. At least the front walk is ungated. I admire the gardener's work, planters overflowing with fall mums, yellow, orange, burgundy. A bamboo fountain centers the entry way, and the water splashes into bright blue rocks. I'll sit here and read a book on this bench if Bill doesn't answer the door or his phone. I ring the door bell.

Bill opens it, wet from the shower in one of those towel-wraps.

"Hi, Jo," he says. "I had to shower before Nory gets back. Sorry I got caught at the principals' meeting for so long, and then the superintendent called us all in to talk about the bond issue on November's ballot. Next thing I knew, the morning was gone. I caught your voice mail after lunch."

"No harm done." Why am I always deferential to Bill? If he pressured me, I could work at another school. Better yet, I could retire early, move, live free! No, I wouldn't move. Not with this fierce new debt to Suz. . . Zoozle.

"So what's this big news I missed out on? I'd just as soon we talk about it here anyway, without Mitch and Kaye and your daughter. Let me slip on some shorts."

He disappears, and I admire a sculptured dolphin signed by
Weyland.

"That's a piece he did for us. Like it?" Bill returns in a fresh
blue-Hawaiian shirt and khaki shorts. He stands next to me, obviously
awestruck by his own riches.

"You forgot to mention Phillip." I don't want anyone to forget
Phillip.

"Who? Phyllis? Was that the black woman at the funeral? I
wondered what someone like that was doing there."

"No, not her. That's Chloris, who by the way is a gem of a
woman." Bill snorts and raises his eyebrows. I go on, "Phillip, as in the
grief counselor. The one at the hospice. We met him at the funeral. He
has the big dog, Jacques?"

"I remember the dog. Why would Phillip be at Mitch's?"

"It's a long story."

"Let's get back to your big news. I've only got an hour. Nory has
us lined up to meet with a builder about a new addition to this house.
She's off to the vet with the cat. She'll be sorry to have missed you.
C'mon, let's sit on the terrace." He slides open the verandah door.

We move to a redwood deck overlooking the palisades. A path
follows the cliff down to the sea. It's low tide and the sound of the surf is
a subtle whisper. I quell the jealousy that simmers at his privileged life.
He followed his path to success with unwavering belief in himself, p.e.
teacher to principal. It didn't hurt to marry a rich girl either. No wonder
he went to Stanford.

"Wine?" asks Bill.

"No, thanks. I have some grading tonight." I'm abstaining along with Phillip and Zoozle; I'm not comfortable telling my brother this detail. He'll only harangue me about my daughter's problems.

I pull the paper out of my purse. "This is what Winona found in her Bible this morning. Daddy gave it to her, and she forgot about it. You know Winona's Bible, and if you didn't notice, she's losing her memory."

Bill grins. "We have some nut cases in the family, don't we?" He studies the notebook scrap. "And you think this is significant because?"

It's hard for me to keep my temper. "Look at the possibilities."

"T48? S?" he reads. "C'mon, Jolene. I see a note that maybe Dad wrote, it doesn't look like his writing, or he made it under the influence of morphine. I don't see that it means anything."

"It might."

"Such as?"

"Well, we brainstormed a lot on this, thinking maybe a tax code or something. In the end, Mitch suggested and we agreed it probably was Dad's dying wish to say 'Trailer for Suzanne.' Remember Suzann said Mitch and Winona knew about it? Maybe Daddy wrote this after talking to Suzann that day."

"That's a stretch." Bill stares out to sea. "Besides, the trailer is long gone."

"Phillip faxed a copy to a handwriting expert along with an exemplar of Dad's writing. We want to confirm it is Daddy's writing." I smooth the paper, remembering Daddy's smile, even as he passed from us, he smiled.

"So you do that, what about this arbitrary code? It would never hold up in court." He summarily hands the paper back to me.

"You'd take your family to court? Won't that look good in the headlines, 'Local Principal Sues Family over Father's Estate." I get a mental charge from the shock on Bill's face. He loves publicity and has a reporter on campus at least one day a week, like a quota for news coverage. He goes crazy when *his* school, Del Loma High, gets negative publicity. "Don't think I wouldn't take this to my local journalists, most of whom I wrote college recommendations for in their time of need." Not to mention the fake Facebook pages they've made mocking you, oh mighty principal who thinks he's beloved by all, I think maliciously.

Bill doesn't answer.

"Why would you do that, Jolene? Your daughter is a drug addict. It's like throwing money down the corner sewer to give her money."

I'm about to say something I shouldn't, when the door to the deck opens, and Nory steps out, holding a Siamese cat. "Hello, Jolene. Maroney got his shots and is ready for the kitty hotel when we go to New York City with the choirs for the holiday competitions." She puts the cat back inside and joins us on the deck. "Where are you traveling this winter break?"

"I haven't looked that far ahead. First, Bill and I are working out some issues from Dad's estate."

"I thought that was settled."

"It was," I hesitate, "until this morning. We found some new evidence to support my daughter's claim on the trailer."

Nory takes off her sunglasses and sets them on the table, lets her long hair down from a clip. She looks at her watch and at Bill. "Oh, interesting. Look, I need to clean up a little before the contractor arrives." She doesn't ask to see the evidence or to hear more about it. She clamps a manicured hand on Bill's shoulder, the bright orange polish accenting his blue shirt like a parrot's beak. "Don't forget what time he gets here," she says before swooping indoors. Maroney swirls around her ankles and she picks him up, kissing his nose.

Bill goes inside, talks a minute with Nory, and comes back with a magnifying glass. He examines the note under the magnifying glass.

"I still don't see much here, Jolene. And as I told you, it won't hold up in court. Don't be silly."

"Bill, we've had our ups and downs, but we're a family. I want Dad's death to help us come together, not to drive us apart. I feel as if I hardly know you anymore." I'm through kissing his feet. "I have some good news about Suzann." I'm not ready to talk about the other news, not so good, too damning to me as a mom. "She's drug free, has new friends, and is really starting over. She could use our full-hearted support. At her age, she needs to live on her own, not with me, not with Winona. Can you imagine living with Winona? Can you imagine your successful New York kids coming home to live with you and Nory if the stock market crashes again? The economy isn't exactly working in their favor, you know." It is an idea evidently so appalling that Bill sucks in his breath.

"And you want me to do what?"

"Offer Suzann compensation for the trailer?

"Based on this? That's ridiculous!" He shakes the paper under my nose. "What about the other grandkids?"

"Suzann was the only one who had any real connections to her Grandpa Joe. They were so close, no matter where she lived and what she was doing. She called him. He called her. He offered her his love all her life. She came to the hospice. She spoke at his funeral. Besides, who has to know?"

"You just said there are no secrets in a family."

He must have forgotten the secrets I kept for him when he didn't share our childhood chores, the long hours I worked and my childhood evaporated, all the duties I covered for him.

Bill walks to the railing of the deck, his shoulders tense, his back straight. He turns to me. "I am not agreeing to this blackmail."

"Are you afraid that the power is shifting?" I amaze myself with this tone.

"Don't go there. I've always wanted the best for you, Jo. I've kept a lot of parents off your back, at school, things you don't even know about with complaints about your teaching style and your rigidity. You think I'm the villain here? I'm not. I worked hard for everything I've achieved, and don't ever forget that." He paces the deck, thinking.

"This is what I can do because we are a family, and it looks like Suzann could use a break. Nory and I have a duplex in Imperial Beach we've had trouble keeping rented. Let's put Suzann in there for say three months, rent-free, subject to inspection for drugs. I don't want to lose this property for one screwed-up niece."

"Six."

"Six?" He shuts his eyes in disbelief.

"I take it back, a year. That trailer would have been a God-send to her. Rent-free duplex for a year. Search all you want. Drugs are out of her life." As I say this, I hope I believe it. "She'll keep the place up for you, and you can make good on a promise from Daddy. It's a lot less than full payment in cash for the trailer."

"You're tough as nails."

"I learned it from you. And our mother."

He laughs as if I'm kidding, but we hug.

"One more thing before I go, Bill. I forgot to tell you that we found Dad's stolen belongings. Everything is safe in a storage locker. Zoozle tracked them down."

"You're using that ridiculous name now too?"

"Don't call it ridiculous, and yes, I'm going with my daughter. What's the harm? Can't you at least say it's good we found Dad's stuff? None of it has monetary value, but the pictures are there. A lot of our childhood has been resurrected. It's important, don't you think, to have our photos and letters and all that history?"

Nory pops out the door and clears her throat. Bill nods. "We're wrapping things up, honey."

"I hope Nory agrees to the condo deal," he says in a low voice.

"Tell her there's a tax write off. She'll get it." I grab my purse, walk back through the house, air kiss them goodbye, and jog back to the car. I'll call Zoozle this evening. Even with all my new skills, I can't drive and talk.

CHAPTER 31: ZOOZLE

Free. That's how I feel. Mel is out of my life and there's hope that I'll be out of Winona's if Mom handles Uncle Bill and quits bowing at his feet, like she's part of his rock-star entourage. Funny that she hasn't called yet, which makes me think she chickened out of going over there. She hates confrontation. I won't think those thoughts. We're starting over together. She might love me. She will help me.

Yesterday's wait for the Uncle Bill no-show made my blood boil, but Mom and Phillip spent the time talking with Mitch and ooohing and ahing over Grandpa Joe's albums once we got the truck loaded. Mike and Norm were sweating buckets, which cracked me up. Mitch laughed too.

I have nothing to do today except job hunt. It's a bodily malfunction, genetic circadian rhythms at work, that I'm up at my usual early hour, as if I'm off to teach at 6 a.m. Instead, I'm checking out the classifieds when I get a text from Sandy Griffin, "PMP," followed by "CM." Peeing my pants? See me? I reply "ASAP," and she follows with "HQ8." I assume HQ is the dance studio. I'll find her when practice ends at 8.

My VW has other plans. It will not start. I try to push it and jump in, but the engine won't turn over. I'm hitting the dashboard with my open palms. The city's lack of decent rapid transit never bothered me until today.

I can't call my mom, who's already taken off more days this semester than she has in her entire career. My calls to Eric and Chloris go straight to voicemail. Mitch has that bad back. I could walk over to Sal's and check in with the boys, remembering even as I think it that Sal Junior and Gil are rarely out of bed until noon since Gil works the night shift at UPS, and Sal, Junior parties late. Winona is no help, having no car or driver's license either. I scroll through the numbers on my cell. Lordman. I hate to play the helpless lass with him. Times are desperate, and he usually works afternoons.

He answers his phone with a groggy, "Lo? Who the hell is so stupid?"

"Zooz."

"Christ, Zoozle, it's barely daylight."

"My car won't start, and I need to get to campus. Something's up."

"Christ. Okay. Where are you?"

"IB. You'll see me. Take Palm to Fourth and then right on Elm. I'll be out front. You can't miss the pink apartments."

"Great. Pink as in Pepto Bismo. Bring some, okay?"

I lock the VW down the block and go back to wait. Poochie runs around the yard, but I have to throw him back inside when he starts barking at pigeons in the palm trees. I bring the classifieds out to look at while I wait, thankful that Winona still takes a daily paper. A job, an apartment, or a house for lease are on my list. In Hillcrest, there's a business office for rent about five blocks from the deli. Wouldn't that be the greatest, if I had a business? I disliked Ms. Garant, I liked Bert Rapshon, but the whole idea that I was their little slave got to me. Maybe

I could run a copy shop? Or a dance studio? A dance studio would be a dream.

I start listing the things I'd need for a dance studio besides a building: mirrors, barre, chairs for the mommies, curtains for changing, exercise mats, lockers or cubbies, a bathroom. It's a long list. It passes time to dream a little.

Lordman pulls up at last in his PT Cruiser, metallic red with flames on the front. I get in and ignore his flannel pj bottoms, a white t-shirt, wife-beater style, which would be gross except his arms are so fine. He hasn't shaved. He looks grumpy until he smiles.

"Wait," I say, and run in to grab a driver's coffee thermal mug and a Pepto Bismol tablet from Winona'a cache of cure-alls. He likes his coffee strong and black.

I hand him the tablet, which he chomps and swallows, and then he takes the mug, and he smiles that Lordman smile again.

"Thanks, good lookin'."

"You big silly. You're saving my life." I explain about the texts from Sandy.

"You sure you want to go back out there?"

"What do I have to lose?"

"Correctemundo. You're a rocket, Zooz."

"I wish." That reminds me of my list, and I talk as he pulls onto the 805 going about ninety. "I was making a wish list. What I would do with a million dollars, that kind of thing." I watch the cars we're passing.

He puts the coffee thermos into the holder. "Baby, what I wouldn't do if I won the lottery."

"Such as?"

"Get out of that stinkin' deli. I'd open a pastry shop."

"I'd open a dance studio."

We look at one another so long that I have to grab the arm rest when he brakes suddenly in traffic.

"We could have a coffee bar with pastries out front of my dance studio. Feed the mamas and exercise their kids and then feed the kids something good for them instead of empty calories. Wouldn't that be awesome?"

"Awesome and expensive. Who has any money for a start up these days? But I don't want to live with my nutso mother forever." Lordman has stopped smiling. I can see the calculations coming out of his ears.

"It's better to dream than not to, Lordman."

"Got that right. Where do I turn anyway?"

"Take the next exit and go to Lot J."

"Want me to wait? I don't work 'til afternoon."

"Would you? You don't have to. It might take a while."

"I would. Not for anybody, but I'd wait for you." There's an undercurrent here, a message I'm reading but not believing.

"Here, go over the classifieds." I hand him the paper, which also has my wish list along the side. "I'll call you if I'll be later. I can beg a ride off Sandy if you have to go."

"I'll be right here, babe." Gaylord leans his seat back, adjusts his shades, and appears to fall asleep with the paper in his lap.

Walking across campus as the sun rises brings memories that hurt. I want to be with my team, I was the right woman for the job, and the stupidity of youth not to mention Mel's dirty tricks should not have cost me my job except the whole working for a boss part of it.

As I approach the dance studio, the door is open; the sound of my sandals clacking on the polished floors overrides any music or noise from inside the room. Sandy runs out of the studio to meet me.

"Ms. Zimmerman, you are not going to believe this," she whispers as she hugs me. "Look, I've got this text. Lacey sent it to the whole team instead of just to Veronica."

The text says "G/f gj, rid of msZ"—so what?

"I think this means Veronica and Lacey set you up."

"Easy to say, hard to prove. And I signed a letter of resignation."

"Yeah, but Veronica printed those posters, Ms. Zimmerman. She bragged to us. I bet it's even on tape. She's so stupid." She pulls out the infamous copy of Mel and me.

My cheeks are flaming with embarrassment. "We were sleeping. I didn't know anyone took pictures. I turned down major money to stay out of that stuff." I don't mention I tried to kill myself to stay out of that stuff.

"So, maybe Ms. Garant would reconsider if she knew one of her own dance team members shafted you."

"I doubt it."

"Let's find out. I'm with you."

Sandy steps into the studio. The girls are warming up. I feel the jab of nostalgia for what could have been.

Ms. Garant peers into the hallway, her tight face looking polished to a sheen this morning. She's in a black leotard with a pink tulle skirt. Her abdomen bulges. I guess she had to choose between the Botox and the liposuction. She steps back and sucks in her gut when she sees me leaning against the wall.

"I don't believe we have further business with one another, Ms. Zimmerman. Ms. Griffin, please join your team mates." She turns towards the door.

Sandy doesn't budge. "Ms. Garant, I know you hate our cell phones and all this modern junk, but I wanted to share this message with you and Ms. Zimmerman."

Ms. Garant hisses and starts to walk away when Dave Inman hurries by to his office. He has Mr. Luster on his heels, yelling about suing the school for exposing his daughter to a filthy pervert.

Sandy proceeds, "Mr. Inman, Mr. Luster, could you join us?" She calls loudly enough that the dance team appears at the studio doorway and several, including Lacey and Veronica, sidle into the hall where they lean smirking against the wall.

Sandy holds her phone and pulls up the text message. Ms. Garant looks baffled; Mr. Inman, intrigued; Mr. Luster, bored. "This means those posters were a set up. I'm not saying Ms. Zimmerman is some angel, but she was a good dance teacher and it wasn't her past that caught up with her; it was a witch hunt led by. . ." She turns and stands in front of Veronica, "led by Veronica. Look, here's the web site. It's a porn site with pictures of us, our dance team and our dressing room. Want to talk about perverts? There's one." She links arms to hold Veronica in place.

Veronica defends herself. "It was Mr. Inman's idea to put the camera in our dance studio."

Sandy pulls Veronica to Ms. Garant, who hasn't said a word. "But Veronica used the tapes to ruin everything, our whole dance season, Ms. Zimmerman's career."

Veronica denies every word. "I wouldn't do that," she says. She walks back into the studio, slamming the door, when Lacey's resolve crumbles.

Lacey is saying she's sorry to the whole world, but Veronica said Dahlia promised her the advisor's role when Veronica turned twenty-one since she had stage experience in Salt Lake City. "Remember, Ms. Garant? Veronica's birthday was in October. But you decided Ms. Z was some hot shot. So Veronica started uploading our practice tapes and some locker room shots to that web site. It was that Mel girl who gave us the idea."

Ms. Garant turns to Dave Inman. "What do you think, Dave?"

"I think we had better consult the chancellor and his legal team." Dave comes over to stand by me. "I'm sorry, Suzann. We may owe you an apology. You will hear from us soon, once we untangle this web of intrigue."

I stand silent and shocked. Me? With a new, level foothold in the world? Lordman is waiting in the car and my mom will go over the moon when she hears this news as I did last night when she called to tell me about the duplex deal she worked out on my behalf with Bill.

My dreams may come true.

CHAPTER 32: ZOOZLE

In Southern California, our summer ends as late as Halloween. It is definitely autumn now, crisper, cooler, without the fog we get in the summer months. The November evening sun is glaring in my eyes. The air carries a faint note of iodine. The seagulls are noisily stirring up a kelp pile.

Leaning against Lordman in a porch swing on the duplex's roof, I have my feet curled under me; we are listening to the surf at low tide, its subtle murmur. The others are downstairs watching Charger football.

Lordman and I decided to host an early Thanksgiving potluck. We've improvised enough dining space from a ping-pong table, set with thrift shop dishes and a couple of yards of fabric, orange-and-brown leaves outlined in gold. Chloris and Auntie made a centerpiece of pumpkins and gourds, leftover from their mammoth pot of squash soup.

Mom is outside with our goofy rescued labradoodle, Fluffernutter. The dog is three, so no longer a pup. She's right for us. The day after we moved in, Lordman and I got online and looked for a dog to rescue. We wanted about ten of them. Until we get a house with a big backyard, one is enough. Lordman and I took one look at Fluffer's silly smile and mellow eyes, her wagging tail, and she was ours. The name is the first of many compromises we've learned to make between my energized do-it-now agenda and Lordman's calm, cool, collected nice guy. He laughs with everything, especially me.

My mom looks younger, more relaxed. She has taken this semester off to heal with me, attend sessions, deal with her grief and her guilt, our relationship. I wanted Phillip to be here today too, but Mom says one day at a time, one step at a time.

She is building what looks like stairs in the sand. Fluffernutter is putting his paw through them as fast as she creates them. Add water, I think, add love. Make cement. I wonder if Phillip told her that story? I miss him. Chloris joins her on the beach. They are singing while they build new stairs, first a line by Chloris in Somali, then they repeat it together.

Someone has opened the oven, and the scent of the turkey cooking spirals up to us. Lordman's specialty stuffing smells of sage and apples. I'm too comfortable to move when Mitch and Kaye pull up in Mitch's new red Jeep. He gets slowly out of the car. Mitch carries three pies up the outside stairs.

He sees me wave so he comes up to the roof, while Kaye balances a casserole dish and offers her arm to Winona.

"Here's the mincemeat pie from Winona," he makes a face, "and one pumpkin, one apple from Kaye. Don't mix them up I beg you. With Winona's memory problems, who knows what she put in for mincemeat."

"Never fear. I'll keep them straight. Everything has been so crazy with our new studio opening," I pause and grin at Lordman who hops up and does a soft shoe, "and the move from Winona's and all."

"Your job gave you some compensation?" I nod. "I like the way you're handling this place, Suzann. Bill came through too, didn't he?" Mitch gazes around the corner of the porch out at the beach. "Jacques will love visiting you."

"Um, sure," I hedge. It's not my place to blab Mom's beeswax. "Mom's outside with Chloris and our dog. Let's go in with the pies." I skip down the stairs and through the side door, with Mitch and Lordman following. Kaye and Winona have edged inside the front door where they stand by the wall.

"Kaye, Winona, I want you to meet my friends: Chloris's Aunty Chandrace, Eric and Chris, and this is my business partner, Lordman, and this is Lordman's mom, Sharon Blanchard." Everybody nods. Welcomes sing out.

"*Soodhawow,*" says Auntie. "That's Somali for welcome. It is a welcome day, is it not?"

"I think I'm more than a business partner," Lordman nuzzles my neck.

"Everybody's coming, even Uncle Art, Uncle Bill, and Nory. Can you believe that, Mitch?" I ask.

"Really? Joe used to say your uncles couldn't handle the whole family at once."

Grandpa Joe's name hangs between us, and we are quiet. Mitch says he'll join Mom on the beach. He wants a walk before a big meal.

Laughter bubbles up in me as Nory and Bill come up the walk, Nory with an armful of flowers, Uncle Bill carrying a Honey-Baked ham and a briefcase. Oh please, I think, no business on this joyful day.

Uncle Bill and Nory come in smiling at everyone, set down their offerings, check the property for damage in surreptitious glances, and Uncle Bill flips his briefcase open on one of the benches by our table.

I look inside where there's a set of envelopes, paper clipped together. Bill pulls one out and hands it to me. "These were to be distributed when the estate was finalized. Dad wrote them in hospice. This is the last thing left to do on the estate."

The handwriting of each name on the outside is my mom's. It says, "Joe asked me to write some thoughts for each of you. He laughed and said these were his final pearls of wisdom." Inside each one there's a message from Grandpa.

There are three other notes, Art's, my mom's, and Winona's. Uncle Bill has secured his already or didn't get one, I think with a rush of unnecessary hostility.

"Could we deliver these after the blessing at dinner?" I ask.

Bill says sure and puts the briefcase into a closet. "Let's put these out like name cards," he says, setting each on a plate, side by side.

We are blessed. We are back together as a family, not a perfect family, because there is no perfect. But it's more than was possible even a month ago. Lordman comes up behind me, puts his arms around my waist, and I lean back into him.

What will be Grandpa's last words to me? I open my envelope and trace each word with my finger. I hold the paper to my heart, where the pain of loss and love sprouts again. "Today's as important as forever."

I hope that's the message for each of us. What advice is more important than that?

About the Author

Eileen Granfors lives in Santa Clarita, California, although she and her husband hope to move to Galena, Missouri, before too long to enjoy the peaceful country life.

Eileen is a proud UCLA alumna, who taught English at the high school level.

After a long career in teaching, she turned to writing. She has published numerous short stories and an anthology, *Flash Warden and Other Short Stories*, and a volume of poetry, *And More White Sheets*. *Some Rivers End on the Day of the Dead*, a coming-of-age multicultural look at the Hispanic tradition of the Day of the Dead, is her first published novel. She is working on its sequel, *So You, Solimar* as well as a prequel to the Dickens' classic, *A Tale of Two Cities*. This book, *Stairs of Sand* is her second published novel. Although it was among her first writings, Eileen revised the book extensively over a period of six years.

She uses short forms of fiction as methods to conquer writer's block and to hone her word choice. She also recommends coloring books for those dreaded days when the words won't come.

Acknowledgments

I am grateful for the astute help of my editor, Kathleen Penrice, and my ever-faithful, ever-honest reading circle—Caroline McCoy, Yvette Johnson, Anna Boorstin, Jeannie Bloom, Helen Meek, and Immy Kwon. Thanks to my teachers in creative writing at UCLA Extension: Cecilia Brainard, Van Khanna, and always, my most patient and optimistic champion, Eve Lasalle Caram. Special thanks to Yvette Johnson for her beautiful poem, a gift to me as I struggled with this novel. Thanks to Dougal Waters via Getty Images for copyright and the cover photo and to Create Space for their terrific customer support system. Sending hugs and love to my entire family, who have cheered for me to continue to tell my stories. And to anyone living with Borderline Personality Disorder, trying to make sense of life, this I know and believe: You can overcome your demons.

11857812R0016

Made in the USA
Lexington, KY
05 November 2011